the
TRESPASSERS

the

TRESPASSERS

≈ ≈ ≈ *ROBERT ROPER*

Ticknor & Fields NEW YORK 1992

For information about permission to reproduce selections
from this book, write to Permissions, Ticknor & Fields,
215 Park Avenue South, New York, New York 10003.

Library of Congress Cataloging-in-Publication Data

Roper, Robert, date.
The trespassers / Robert Roper.
p.   cm.
ISBN 0-89919-987-9
I. Title.
PS3568.069T74   1992
813'.54 — dc20   92-13043
CIP

Printed in the United States of America

AGM   10   9   8   7   6   5   4   3   2   1

For Michael Doise
sweet-natured student of hearts

Man has no Body distinct from his Soul; for
that calld Body is a portion of Soul discernd
by the five Senses. . . .

The lust of the goat is the bounty of God.
The wrath of the lion is the wisdom of God.
The nakedness of woman is the work of God.

Wm. Blake, *The Marriage of Heaven and Hell*

Ah, these manly he-men, these flaneurs, the oglers, these
eaters of good dinners!

D. H. Lawrence, *Lady Chatterley's Lover*

At a quarter to five a car could be heard coming down the dirt road from the direction of the quarry, and Catherine Mansure and her young son, Ben, went out to meet it.

A dusty dark blue Volvo, a good twenty years old, entered the turnaround circle in front of their house and made two complete circuits, its driver calling out joyous hellos, before parking in just the wrong place (where it would block any cars coming later). Catherine directed that it be moved.

The driver, a good-looking man in his early forties, with curly dark hair receding above his temples, reparked his car with excessive, ironic apologies and hugged Catherine for almost a full minute. Afterward he shook hands with the boy, mock-formally. He had brought a leather bag and a bottle of wine.

"The mansion looks . . . decrepit, as usual," he said, and then he laughed, making a chesty sound. The house in fact looked superb, cool and freshly whitewashed in its nest of tremendous oaks. "One of the great California houses," he continued. "I don't see why I can't own it." And then he laughed again, taking Catherine's hand, and said, "And you look terrible, too."

They walked toward the house that way, holding hands, and Catherine's son walked on her other side, all the while looking across at the man with an expression of intense unemotional interest. Just as they were going up the few brick steps to the ponderous oaken door the boy peeled away.

"First things first," said the man, whose name was Bob Stein. They were just inside, and he pulled a typed manuscript out of his leather bag and handed it to Catherine with an embarrassed grin. "I don't want to see it again or talk about it all weekend, although of course I expect a typically sensitive, thorough critique later on, something that pulls no punches but that doesn't destroy me, either. That's not asking too much, is it?"

Catherine laughed, taking the pages.

"Good," he said, finally relinquishing his grip. "And now we won't talk about it anymore, not a single word."

The evening was splendid. The windows of the large parlor in which they sat were thrown wide open, and the smell of oaks and of the nearby grassy hillsides invaded. From time to time Catherine could hear sounds from below the house, where the various outbuildings stood. Ben would be playing down there, and she found herself listening for his voice rather than attending to Bob Stein, who, after all, was an old friend who had long been absent. But now she made herself conscious only of this friend: she was aware of him suddenly as a dark-haired, green-eyed man with a mustache, a fairly healthy specimen all told, though somewhat pale and with forehead nervously sweating.

He sat in the corner of a vanilla-colored couch, with one shoe resting on edge on the floor, the other on top of the first. His short thighs, which she remembered as being uncommonly thick, faun-like, filled his upper pantlegs to the bursting point. He held a glass of white wine balanced on one hip. Catherine had forgotten how hairy were the backs of his hands: the first section of each finger was covered with intensely black, soft-looking hair, and in one little thatch nested a silver ring with a jade setting.

Catherine was thirty-five, a tall, full-figured woman with a complexion comprised of subtle colorings, fadings and freshenings constantly ongoing. Unlike her mother and older sister, also redheads, she had found herself able to live in the sun, was not fatally pale and prone to burning; and maybe just for this reason she was always half crazy about this or

that activity, anything requiring her to use her body strenu-
ously. Just in the last few years, since she and her husband,
Rick, and their son had moved up to this famous house in the
coastal mountains, she had become passionately enamored of
gardening, both vegetable and flower; and now her other
physical enthusiasms, her mountain trekking, horseback riding, tournament tennis, and so forth, had been pushed aside.

Bob was talking about some friends of theirs, people they
had known at Berkeley (they had both gone to the University
of California, although in classes seven years apart), and
about a woman named Maryanne, "She's very disappointed
in you — very," he pointedly remarked. "She says that you
had promise in a hundred different ways, but that you settled
for being a wife, and a rich wife at that. You were always a
model for her, and now you're a sort of negative icon. A
cautionary figure, so to speak."

"Me? I was a model for somebody?" Catherine laughed
warmly. "I don't mind being called a negative icon — that
sounds like fun — but Maryanne never paid me any attention, so I don't see how I could have been her model. Anyway,
any positive-iconism I had was simply stolen. Just a dim
reflection of Rick's."

She seemed amused to have this report, not offended in the
least, and Bob Stein himself was mildly put out, having
hoped, it seemed, to provoke a retaliation.

"Rick was the star," Catherine continued, "the fabulous
idol. I was just the abject worshiper he happened to choose.
No one ever noticed me before he came along — absolutely
no one."

"No, Catherine, that's not true. Everybody noticed you.
You inspired more ummm . . . eager yearning than just about
anyone else, any other girl I can remember. But you couldn't
be approached. Everyone knew you'd been anointed, that you
belonged to the king. We had to step back and let him take
you in his own good time."

Catherine smiled, but this was in some ways an accurate description of what had happened, and color rose in her cheeks. She had been tremendously naïve (she now believed) in her college days, innocent in a way and to an extent not easy to account for, either in terms of her background (a fairly standard suburban childhood, with high school teachers for parents) or of a lack of intelligence. It was in this pathetic condition, as a generically wide-eyed, vulnerable pretty girl, that she had fallen under the spell of her future husband. Rick was then incarnated as a charismatic graduate assistant, after a legendary college career (also at Berkeley). A leader of student strikes in the sixties, he had come to occupy an unusual position in the Department of Comparative Literature, under whose auspices he delivered the occasional lecture while conducting a film program of an extraordinary, campuswide popularity. Catherine and her friends, and just about everyone they knew, had had to connive and conspire to get admitted to this course, where there obtained, as she now recalled, an atmosphere of excited experimentation, an electric mood of Sorbonne-like improvisational glamour. Rick in his street-guerrilla garb, with a tweed sportcoat and dashing scarf thrown in for good measure, exercised a powerful fascination: somehow he combined intrinsic interest, male beauty, "high academic standards," and an implied critique of all formal instruction in a single compelling figure.

"Rick was the star," Bob allowed, "no doubt about it. Funny how he got around the problem of a 'cult of personality' — it was just that he was so superior, we were all moved that he would actually condescend to make contact. Even then you knew he belonged to a larger world. You half expected him to be called away at any moment, swept up into a sphere forever beyond your reach. But you're wrong, Catherine," he admonished, "you underestimate your own powers. When Rick took you up it only confirmed what everyone else already felt about you. We kicked ourselves for not having recognized you sooner."

Catherine shook her head, and she said with cheeks only slightly less suffused with color, "You know, Bob, it's a good thing you're a writer of fictions . . . I never recognize myself in anything you say about me. It's just the purest, most imaginative sort of invention."

"No, Catherine. I only tell the truth — only the truth. It's just a deeper truth than you're used to, perhaps . . ."

Half an hour later, realizing that she needed to get supper under way, she showed Bob to his rooms. They were on the third floor of the three-winged, many-chambered house, with its curious curving hallways, its massive, half-timbered interior walls and profusion of elegantly leaded windows, and from his west-facing balcony Bob beheld a view of the entire southward sweep of the Santa Cruz Mountains, mile after mile of virgin-looking forest. After a moment of appropriately shocked contemplation he wondered out loud whether this was "all Mansure land — part of the old colonial land grant, or something of the kind. As far as a man could ride a horse in a single day, or was it a month?"

A *half mile* from the house was the quarry, a going concern, and the estate also supported a thriving native plants nursery. Rick's great-aunt, Gerda Mansure, had established the nursery, and she likewise brought the quarry back into operation after years of disuse. But aside from the quarry and nursery the property consisted of 2,400 wild, largely unimproved acres, most of them densely covered with coastal forest. On the high ridges stands of live oak could be found, with something of the character of the cork oak forests of Tuscany; at lower elevations grew Douglas fir, madrone, tanbark, and bay in a complexly interwoven forest; at the lowest, along the creek bottoms, stood copious groves of redwood, much of it never timbered. Catherine had hiked or ridden a horse over most of the property by now, but she was still in a condition of ecstatic amazement about it all: she felt as if she hadn't yet taken its measure, and indeed, she was still discovering unsuspected features, secret watercourses, mysterious canyons, ponds not indicated on the topo maps.

A network of fire trails crisscrossed the land. By county ordinance these were to be kept open year-round, and it had fallen to Catherine to supervise the effort. Usually she recruited a crew of several men from the nearby town, Cuervo, and worked with them throughout the spring.

Gerda, the great-aunt, was still very much the mistress of "Longfields," however. Now in her mid-eighties, still formidably active, she was the daunting matriarch in all but biological fact, full of crotchets and granitic opinions. Childless after three marriages ("really four, if you count some funny business"), she had outlived or simply worn down all her enemies, and to her astonishment and dismay now found herself alone. The sole purpose of her life over the last fifty years had been the preservation of her property — and most emphatically it was *her* farm, not her second husband's, certainly not that of any of her egregious Mansure in-laws. The "unspeakable Mansures" had battled her in court for years, counting on her often parlous finances to work in their favor eventually. Their motive, as she insistently saw it, was only to "steal from me this property, which is mine. And I haff not allowed that — no, not yet."

But finding herself alone, having no consanguineous kin of her own (she had lost touch with her few cousins in Germany), recently she had softened in the direction of Rick and his little family. They were invited up for a single week one summer, and they never left.

"I don't care for Rick," Gerda would say. "Maybe I only like that he isn't so bad as his father. And I'm afraid for little Ben. This beautiful boy has something cold in him, I think. He reminds me of Regis, the second-oldest uncle. Too much of a careful mind."

"But Gerda, don't you like me, either?" Catherine protested. "Why did you ask us to live with you in the first place, if you don't like any of us?"

"Oh Catherine. I like you well enough, you know. Yes — I suppose I do."

"And how can you not like a child, a boy of only seven years? Especially when he loves you with all his heart? Look at the pictures he draws of you — he makes you the biggest of any group, bigger even than the redwoods. Look at Rick and me. We hardly reach to your knees."

"Yes, I can see the pictures, Catherine. And I don't say that I don't *love* the boy. No — I never said that."

But this was the sort of thing one had to expect from her. Blunt, spontaneous expressions of ambivalent feelings, or worse. It had taken some getting used to.

Catherine had never thought that they would stay, and she remembered well Rick's initial reluctance: he looked upon his great-aunt with rather bleak amusement, having been persuaded, after years of hearing the other side, that she was nothing but an obstinate and untrustworthy opportunist. The gravamen of all the suits and countersuits was that she had contested her husband's legal will, specifically the provisions of it ordering a two-way division of the mountain property known as Longfields; she wanted it all, every last acre, for herself, and she had proved extraordinarily resourceful in her struggle to achieve this questionable end.

"But Gerda," Rick said to her once — it was the only time Catherine heard them discuss the matter — "you have to admit that you were wrong, and that you lost. All the other acres, everything on the eastern slope, now belong to Regis's sons, which is the way Uncle Willy wanted it. After all, that's what it said in his will."

"My dear Rick," Gerda replied coolly. "Someday you may understand me. But probably not. Willy wanted only one thing, that his great, beautiful forest should remain undivided. I and my poor lawyer did our best to achieve that, but we were beaten in the end. We were cheated, really. The Mansures wanted also to remove me from this place of mine; it was *they* who wanted the whole forest, even this old house, which I designed and built myself."

"That's funny — I always heard it was Julia Morgan, the famous San Francisco architect, who designed your house."

"No. Julia brought her plans down here for me to examine. I took one look at them and laughed. And then *I* built my house. Which is as you see around you."

≈ ≈ ≈

For Catherine, this was all somehow a matter of only slight interest. In a remote way she was an admirer of great houses, baronial properties, and so forth, and she could see how families might fall apart over such issues. Her own family, however, had had little enough to pass onward (or to inherit, for that matter); they were not "great," no, not distinguished in any way.

Her father, a teacher of high school chemistry, had failed entirely to accumulate, not so much by design as by stubborn, insuperable temperament. In his thirties he developed a new electrochemical process, with applications in many fields (primarily electro-discharge machining), and had he but taken a few simple steps, all the patents, and also a small fortune, would have been his. But as it was, the lab where he worked enjoyed all the benefit. But her family had never aspired in that way — really, they never aspired in *any* way, except toward security, normality, toward sensuous and intellectual diversion on a moderate scale. Her parents had worked hard, then had gotten on to their pensions. After which they traveled widely. In their late fifties they went all over the world, and they were still, in their mid-sixties, taking off gamely for Nepal, for the Caribbean, for various destinations in South America.

Her mother had been a "great beauty" in her youth — so everybody said. Yet she settled for marriage to a mere chemistry teacher. Then she bore her daughters, raised them well, and became a teacher herself (of high school French and Spanish). She was now a passionate bridge player, with some six hundred master points. Lately she had begun to spread out physically, becoming rather jolly in the process.

It was all a question of inheritance (Catherine had recently come to believe): not of material inheritance, although that was important, but of innate character, inborn spirit, iron and ineluctable destiny. Her generation had somehow failed to make the great change they planned, the "revolution" that would have freed them from these old, iron laws; and in the wake of that failure, the old ways, the ancient, inescapable strictures of fate, had come into play with a renewed vigor.

Rick had been the very type of the new man, the liberated sort who would fashion a new world, one running according to new laws (or possibly, according to none at all). And Rick, to his own amazement, had ended up much as his uncles always wanted. He was now a defender of the family interests, of its various and complex holdings. The radical student, the romantic, relentlessly deconstructing young professor, was now a sitter on corporate boards, a dweller in impressive offices.

"It happens right before your eyes," he had said to her, "you're painfully aware of it all. It's not like you wake up one morning and no longer care about looking ridiculous. You're still susceptible to the old irony, you know ... you still see things in the round, and you can barely act, because you're so 'conscious' of it all. Not that being conscious means all that much in the end. It's just the cross you have to bear, and you begin to suspect that all those unthinking clods, those reactionary pillars who came before you, probably had it too. They just didn't complain about it so much."

Rick the radical journalist (he had written two books about Latin America), the self-defined "Maoist-Debrayist," who still considered himself a socialist in some final sense, supervised an entire division of the Laurel Foundation, the Mansure-dominated corporate aggregate. He had a good head for business, everyone said, and he was doing Laurel "a whole ton of good," according to his uncle Regis, his immediate superior in the hierarchy.

And Catherine had to ask herself: had this been Rick's destiny all along? Or to put it more precisely: was there any reason to doubt that this had most *certainly* been his fate (if not actually his aim), that he had been prefigured, prewired, preprogrammed to do exactly such work? "Blood will tell," as they say; or as Bob Stein recently put it, "Even then, you knew he belonged to a larger world."

That *evening* by half past seven, Rick had still not come home. Everyone else sat down to dinner, leaving a place at the foot of the table. Gerda habitually sat at the head, and the platters of food as they came out were shown her first. The precise way she had of puckering her lips, as she peered doubtfully at a tray of chicken breasts à la Dijonnais, never failed to excite a kind of irritated pleasure in Catherine.

"I've seen this before," the old woman remarked. "These are your juicy little morsels, with too much the spice."

"No, Aunt Gerda — they're not so hot. You liked them well enough before."

"Yes. I liked them all night, as I remember."

Bob Stein had taken a shower, and his cheeks were pink and blue from a close, careful shave. He had insisted on sitting next to little Ben, because "we men have to stick together." Ben had so far answered, in his high, monotonic voice, questions about baseball, football, horseback riding, and his favorite subjects in school.

Each time the boy made another precise, detailed response, in that voice that was bizarrely like a computer's, Bob's eyes widened, and he looked to Catherine as if asking permission to laugh.

"But if you don't like football," he said, "and you don't have a tennis court here, how do you have fun? Don't you like to play games?"

"Yes. I like a lot of games . . . I like chess, although chess isn't really a game. It's a sport. That's because it's physically demanding, as well as mentally hard."

"So — who taught you to play chess? Do you really know how to play?"

"My father taught me the moves. Then I read a book called *Logical Chess*, by Irving Chernev. It's got all the great games in it. He explains every move they make."

Bob looked over at Catherine again; he could hardly refrain from rolling his eyes, it seemed, from shaking his head in wonderment.

"You painted a beautiful picture today," someone else now observed. "I think it's my favorite picture, Ben, because you used so many different colors in it."

The speaker was a young woman, Karen Oldfield, who had recently moved up to the farm, taking employment as a sort of governess/chauffeuse. Normally she ate in her own small cabin, down below the house, among the barns. But tonight Catherine had invited her up to the house, hoping to provide a larger party for Bob.

"He painted it in just five minutes," the girl continued, "it seemed to fly right out of him, when we went up on the quarry road. He got the blue-gray of the stones just right, and the blue-green of the pond. And the mountains and the sky, too."

"I like it there at the quarry," Ben explained. "The rock dust smells sweet. And sometimes it gets in your mouth, and then it makes your teeth squeak."

Bob Stein smiled, shaking his head. Again, he gave Catherine his look, meant to convey profound amazement, frank astonishment at her son's odd acuteness.

Catherine had gotten to like the young governess lately. She was a local girl, a recent graduate of the canyon schools, very pretty and fresh, and with a certain composure. She had no boyfriend, and she created a tremendous stir when she first moved up to the farm, where the quarry workers and other young men caught sight of her. Though born and raised in Cuervo, as were many of Catherine's other workers, she had been practically invisible, almost unknowable, in her life in the squalid mountain town; the boys who grew up with her, some actually her classmates, suddenly found in her many remarkable qualities, which the move to the farm had magically revealed.

"If I were twenty years younger," Bob Stein declared, "and if you would let me, Karen, I'd take you away from all this. Carry you off to Florence, in Italy, where they'd appreciate your special beauty. Catherine, who was it who painted that Venus — you know, the plump, lazy one, lying on a sort of sofa? With the copper-colored hair?"

"I don't know, Bob. I'm afraid I'm not up on my Venuses. Are you thinking of Raphael? Titian?"

"Yes, Titian, that's right. Very good, Catherine. Titian. It's the Venus of somewhere or other." Turning to the young woman he said, "Now let me tell you something, my dear. I don't say these things to just anybody, you know, but you're the very type of a Titian-haired beauty. Do you understand? Have you ever even heard of Titian? Or of the quattrocento? An old Italian painter, a dusty relic, and there's no reason you should know about him — but he had a favorite model, someone he put in all his great works. And she looked just like you. Don't you agree, Catherine? Isn't the resemblance extraordinary — even uncanny?"

"Oh, uncanny's definitely the word, Bob. That's the only way to describe it — uncanny."

"Well, now — you see?"

Pouring himself more wine, he continued, "I wouldn't say this to just anybody, you know. Now if someone ever asks you, later in life, if you've ever been outrageously complimented, just say that the obscure novelist Bob Stein, slightly in his cups one evening, recognized in you the form of the goddess. Say he saw in you the very image of classic, ageless beauty. And that he asked nothing but to be allowed to worship at your feet. To be free to praise you, in all the old, awestruck ways."

The young woman, in response to this unexpected effusion, looked positively stupefied for a moment. But soon she recovered her composure. That modest, girlish dignity, that natural self-possession, which distinguished her even more than her sweet prettiness, returned as she said:

"Thank you. Thank you so much. That's a very nice thing to say — *very* nice. And I will remember it. I know that I always will."

"Well, I mean it. I really do."

Then Bob looked anxiously over at Catherine: did she, at least, not take his meaning, did she not construe his subtle, impeccably facetious intent? In the past, she had always been dependable when it came to such things, to interpreting his most self-mocking declarations to strangers (especially to young women); and now, to reassure him, she smiled back in a dry way, meanwhile handing him the bowl of garden greens.

≈ ≈ ≈

Two hours later, when dinner had been over for a long time, Rick finally came home. They heard him shuffling through the entrance of the quiet house, dropping his bags and hanging up his coat, and then he appeared in the dining room, where Bob, Catherine, and a drowsy Gerda still sat at the maple table.

"Here he is. Here's the great man, after all," Bob said, standing straight up.

"Hello there, Bob. Glad to see you. Really sorry I'm late. But it couldn't be helped."

They shook hands firmly, almost violently. Rick kissed Catherine on the cheek, then half sat, half stumbled into his chair, the picture of after-work exhaustion. A lithe, handsome man who would soon turn forty-five, he gave an impression of powerful energies only momentarily baffled — formidable capacities temporarily undermined.

"Hard times at the office, eh what, chief? And then that damned commute," Bob said. "Getting worse all the time, isn't it? Godawful."

Rick smiled. "Be without sympathy, if you have to, Bob. Kick a poor fellow when he's down. You who's never had any kind of job; who doesn't even know what the inside of an office looks like."

"Rick, would you like a glass of wine? Or maybe a scotch?"

"Oh, definitely scotch, Catherine. And make it a big one."

Rick had eaten at the office, he apologized. He had failed to eat anything earlier in the day, and then at around five-thirty, suddenly feeling terribly weak, he got his secretary to order in a salad. "Otherwise I would've passed out. Just fallen on the floor. I felt weird the whole day . . . But you can't believe what a zoo it was up there today. An unending round of meetings, conferences, and the like, with nothing really getting accomplished. And everyone needing my attention, for some reason."

Rick was an avid runner. He still participated in the odd 5 or 10K race, although his marathoning days were over, he regretted to admit. His runner's pallor sometimes made him appear almost ghoulish, yet in fact he was impressively fit — physically in the greatest possible tune.

"Bob, have you come alone this time? Didn't you bring anyone? I still remember what's-her-name . . . you're not still seeing her, are you? Or the other one, the leggy blonde?"

"Old what's-her-name, Rick? You mean, old so-and-so? I don't think I am. But it gets hard keeping track of them after a while. Or is that what you're trying to imply?"

Rick smiled. Catherine now supplied the name of the woman in question — Veronique — a "good friend" whom Bob had once brought to Longfields for a visit.

"I haven't seen her in over a year, Rick. I think she's gone

back home, back to Paris. I don't know if I ever told you —
she was married the whole time. And with kids into the
bargain. Somehow this never came up between us."

Bob had been seriously in love with his Veronique. At least,
so he told Catherine at the time. In recent years she had tried
to resist, but had finally succumbed to, the conclusion that he
purposely sought out such situations: partners already hopelessly out of his reach.

"Yeah, she had her way with me, Rick," he went on. "We
had some fun, though. It's just that for her, it was only a
vacation. She had a real life to go back to."

"Well, Bob," Catherine put in gently, "you were having
your own little vacation, weren't you? And I can't believe you
never talked about her being married. And having kids. It's
simply not to be believed."

"No, we really never did. But I'm not complaining . . . I just
think it's sort of ironic, don't you? Here I spend my whole life
worrying about 'using' women, whether I'm exploiting them
somehow, and then I get used myself. You know me: I've
always tried to please my women, always. First it was Mom,
then my sisters, then my teachers at school. I only became a
writer because they said they liked it better — said it sounded
more romantic. I'm like Picasso that way, I guess. He used to
claim he never would've become a painter except it helped
him pick up girls. The pretty ones went for the artistic types,
he noticed. You know — the musicians, the poets."

Rick asked about Ben, who had been sent to bed. Karen
had also returned to her cabin, to Bob's disappointment. The
conversation turned, by means of Bob's questionably sincere
expressions of interest, to the matter of Rick's new work, his
recently undertaken responsibilities for the Laurel Foundation. Bob was completely ignorant of the business world, he
claimed; his threadbare, introspective writer's life had left
him as uninformed about such matters as it was possible for
an American to be.

"But tell me what you really do, Rick. I mean, what happens in your glass tower up there? What were you doing at, say, three o'clock today — what was really going on?"

"At three o'clock, Bob? You want to know about three o'clock? Well, I was probably on the phone, talking to L.A., at three o'clock. I'd just come back from the gym. We have a facility up there, a pool and indoor track, that sort of thing. But at three-fifteen, something did happen . . . this guy named Raab, a Young Turk from the tax division, came over. He's one of Uncle Willy's protégés. He had to see me all of a sudden, couldn't wait . . . he proposes buying stock in some little company, one of these older business-programming outfits, with minimal commitment to the home-computer end. They've been having trouble getting new product on the market, he says. Then he starts explaining the tax advantages to me, telling me why we should make the purchase right now rather than in six months, for example. But as he goes on and on, I start wondering why he's come to me at all, since people above me usually make these decisions. Or if he feels he has to lobby it around a bit, take it to someone in the family, why not to one of my uncles? Does this signal a swing in my favor, I wonder. Or, on the contrary, has he come to me, the least significant and influential of the full-bloods, to get an approval that doesn't mean much, that's commensurate with the fairly low order of importance of such a strike?"

Rick sipped his scotch, and leaning back in his chair, he now fixed Bob with a "corporate" look, icy-cold and no-fooling. Then by an almost imperceptible modulation of expression, he communicated something different, that he was aware of how he appeared, of how he must be sounding, of how Bob would surely be taking this, already formulating a telling case, for the benefit of their friends back in Berkeley: "And you can't believe the change in Rick, he's become the complete corporate animal. No sense of humor, none at all. Not that he was ever able to laugh at himself, of course . . ."

"Should I go on, Bob?"

"Please, Rick. Please do. Fascinating stuff. Absolutely riveting."

"So . . . I asked Raab about it. Straight out. And he acted rather surprised. Utterly taken with my candor, you understand. Normally, he would've gone to one of the uncles, he said, but Ferdius and Bill are both out of the country; and feeling that time was of the essence, he simply came to me. Then he goes on about tax credits and the like, and it occurs to me that I've misunderstood the magnitude of what he's proposing: this isn't just some quiet little buy, it's an outright gobble of the whole damned company. A takeover of a kind. But that has ramifications I'm not qualified to evaluate. Effects on our other markets, on our other divisions, and so forth. Then we have to consider that the other family members, some of them quite old by now, will almost certainly oppose such a move. My aunt Willow hates all chemical and technical innovations of the last forty years, you know. If we push such a thing through against her wishes, she'll become intractable in ways that could drive this Raab, a meticulous tax type, to suicide. So maybe he just thinks I'm more rational, for a Mansure. Or maybe he's feeling me out, seeing if we can't make big medicine together, somewhere down the road . . ."

As Rick pronounced this last phrase, "down the road," he gasped, actually turning pale. A look of complete surprise, almost of wounded innocence, crossed his face, and he stood up from the table as if sprung from his chair. Saying not a word, and staring fixedly in front of him all the while, he hurried out of the room.

"Rick? Rick? Are you all right?" Catherine exchanged a look of puzzlement and concern with Bob Stein, who only an instant before had been stifling a yawn. She also stood up from her chair, although somewhat more slowly. Then calling after her husband, meanwhile shaking her head in perplexity, she followed him upstairs.

C*atherine found* Rick in their bedroom, and after getting him to lie down she opened all the windows, because he complained of feeling suffocated. But the night air only made him cold. He was deathly pale, having just vomited three times. She wiped the moisture from his forehead and got a quilt from the closet, but he kept shivering for several minutes.

"Is it the flu, Rick? Is it something you ate?"

"I don't know. Some people are sick in the office though."

She asked if he wanted her to call his doctor, but he didn't think that was necessary. The nearest medical facilities were thirty miles away, far down the mountain, in Palo Alto.

"Jesus — I'm so fucking cold . . ."

"I'll roll out a sleeping bag on top. That should help."

"Whatever."

Soon he stopped shivering. He looked completely exhausted, lying on his back under all the blankets, with just his head visible. Whenever he became sick, he seemed to lose half his bulk; though a fairly tall, somewhat imposing figure, with broad bony shoulders, he weighed only one hundred eighty pounds at best.

"Bob will find significance . . . think I'm afraid. Think I'm running away from him."

"Running away? Afraid? What in the world are you talking about, Rick?"

"He really irritates me sometimes, you know? The little schemer. The sneaky little prick."

"You're just sick, Rick, that's all. Relax, will you?"

His eyes remained closed; he seemed too weak to open them. Catherine, sitting quietly by his side, was after a moment affected by his incapacity, strangely stirred by it. When they first lived together, many years ago now, in Guatemala, he had suffered from tropical fevers and other ailments; she had nursed him diligently, always eager to do so, somehow almost relishing the task. He had simply given in to her then, and seemingly to fate as well, in a fashion quite unlike him otherwise — had lain passively, helplessly in her arms, with all his hard, accomplishing spirit temporarily not in evidence.

"I'm okay," he said after several minutes. "You can go back now. Go on — go back to Bob."

"No, I think I'll stay here a while. Should I get you a pail out of the bathroom?"

"Maybe you'd better."

When she came back with the pail, he turned his bony-browed face her way; in this manner, he acknowledged her effort. As his hairline receded, his brow had come to dominate his features even more. It seemed now as if his entire personality were gathered there, in the smooth, finely modeled swell of forehead.

"Rick, Maryanne called us today. Just out of the blue . . . and then it developed that she'd heard about Bob, that he was coming down, and didn't want to be left out. She asked if she could come down this weekend, too. Tomorrow, or maybe on Sunday."

"Maryanne?" Rick seemed utterly perplexed for a moment. "Oh, God, no . . . not *that* Maryanne. Tell her no. For God's sake, tell her she can't come. Not now."

"It'd just be for the day, Rick. She can't stay the whole weekend, she says."

"Please — tell her I'm sick. Tell her it's, I don't know, cholera. Say we've got an epidemic going here."

Another of their oldest Berkeley friends, Maryanne had phoned just before dinner, just as they were sitting down. She proposed a sort of reunion, a gathering of the old crowd. She hadn't seen Rick or Catherine in almost two years, and she had visited at Longfields only once before that.

"She's calmed down quite a bit, Rick. That's what Bob says, anyhow. That she's much easier to take."

"She can't have calmed down all *that* much. Hers was a terminal case, Catherine, a lifelong affliction . . . Where the hell is that pail, anyway?"

Catherine soon returned to the dining room. Bob Stein had gone to bed, as had Gerda. Catherine stayed awake till after two that morning, sipping tea and reading the manuscript Bob had brought her.

≈ ≈ ≈

She had a history of reading his books-in-progress: he insisted on it, actually demanded it of her. He depended on her opinion of his writing, he said, more than he depended on anyone else's, and he sometimes went so far as to incorporate her suggestions into the published texts. This literary intimacy was the remnant of a larger, much more encompassing closeness, the memory of which it both evoked and assumed.

There was a time some years ago when they had all been close, when Bob, Catherine, and Rick had formed a sort of threesome. The heyday of this all-but-romantic triangle had come in the late seventies, right after Catherine's student days. Bob, still a graduate student, had begun to give signs of chronic thesis-struggle. Rick, meanwhile, had become thoroughly sick of the university; he had been there forever, it seemed to him, pretending to teach, pretending to know something. With the idea of providing Bob, as well as himself, with a way out, a means of escape, he accepted an offer from one of his uncles, who had long been enticing him to leave the academy. He would go down to Guatemala, to the jungles on the southwest coast; there he would help reorganize a large, chronically unprofitable banana and avocado plantation, a holding long in the family. Bob Stein could come along, too; he could stay as long as he wanted, living practically for free.

Catherine was also expected to come. Indeed, it was in Guatemala that Rick and Catherine suddenly married — not for any of the ordinary reasons, not out of romantic impulse certainly, but largely to avoid giving offense. The Guatemalans among whom they lived were deeply Catholic, traditional in all respects; they had heard nothing of the advanced attitudes toward matrimony then current in places such as Berkeley, California. Later, however, when Rick and Catherine returned to the States, they were a little ashamed of what they had so rashly done; for some years they spoke of the marriage as a kind of prank, as something not wholly intended.

It was in Guatemala, also, that Catherine achieved a more realistic understanding of what it meant to say that Rick was a Mansure: a scion of that illustrious, multipropertied family. The plantation he had been sent to run, which was called Escambeche, at first seemed nearly coextensive with the province in which it was located; it comprised whole mountain ranges, jungles, rivers, as well as three Indian villages, whose inhabitants, when Rick first came to meet them, greeted him like the junketing son of a distant king. Rick fulminated against these tiresome vestiges, of course, these absurd feudal trappings; he would not have people bowing and scraping before him, no, not Rick Mansure. Soon, however, he came to feel the full, ponderous weight of the economic relations this behavior expressed; and he set to work grimly, in a very Rick-like way, hoping to correct all that was wrong.

"It beats me," he said to Catherine, "how people can live like this, how families can tie up their destinies for generations with a monumental, unmitigated failure. The bookkeeping practices, the line-of-command confusions, managerial absurdities of all kinds . . . this is an economic structure that's literally sick unto death, seriously on the verge of collapse.

But I don't think I'll let it fail, not just yet. Later on, we can turn it upside down if we want. Make a little revolution here, in a strictly economic sense."

The Guerrilla Army of the Poor, called the AGP, had been fitfully active in the region. Rick knew all about the AGP, in fact he approved of the line it took on most issues, including retrocession of foreign-owned holdings. For the time being, however, he was content to play a role rich in irony: he, the academic Marxist, the supporter of progressive movements all over the globe, would masquerade as a *latifundado*, as an old-fashioned profit-seeking, reform-minded estate owner.

Catherine, too, found herself playing an unusual role: she was cast as *la doña del jefe*, the Beautiful Chatelaine, a sort of Lady Bountiful in blue jeans. Nothing was expected of her in the way of effort, and she might have spent all her days simply seeking amusement, as her predecessors, the wives of the previous estate managers, had done. She spoke Spanish fairly well, having studied it for years in school, and she could communicate with the people, especially with the women. Those of mixed blood, the Creole wives and widows, positively doted on her, immediately tried to make a pet of her. They encouraged her in the direction that they would have followed in her place — toward family, comfort, amusement — continually wondering why she, with such a handsome husband, did not yet have any children, at the advanced age of twenty-two. But it was the Indian women, the pure-blooded ones, whose husbands worked the menial jobs on the plantation, who really captured her interest. They carried their babies on their backs, swaddled in gorgeous, handwoven tribal fabrics; they lived in an ancient, simple-seeming way, meanwhile practicing an impeccable hauteur, whose essence seemed to be a calm acceptance of their tragic human helplessness (a helplessness, however, with connotations of murderous strength). These women never doted on her — indeed, they hardly deigned to notice her. But their re-

moteness called out to her. Somehow it made her ashamed of
her own good nature, her casual, openhanded agreeableness.
Not wanting to seem like the typical *norteamericana*, the kind
who makes of herself a parody Indian, in borrowed manner
and dress, she kept a certain personal distance, meanwhile
conspiring to learn as much about them as she could.

Rick encouraged her in her interest. He liked that she was
making many friends, that she was doing something to "im-
prove conditions." There were two small, ungraded schools
nearby, both badly in need of books and other materials.
There was also a medical clinic, very poorly stocked and
indifferently run. Five days a month, a medical student traveled out from Guatemala City in hopes of bringing a modicum of relief, or perhaps just of learning through practice;
and Catherine began to assist him. Soon she felt competent to
give injections and examinations, and she began to diagnose
and treat the common childhood ailments. Then she under-
took a rather grand project: she personally supervised the
construction of a new water system in Panjeb, the most remote of the villages, where the children had diarrhea all the
time, and where the rudimentary sewers also needed replac-
ing. Rick liked to joke that "she thinks she's joined the Peace
Corps — with the one pertinent difference, that her husband
owns the country."

"Oh, Rick," she would answer him, "I don't care if I seem
absurd. Is that what I am, absurd? If you can let people call
you Don Ricardo, then I can plot a few new sewer lines, I
guess. I've always been a bit of a fraud when it came to having
a 'correct political analysis,' anyway — you've always said
so. Secretly I'm just a bleeding heart. A do-gooder."

"Well, you just go right ahead, dear — go right on. Whatever makes you feel good."

Bob Stein finally arrived at Escambeche; he did not stay for
long, however, only for about a month. He remarked on the
great changes in both of them, and then, when he returned to

California, he quickly produced a novel, clearly inspired by his four weeks' stay. It was a long, funny book, still Catherine's favorite among his works. He described the situation of two young Americans, both political radicals, who travel to Central America, there to undergo various seriocomic experiences; the man, the son of a wealthy California family, suffers a sort of nervous breakdown, as his rigid, book-learned ideology confronts the multiform reality of "Cualtenango."

The woman — Catherine read her own portrait with mingled amusement and exasperation — impulsively tries to help the *campesinos*, who are largely baffled by her inexpert efforts. Though wrongheaded about everything, she quickly makes friends, instinctively builds rapport, and the local Indians soon come almost to worship her. In the last third of the book, the heroine experiences a "sensual awakening" as well, which leads to an illicit affair with a Cualtenangoan writer, an indigenous intellectual-cum-revolutionary.

"But *you're* this guy, Bob," Catherine later complained. "You've made him look just like you. It's like the lover in all of Lawrence's novels — somehow, he always sounds just like the author. But tell me, does this mean you've been sweet on me all these years, Bob? Is that what you're trying to say?"

"Well, we know the answer to *that* one, Cath. Don't we?"

Then they both laughed, Catherine a little more uneasily than Bob. But she continued: "What about this, though — what about poor Rick? Look what you've done to him here. This has to hurt him — has to. It's a betrayal, Bob. Not a big, four-star double cross, but a betrayal nonetheless."

"Well, did Rick ever say that? Did he ever actually say to you, 'Bob Stein's done something awful, stabbed me in the back, and I hate him for it, because it really hurts me'?"

After a moment Catherine replied, "No. But you know Rick. Just because it *did* hurt, he wouldn't say anything."

"Well, but that's just my point. I *do* know Rick — I think I know him quite well. And that's exactly what I was trying to say about him. About my character, I mean, the character in my book . . ."

Rick had his revenge, however. Two years later, he produced his own little book, called *Escambeche*. It sold approximately forty times as many copies as had Bob's. Not a novel but a diary, with chapters of political analysis appended, it recounted Rick's attempts to modernize his family's plantation, which, in his fluent telling, was not simply a great property, an estate his uncles happened to own, but a magical world replete with painful memories of his own dead parents. (Rick's mother and father died when he was only six, in a car crash in Juan-les-Pins, in the south of France. He had been raised mostly by his uncle Gower and by Gower's wife, Annalouise.) To Catherine's surprise — she had never before heard Rick say a word about any of this — his parents once vacationed at Escambeche; indeed, they had gone there on their own honeymoon, in 1937–38. In his book, Rick described interviewing a number of the old-timers, people who could still recall the visit by the young, handsome American newlyweds, who had brought along "many bags of golf clubs, Señor, although, as you can see, we have no fields for play here in Escambeche." The contrast between the glamorous, otiose couple of the thirties and Rick and Catherine themselves — grim, driven radicals intent on remaking the world — was developed most skillfully, and Catherine was left wondering whether she would ever really know her husband, ever be taken into his deepest confidence.

"But *why* do I have to read about such things in a book, Rick? How could you *not* have mentioned them when they're so important to you? When you were thinking about them the whole time?"

"But I wasn't, Catherine — not at all. I hardly thought about it the whole time down there. It only became important when I found myself writing . . . that's the way it goes sometimes, you know, you need a pretext. But I hardly remember my parents, to tell the truth. Even before they died, they were always leaving me, always traveling overseas. My father had a special interest in the family shipping lines, and that got him to Europe. And Mother was half Spanish, as you know. She liked to visit her family — I think they lived in Seville."

"Rick, don't you dream about them? Aren't they in your soul, deep down, right at the very center? Aren't you desperate to know all you can about them, every last little thing?"

"No, not at all. In fact, I probably know too much about them now. More than enough."

Rick's book was a great success, in any case. It saw publication in two paperback editions in the first year and was translated into six languages, and it sparked a debate in certain left-wing circles. Poor Bob Stein, whose own book had sunk quickly — it had been widely read only in Berkeley, and only in political Berkeley, at that — never quite forgave him.

T*he next morning,* Saturday, Catherine arose before dawn, by habit. Though she had had only little sleep, she dressed automatically and hurried down to her gardens, in a wide, sloping meadow southwest of the house. She turned on her hoses and began to water. The winter and spring had been dry, and at the end of May she was beginning to see her abundant terraces in a new way: as the typical folly of the overfunded, overambitious amateur gardener who never considers local conditions, who never imagines a drought. The prodigious spread of her terraces had come to seem anomalous; the deep green life of them was almost shocking, poisonously vivid, like a velveteen cocktail dress in a room full of choir robes.

The sun had not yet cleared the hill. Around seven, Bob Stein ambled down from the house, having found no one else awake there; for a long time he simply crouched outside her garden fence, wordlessly watching her work. At one point, he began to whistle "Old MacDonald Had a Farm"; then he stopped.

"What is it, Bob? What's on your mind, anyway?"

"Nothing, Catherine. Absolutely nothing. And I like it like that. I just enjoy watching you, that's all. Especially in rubber boots."

"And muddy pants? And gloves? Is this a fashion statement you can understand, Bob? Is that what you mean?"

Sometime later, after they had walked back to the house, Bob announced to Rick, who had come down to join them at breakfast: "Your wife is a wonder ... a marvelous being, Rick. Everything she does is right, perfect in some special way. When we were down in her meadow I suddenly saw her gardens for what they really are: shrines, potent emblems, symbols of the earthly paradise. All the local spirits had gathered there, I swear, attracted by her passion, her concentration. Whatever she does has a seductive quality, a naturalness ... a stirring sufficiency. It's deeply beautiful, although I mean even more than that ..."

Rick merely sipped his coffee, neither agreeing nor disagreeing. He had heard Bob on this subject before. When Bob was in his intensely lyric mode, he might say the most fulsome, embarrassing things, in a tone only marginally sardonic; one had to let him rattle on, there was simply nothing to be done.

"If I could get just a fraction of the weight she has in everything she does ... well, I'd be happy. I'd be satisfied, finally. One baby zucchini, one sprig of lavender from her garden, has more conviction than all the words I produce in a month — or a decade, for that matter. When she decides to do something, the impulse just flows out of her. It instantly takes its most suitable form. I, on the other hand, have to strain and pervert to get any impression of reality. Then I distance myself from it — I pull back, to show how 'aware' I am, how wise to my own pathetic tricks."

Catherine, not quite sure what he meant to say, pointed out that growing vegetables and writing novels were different occupations. She might seem "natural" or "sufficient" in what she did, but only because she attempted so little; she had always lacked ambition, as they all knew, just as she had always lacked any particular talent.

"No, Catherine," Bob insisted. "A thousand times no. Some people are just blessed with hands that can build, hearts that understand. Life takes a more interesting shape around them. I knew this about you from early on. I remember how it always used to amaze me. You seemed to know by instinct just what to say, what to do in every situation. People became less neurotic around you somehow ..."

Rick, reaching some sort of limit, cleared his throat dryly. He looked faintly green this morning, after his night of stomach trouble. Having noticed Bob's new manuscript, which had been left on Catherine's bedside table, he asked if this represented Bob's fifth "little comedy" — or was it his sixth?

"Only my fourth, Rick. Only number four, I'm sorry to say. After so much painful striving, there should be twenty volumes by now, at least . . . but there aren't. Too bad. I had always hoped to be prolific. I'd always wanted to be bold and facile — more like you, I guess."

"Facile? Is that what you think I am, Bob — merely facile? Well, I don't take offense. It's just not in me anymore. I have no writer's ego left, none at all. It got flayed out of me, on my own number three."

"Oh, but I *liked* your number three, Rick — really. A little thin, perhaps, but clean. You had really mastered the diary form by the third go-round, I thought. You'd finally triumphed over the material."

Rick, after a thoughtful moment, smiled crookedly. His third book had been treated unkindly by the critics, even by most of his former political friends, who called it repetitive and stale. They had seen evidence of "neo-conservative drift" in its arguments. After three books written in less than two years (the last having appeared in 1983), he had published nothing.

In a calm, they-know-not-what-they-do tone of voice he now declared, "It may have been obvious to you, Bob, that I only had a couple of ideas, a couple of things to say. But I had to discover that unhappy fact for myself, by writing them over and over. And now — I've left the field to my betters. To the true masters."

"Rick, I really did like number three. I even teach it in my Deep Journal class, the one I give at the Extension. All the scribbling housewives love it. The secret, passionate amateur writers — they're all most deeply impressed."

"Well, I'm honored, Bob. How kind of you to let me know."

Young Ben, followed by his governess, entered the kitchen at that moment. They had already eaten breakfast, Karen told Catherine. Ben asked if he could play video games on Rick's computer; Rick made no response, but Catherine said that they would probably be doing something else this morning, maybe going for a horseback ride. (Ben had his own ponies.) He seemed neither excited nor disappointed to hear this; he stood motionless just behind his mother's chair, pursing his lips and blinking, an arm thrown idly across her back.

When *Maryanne came* (despite Rick's opposition, which had lessened when he began to feel better), Catherine had already finished Bob's manuscript. But she told him that she still had some chapters to read; she was puzzled, didn't know what to say to him, and wanted more time to compose a response.

"Oh, it's bogging down, is it?" he worried. "Getting thick?"

"No, Bob, it reads very well. But it'll take me a few more days. What if I mail it back to you, with comments?"

"Of course, Catherine. Whatever you say."

She could feel his intense disappointment, however. He could hardly let himself breathe before knowing what she thought of his manuscript. Among his other odd misconceptions of her, he considered her to be a "truly objective reader" (whatever that was); as he had said to her, "I count on you to respond just like a regular person. It's one of your best impersonations."

On Sunday he said, "I know it's unfair of me, Catherine. Believe me, I wouldn't do this to anyone else. But you're one of the few people I trust anymore. As strange as it sounds, I believe implicitly in your integrity."

"You ought to believe in your own more, Bob. You've never shown me anything that wasn't first rate."

"Well, that's because I pick what I show you so carefully. Most of what I write is trash. Really awful stuff."

Maryanne, whom Rick had quarreled with some years before, arrived in a dither, complaining about her absurd work schedule. She had been in the office even that morning, and by the time she returned to Berkeley that night there would be half a dozen phone messages, all work-related.

She had gone to law school at the advanced age of thirty-four; previously she had been a private school teacher, a social worker, and a therapist of a sort (one with a master's in public health). She had quarreled with Rick during the period of her most intense, most unforgiving feminist self-discovery, which for her had come rather late. It was curious, then, that she now found herself in a booming law practice limited to divorce actions, and that her clients were almost all men.

"I just do a better job for them," she said. "It's like being a male novelist, Bob, and writing about women. You just welcome the artificiality of it. If I was representing my own sex, I'd be too invested all the time, too aware of the painful issues. This way, it's a matter of doing a clean, efficient job, nothing more. Even so, I do get to caring about the poor bastards sometimes . . . some of them don't deserve the messes they've made of their lives."

"But Maryanne," Bob reminded her, "these are *men* you're talking about. These are *oppressors*. Why should they get a fair shake in court, after all?"

"Nobody gets a fair shake in court, Bob. That's not what it's about. Divorce is a disaster — it's a way of letting your own blood, of slitting your own throat. Sometimes one or the other party is clearly monstrous, and then it's probably justified, but only probably. In sixty, seventy percent of my cases, I'd say, the horror and humiliation have no conceivable rationale. These marriages could be stitched back together, if there was only the will."

Maryanne, who had gotten more style conscious in the last few years, now had little in her bearing to suggest the radical of the early seventies. She was even taller than Catherine, a willowy, small-chested woman, a bit weak-looking. Her large, oval gray eyes had a moistly dreamy cast, and Catherine thought her very attractive. In the old days, she always hid these tender, winning eyes behind spectacles.

She had never married, though for the last several years she had been living with one man. The great love of her life, odd as it was for Catherine to contemplate, had probably been Rick Mansure; back in the old days, when Rick was the great campus figure, there had been a one-sided, intense, and enduring bloom of interest. Maryanne, always contending, always debating, irritating in her dialectical energy, had made of herself an indispensable adjunct, a sort of theoretical conscience to Rick's authoritative maximum-leader. Rick had smiled upon her, unpredictably, just as he had also smiled upon Bob, who, though undistinguished in most ways, had had the knack of keeping him interested.

"Catherine, where is Rick, anyway? Where's the great one?"

"He's upstairs, Maryanne. Working on his computer. He's not feeling too well. He's been sick on and off all weekend."

"Oh, I see."

Maryanne would not be offended. Or if she was, she would not show it. She had long ago accommodated herself to the idea that Rick no longer cared for her — that he could be expected to greet her coolly, if at all, after long spells apart.

"If he wants to avoid me, well, that's fine. But I'll tell you what I want to do. Let's go off somewhere. Let's go exploring. Let's get your horses and ride down to the big forest — you know, the really wild part, halfway down the mountain."

"But we were riding down there yesterday, Maryanne. I'm afraid Bob's about horse-ridden out. The old cowpoke's saddle sore."

"Let's walk then. I don't care. I remember it from last time. It was exquisite."

Bob, wearing a daypack, led the way. (He knew the route from yesterday.) He wore shorts despite Catherine's warnings about poison oak, and he pushed his way through the brush with his pale, shaggily hairy legs churning comically, like some muscular wind-up toy. Maryanne and Catherine hung back a few yards, and in the easy going along the fire trails they covered the usual subjects: Maryanne's love life; the fates of several friends they had in common; Maryanne's frustration at not being able to get pregnant, now that she half wanted to be a mother. In the warm, humming quiet of the May morning they achieved a comfortable pace, the flow of their discussion not unlike this unconscious physical effort.

"I don't know how you live out here, Cath — I think I'd go crazy. It's just too perfect. I can't take beautiful surroundings day in and day out. They don't correspond to my interior landscape."

"Rick has something bothering him these days," Catherine responded, not very appositely. "He's entered another of his hard phases — when absolutely everything about him gets hard. Even his body gets hard, wooden . . ."

"There was always something about him. Some remote inner place," Maryanne said, "that nobody else went to, except maybe you, I don't know. What is it in women that makes us respond to such characters? Some genetic flaw? An ancient adaptation that just doesn't work anymore? I'm speaking generally, you understand . . . I don't really know Rick anymore. I try to remember what it is that I did to him, what made him decide he couldn't stand me, and for the life of me I can't. Somehow I just impinged. I got too close."

Catherine replied consolingly: "Rick's just strange. He doesn't have friendships, not in the way other people do. It sounds horrible, I know, but he can suddenly become completely rational, step back and say that something just isn't working out, that it's gotten unproductive. Then he shuts off. God, it frightens me, but I think Ben's like that too . . . it's that way of breaking everything down. Always analyzing feelings, and not allowing too many of them, either. Gerda calls him the little professor. She says he's cold. It's not being cold, though — it's something more. I don't quite understand it . . ."

Maryanne said that there was nothing wrong with Ben; on the contrary, he was a wonderful, surprising boy. She had taught seven-year-olds herself, and she had seen other little boys who were much like him, who had entered that cut-and-dried phase.

"They can have powerful, astonishing minds at that age. They learn to be rational first off, and the other only later. It's their favorite tool. It leads to everything else, in a way. And it gives them a feeling of great control. I think they can be a bit afraid of their big, bursting heads at that age . . . but don't worry, really. Be thankful instead."

The forest, beginning half a mile below the house, had a strange character. By degrees they found themselves in a denser, much more tightly woven woods, where trees grew taller and broader. According to Gerda, a stretch of the forest, almost a thousand acres, had never been logged or otherwise put to use, and it was easy to believe that this, where they were walking, was part of that ancient remnant. The trees were an odd mix. Douglas fir predominated, but madrones, oaks, bays, buckeyes, tanbarks, maples, and alders throve where conditions permitted. It was not a feeling of a park-like, cathedral-of-the-trees sort of forest, but of something rougher, more ragged that one had; great swatches of treetop canopy were missing, as if violently torn away, and in these places the light poured in and allowed brush to take over.

Some blackberry thickets extended over entire acres. The densest parts, where the poison oak and chaparral grew together, held a special interest for Catherine, who, with her trail crew, had often had to slash her way through.

Bob, still out in front, unexpectedly reached an overlook. As the women caught up he began taking in great draughts of air, somehow contriving to look like a sturdy Swiss mountaineer, one exulting in the Alpine freshness.

"What's that smell?" he asked suddenly. "Is it water, or rain? The old trapper thinks he smells water. Just like a mule, he sniffs it miles away."

Far below was a lake. Catherine now pointed it out. It seemed very small at this distance, intensely green in its gray-blue, red-brown forest setting.

"The old trapper has found a pond, all right," she admitted. "But can he get us down from here? Without having us break our necks?"

"Catherine, do you really own all this?" Maryanne asked, looking frankly shocked, almost fearful at the thought.

"Not me, Maryanne. But Rick's great-aunt does ... just about everything you can see in that direction. And in that one, too, I guess."

"Well, but to think that anyone does ..."

Catherine knew a path down from the overlook. After a moment she found the vague beginnings of it, and they carefully began descending the earthen cliff, following the switchbacks worn by deer and other game. They aimed for the pond, but halfway down they lost sight of it, and it took them forty-five minutes more to find the lake through the brush.

"Oh, Catherine. What a jewel. What a treasure," said the intoxicated Maryanne.

"Are you going in? The water's not very cold, you know."

"I'm not sure," Maryanne replied. "Are there snapping turtles, or anything like that?"

The pond, viewed now more obliquely, was greenish-blue in color, tending to black in its depths. On all sides the scrub forest enclosed it, but the western edge was slightly less densely overgrown. A muddy, single-file path had led them around to this side.

On the shore they laid out a sheet, and Catherine unpacked picnic goods from Bob's knapsack. But before they began eating, they simply lay in the sun for a few minutes —

Catherine's determination to dive in quickly, before she had cooled off, foundered on a sudden feeling of shyness.

"At least, I don't *remember* its being cold," she said. "And no — there aren't any turtles."

"I'm not so good in cold water," Bob Stein complained. "It's you women who have an extra layer of fat — that subcutaneous sort of thing, extra insulation and so on."

"I don't have any subcutaneous anything," Maryanne replied, and she proceeded to display her lack of curves. "But at least I'm not a wimp, Bob, like you are. 'The old trapper,' indeed."

"Oh, *am* I a wimp? Is that what I am in your eyes? Only a wimp?"

"Yes. And not even that, usually."

But it was Bob, a few minutes later, who began to undress. Catherine pretended not to watch. But he was directly in her line of sight, and there was something deliciously silly about the way he carefully, surreptitiously shucked each item of clothing, then immediately folded it, leaving in the end two neat piles, with a sock on top of each.

He looked like something not quite human then: solidly built, nervously powerful, and covered from neck to heels with soft, slightly matted black hair. For a moment he stood in the shallow water, facing away from them. Both Maryanne and Catherine were observing him frankly now, Catherine with a grave expression, as if the sight of his feral nakedness were something she could not quite comprehend. Maryanne was even amused.

"Bob, I think you forgot to comb your back today. And your thighs, for that matter."

"I heard that, Maryanne. I hear everything you say, and what you think, too."

When he dove in — really just floundered forward, making a wallow — Maryanne laughed aloud.

"God, we do betray ourselves, don't we?" she said a moment later.

"Well — but how do you mean?"

"Oh, I don't know. He seems like he's only a mind sometimes. A rampaging intellect. But then you see what his head sits on. The spunky little faun of him. The sexy, absurd little package . . . I'd like to go in there and drown him, maybe."

But to go in, she had first to get undressed herself. And it was odd how Maryanne's saucy, twinkle-in-the-eye manner leached away; as she struggled with her blue jeans, then with her sweatshirt, her movements became constrained, almost surreptitious, much like Bob's. She turned the front of her long, creamily white body away from Catherine — away from Catherine, who knew it well, knew its history through and through, and accepted it.

Then overcoming this instinctive, perhaps vestigial impulse to modesty, she bolted straight into the water, taking a few long-limbed, springy strides down the bank; the sight of her narrow white back, with only the slight flare of buttocks suggesting soft flesh, was like an image of nymphs gamboling, seizing the air, claiming the space. Maryanne swam out toward Bob, intent on attack. But at the last instant she veered off, turned onto her back, and circled him lazily. Bob splashed her then, and she spit water at him, and they closed and began to wrestle. The sounds of their battle carried gently back to Catherine, who heard them as if from a distance: the surrounding forest and the looming, brush-covered cliff muffled and almost extinguished the commotion.

Twenty minutes later, as Catherine, now pinkly naked herself, roamed away from the shore, looking for a bush to pee under, she had a great fright. When she saw the stranger standing there — a fair-skinned man dressed in dusty work clothes — she gasped and covered her breasts with her forearms, not out of modesty, but in a gesture of self-defense.

"What — Oh! Oh!" she exclaimed rather absurdly.

"I'm sorry. I'm very sorry."

But he continued to look at her, as if helpless not to. Then he shook his head. And after another moment — the whole encounter took only a few seconds — she whirled away, and she heard him walking off through the undergrowth.

On her bare feet she ran quickly, incautiously, in the opposite direction. She scraped her legs on stiff branches, and when she reached Bob and Maryanne, who were sunning themselves on the sheet, lying peacefully side by side, she burst into bewildered tears.

J*ust someone* from town, someone from town," Rick said airily.

"But how do you know?"

"Catherine, do you really think this forest is ours? That we control it? People go walking in there all the time. Deer hunters, bird watchers. Local kids just fooling around."

"Rick, this wasn't a kid. And he'd been watching us for a long time. I'm sure of it. He looked like a workman of some kind. And he'd been doing something in there that made him all dirty. Building something, I think."

Rick had so little patience these days — he had patience only for his own work, his thoughts. He could not understand, did not want to, how Catherine could be so seriously disturbed having simply run into a trespasser on a remote corner of their land.

"Tell Bob I want to talk to him, will you? Has he left yet?"

"No. And Maryanne's here too. Aren't you even going to say hello?"

No — that was out of the question. It was simply impossible; Catherine had to understand that, had to. He waved her out of the bedroom, his patience now exhausted. Catherine had to go downstairs by herself and make excuses.

"Maryanne, he's just too sick. He's got a stomach virus, something like that. Bob, would you take that bottle of water up? I forgot to."

"All right, Catherine, sure."

"But — why can't *I* go up, too?" asked the now sun-reddened Maryanne.

"Well, because he's just in a funk. He's in one of his shitty moods, that's all. The kind that can last for months."

That night, in bed with her ailing husband, Catherine knew that she wanted to make love: the signs came to her dimly, waywardly, in the form of halfhearted thoughts of sensual moments, of how, for example, it had felt today, walking through the seething woods. She thought that it was rather comical, that her adventure with her friends, swimming in the cold green of the pond, with her breasts and thighs vulnerable to the depths (as if there might be monsters lurking below), should eventuate in this particular urge, this certain type of impulse; why not, after a day of exercise, want to read a good book? Or write a letter home to Mother? Why should there be only *this* that seemed to answer — why not some other, more sensible gesture?

But in any case, she put her hand lightly on Rick's chest. And he, though he knew her moods, took all her meanings quickly, remained obstinately still. Then she touched his hard, unforthcoming abdomen, much strengthened recently by hundreds of sets of leg lifts (he worked out dutifully, often five days a week). Men in their mid-forties, she understood, often began going slack, became gut-heavy, but Rick had consciously decided to go in the other direction; she appreciated his effort, but sometimes a feeling of hopelessness came over her, as if he were only becoming more wooden, insensate as a result, as if the cost of his being so superbly in shape was a certain loss of aliveness. A lessening of response deep down in his cells.

"Rick, you don't want this. Am I right?"

"Yes, Catherine, you're right. I just don't feel like it now. I feel . . . angry, I think."

"Angry? But angry about what?"

"I don't know. I just don't know."

She drew away then, feeling only mildly put out. Lately she had been the initiator of this sort of contact; she often came to him out of desperation, turned to him with a feeling almost of hopelessness. And there often resulted an exchange much like this one: Rick feeling reluctant, imperiously out of sorts, not quite responding, and Catherine somehow feeling compelled to find out why.

"But are you angry with *me*, Rick? Is it something I've done?"

"No, Catherine. I just feel funny. Physically not quite right. I'm still sick, I think. And I'm angry about that, I guess."

"But why be angry, Rick? Everyone gets sick sometimes. It's natural, normal. You don't have to be super-healthy all your life — every minute of it. What are you trying to prove, anyway?"

"I'm not trying to *prove* anything, Catherine. And please, spare me the philosophy, the lecture about 'learning to relax.' Letting things just be, and going with the flow and all."

But after a while, he turned onto his side. Now they were facing each other. Then he touched her lightly on her hip, stroking along her flank, with the fabric of her nightgown caught in his fingers. He seemed dimly present in these fingers — his spirit was elsewhere, otherwise engaged.

"You feel . . . very good," he said, from what seemed a distance. "I love your breasts, Catherine. They smell good, like new fruit."

"Do they? Well, just so long as they don't look like old fruit, I guess . . ."

As if responding to a challenge, he touched her more avidly, became substantially more present. Then they made love for a while; his feeling of exhaustion and her feeling of estrangement somehow became the pretexts, the very reasons to be doing such a thing. And afterward, when they had settled back, pulling the blankets over them, the house became profoundly quiet; Catherine thought that she could hear the night itself, the moonless May night, like a softly settling, endlessly falling fabric of darkness.

S*he wrote* a letter to Bob Stein:

"As you must be aware," she said in part, "your manuscript made me very uncomfortable. I've read all your other books, and when it seemed that a character bore me some resemblance, I was always in equal parts flattered and irritated, but able to 'separate' and to give you some kind of non-subjective response. God help me, I think I can probably do that this time, too, Bob. *But you're going too far now.*

"Knowing you, it seems likely that you need me as a spur to your creativity, that the prospect of completing a manuscript in which I figure, and then of giving it to me to be made uncomfortable, excites you. I don't presume to judge this rather bizarre mechanism, but I must point out the resemblance to the situation of the proverbial dirty old man in the subway car, who exposes himself to young girls — in your case, to only one (old) girl, over and over. Of course, you're well aware of this. I know your enduring need to mock yourself, to betray yourself, which is the other side of your ability to see the ridiculous in everything else. You like to shame yourself a little — just a little — in front of others.

"Without sounding like too much of a prude, I need to remind you that I'm a married woman, Bob. How do you think Rick will feel when he inevitably picks up a copy of your latest and reads about someone named 'Katherine,' who secretly, half-unwittingly regrets her long marriage, who languishes sadly in submission to a cruel, self-obsessed husband who has never 'really understood' her? Someone who has the qualities of a 'primitive generative goddess' (there you go again, Bob, inflating, mythifying), who unwittingly awaits the arrival of an intense, ultra-masculine figure who alone can release her from her tragic suppression? I must admit that I read the early parts of your story with interest, as I am always, like other guilty feminists, intrigued by the theme of the sexually sleeping princess, the woman who needs to be — *aches* to be — ravaged by a dark intruder, a sexual savior of some kind. But then I arrived at your scenes of 'salvation.' Your passages of forceful, shameless hyper-sex, if I may describe them that way. If I say that I was fairly disappointed — not entirely unmoved, but not as stirred as I had hoped to be — I intend no critique of your purely technical, merely writerly skills. The story of 'Kathy' and her lover builds organically, I suppose, pays off on expectations, but the passion that they generate has, for me, a strangely theoretical quality. It's as if you had brought your characters together, prepared the bed for them to lie down in, and at the last moment had to force them to get at it.

"A word about your 'Kathy,' Bob. Please, please stop idealizing women. Stop imagining mysterious, primordial powers within us, exquisite sensitivities and vulnerabilities, treasures belonging to the one sex alone. I know we've discussed this before, because it's always puzzled me, given your dour clarity on most other subjects — possibly, you feel helpless to change at this point, since this is the direction that your inspiration seems to want to take, no matter what. But the result is that your women lack the living-breathing reality that allows one to imagine them ever enjoying sex, for instance. Someone like 'Kathy' can only be worshiped, never loved; and the men who accept her on these terms are fundamentally uninteresting, almost inert. They will always stand a certain respectful distance away, looking up at her, acknowledging by their every gesture her profound superiority. I hardly need to point out that this arrangement lacks a feeling of sex . . . except in a perverse way, it stirs up absolutely nothing, awakens nothing in either the head or the heart. A woman wants to be known, you see, this is a primary drive, usually; known all the way through, if possible, but only by another confused, fluid, hurt human creature. Sex with another cunning, flawed, mysterious being — that's the only way to go. That's the secret . . ."

She continued in this vein, nervously caviling, for twelve closely written pages.

She could never tell him the truth, of course; she could only hint, with her talk of the "shame" he must be feeling, at her actual judgment. The last half of his book was a tiresome, graphic account of "Rheinhardt," the hero, having his way with the estimable heroine; who was so plainly Catherine herself, from her physical characteristics down to her customary turns of thought and phrase, that the model for this paragon felt herself continually squirming. It was much like viewing a masturbatory fantasy, a videotape for example, and recognizing oneself in the central role; being forced to see oneself as the sole, obsessive object of a demeaning and repetitive action. There was precisely the look on the narrator's face (a face Catherine often imagined for third-person masculine voices in books) that she recalled from boring French movies, the kind in which Jean-Pierre Léaud, or some other self-intoxicated confessor, endlessly spills his thoughts head-on into the camera. No doubt Bob's justification would be that he was simply "giving way": refusing to censor his inner voice, surrendering to it wholly. Curious, but this ostensibly honest act, this exercise in literary courage, produced what would surely be his first really commercial work: the resemblance to other affectless, sex-drenched novels of the last few years was too patent not to promise big rewards.

≈ ≈ ≈

A week later, early in June, Rick asked her casually, "Well, did you like it after all? You know — Bob's new book?"

"Oh, it was okay, I guess. Well written, I have to say. But at the same time . . . hateful. Deeply embarrassing to me."

"So — I take it we're in this one as well?"

"You could say so. The main character's name is Katherine, believe it or not. And she lives with her wealthy husband on a great estate. In northern California, I think it is."

"What happens to him this time?" Rick asked. "Does he get a wasting disease? Is he run over by a car?"

"He just sort of fades away, that's all. Everyone kind of agrees that he's not very important. He's gone by the second chapter."

Rick shook his head mock-mournfully. This was all as he had suspected, or perhaps he didn't like it that "his" character had been given such short shrift. "You know, it's the one thing Bob and I never discuss. I've never said a word to him about it, and of course he never mentions it. I'm not aware of anyone in literary history ever having maintained such a long, outwardly warm friendship with the models for his characters . . . it beggars belief. It's not even a question of a *roman à clef* anymore, just a continual, shameless appropriation of our lives, or what he thinks are our lives."

Catherine agreed, but she didn't want to talk about it just now. She winced to think of how Rick would respond when he actually read the new one. "But how are you feeling today, Rick?" she inquired. "What did Goldfisch have to say?"

Goldfisch was Rick's internist. Rick had continued to feel a little under the weather, off and on.

"More tests, he says. Always more tests. He doesn't really know, I think."

"And how's the hand?"

"Still a bit numb. And I'm numb on the other side now, too."

There came a day, four weeks later, when Rick suddenly

announced to her: "I know what it is. I'm pretty sure now — absolutely sure, actually. Goldfisch isn't convinced, and the neurologist says it could still be a tumor, but I think I know. I really do."

"Well, what do you know, Rick? Has something showed up?"

Rick had never told her this before. He was a little embarrassed to be telling her about it now, another secret from his past, from his shadowed, bungled childhood. Well — but he had had polio, yes, childhood polio. He had spent three months in a hospital, in 1954, at the age of nine and a half. They thought he had recovered completely.

"They *thought* you had, Rick? But how can there be any doubt about that? You're not crippled, you don't have one leg shorter than the other, or anything like that. Of course you've recovered."

"No, Catherine — you see, polio can recur. It sometimes returns later on in life, in one's thirties or forties."

He had known for a few weeks now, he said. He'd had a special feeling, a series of strange sensations that at first puzzled him. Finally he realized: these were exactly the feelings he had had that time as a kid. All those years ago, lying immobile in the hospital bed, sometimes for weeks at a stretch (because moving increased one's chances of permanent joint contractures), he had felt in his body a particular way, a frighteningly odd way. And he was only now re-experiencing these sensations. The simplest thing to say about it was that you felt the nerve impulses traveling through your body — going here and there, all the way out to the ends of your limbs. Normally, nerve impulses traveled all in a flash, of course, and you weren't consciously aware of them. But when you became sick this way, you felt every centimeter of their passage through your flesh.

"Rick, is it just this strange feeling you have? Or has someone actually done some positive tests?"

"They're doing more tests now, Catherine. Another tissue culture tomorrow, and on Monday, a spinal tap. And then who knows what else. But I know what they'll find."

On Tuesday he came home triumphant. He was right after all: it was polio, as he had thought. Technically speaking, it was a recrudescence of his childhood infection. All of the specialists, with all their sophisticated evaluations and tests, had overlooked this most obvious possibility until he, the much-abused patient, finally raised it.

"Newsome, the neurologist, actually apologized to me. I couldn't believe it when he did. I'd never heard a medical specialist say he'd made a mistake; it came as a complete shock. The words just flew out of his mouth, then hung there, blazing."

"Rick — how do you feel now? What can they do for you now?"

"Well, I feel pretty weak. But besides the headache from the spinal — which wasn't necessary, as it turns out — I don't feel too bad. I'm supposed to have a lot of bed rest, that's all."

"Oh Rick . . . poor Rick. I'm going to help you get better. You'll see. It'll come out all right. I'm sure it will."

She put her arms around him and pulled him against her, feeling him stiff, wooden, strangely distant, with this bit of bad news to report. His own setbacks, his rare failures in life, had always before left him seemingly slightly puzzled, with a lopsided grin on his face.

"Rick — I'm just glad it's not something worse. Aren't you? We can be thankful for that, can't we?"

"No, it's not something worse, Catherine. And I'll be fine. I'm sure I will. I'm not really worried."

The prognosis was excellent, as the doctors liked to say. Permanent paralysis was unlikely (it was rarely a factor in these recrudescent cases), and they had various drugs now, powerful anti-viral agents, some of them developed in the course of AIDS research. Rick would have to make adjustments in his way of living, of course; he would have to cut back on his exercising, for example, but Goldfisch expected him to be cured in six weeks or sooner.

"It's just the weakness — that's what you mainly have to deal with, they say. A continual quailing in your limbs. But I'm adjusting to that. They say I can work, just not to overdo it. I think I'll start by going to the city three days a week. See how that turns out."

This sense of euphoria, however, of finally knowing what was wrong, didn't last. Even the thrill of triumphing over the doctors soon faded. By the end of July, Rick was unable to go to work at all; he simply lay in bed, too weak to move, for days on end. Catherine and Gerda nursed him, with some help from the girls who worked in the house; and gradually, Catherine began to see that his recovery might take much longer than expected, might go on for many weeks, or even months.

T*he fall came,* and Ben went back to school. Catherine harvested the bounty of her gardens and went often to the town of Cuervo, where she sold her surplus in the health food store. Ben was now in second grade, and after another titanic battle she had gotten Rick to agree to let him go to the local school rather than to one of the prestigious private schools in Palo Alto. Catherine was herself a product of public schools, ordinary public schools. As long as her son was happy and seemed to be learning, she opposed taking him out of the local swim, the somewhat rough-and-tumble world of the kids growing up in the canyon.

"All right, but next year he goes to Winston Academy," Rick insisted. "You promised."

"No, I didn't promise anything, Rick. I said if he seemed to be outgrowing the school or getting bored, I'd consider it. We'll see at the end of the year."

"I just hope you're not going to regret this somewhere down the line, Catherine. When it turns out he wasn't being taught his fundamentals."

Rick took only a casual interest in whether Ben knew his fundamentals, however. It was Catherine who volunteered at the local school, who served on a committee of the PTA, who bothered to get to know his teachers. Rick seemed to be waiting for that day when Ben would suddenly address him as an adult; this interim period, when signs of sometimes startling intellectual development showed against a background of slow, fairly normal emotional growth, was only to be gotten through.

"He's very bright, Catherine, you have to admit that. All

his teachers say so. That we should put him ahead a grade, maybe even two."

"Nobody's ever said that to me, Rick, not that I heard. They say that next year he'll be in a combined three-four class, so he can study math at a higher level if he wants. But that's all."

"Can you imagine what they teach them down there? They don't even have computers. Do they?"

"A couple of Tandys, I think. But he gets plenty of time on computers, I would say. More than enough."

≈ ≈ ≈

Catherine had lost some weight, and when her sister, Muriel, came to visit them that October, much was made of her condition, of the presumed emotional/psychological upset causing this change. Muriel said that Catherine was the one who ought to be in bed, not Rick; that Rick was engineering everything in his customary way, so that he, and he alone, would be catered to. But Muriel had never really liked Rick. She found him admirable, intelligent, and attractive, but somehow not the sort to whom she wished her sister's happiness to be entrusted. Muriel was thirty-nine now, divorced, an associate professor at Tecumseh College, in Portland, Oregon. She was on sabbatical this year and had almost completed her fourth book, a study of twins separated shortly after birth.

"In the late 1870s," she explained to Catherine, "four thousand children were sent to live with foster parents in the Pacific Northwest. Most of them were orphans, and of those we have records of, a hundred and forty were twins. Of these, eighty were identicals. I'm concentrating on the twenty-four pairs that split up before the age of three. In some cases, there are parallel dynasties descended from twins who weren't aware of each other's existence. We see amazing correspondences, familial similarities down into the fourth and fifth generations, and beyond sometimes."

Catherine had read all of her sister's books, and she would read this one, too. She could often see the germ of interest that had gotten a project under way — in this case, it was the question of identical twinship, which had a certain inherent fascination. But then the poor, frail mote of human appeal inevitably got buried, lost under layer upon layer of statistical demonstration.

"Catherine, do you get away anymore? Do you ever go to San Francisco, or to Berkeley? What about all your old friends? You used to be surrounded by interesting people, I always thought. But now you seem alone."

"Do I, Muriel? That sounds bad, all right. But I've got Rick, don't I? And Ben. And Gerda too. You always make out that I'm worse off than I am. I'm in a fallow period, that's all. As soon as Rick gets better we'll start traveling again. We've already talked about it. He's been reconsidering things, trying to sort out the direction he wants to take with his life."

"You know, it's like the sixties never happened for you, Catherine. You're his wife, his loyal helpmeet, and the discussion ends right there. Think of it — you're thirty-five now —"

"Thirty-six."

"All right, thirty-six, then. And you've never had a job. Never hit on what you want to be. If Mother had been a helpless sort, or if we'd come from that kind of class background, maybe I could understand. But I've always assumed that what you did was central in life . . . you find something you like, that uses your talents, and then you make your way in the world. *Especially* if you're a woman. This idea of being a helpless dependent went out some time ago, I seem to have heard . . ."

It was in vain that Catherine pointed out how busy she

always was, how fully occupied she felt: that she cultivated her gardens, sold her produce, and taught a course each spring (Bed Preparation, under sponsorship of the Starry Plough, the health food store); that she took care of the house, supervised the running of the entire estate, and served as wife and mother too. Admittedly, she was a throwback — a hopeless Neanderthal — a disgrace to her sex, as disgraces were currently reckoned. But usually she felt fulfilled in her humdrum, domestic round of life.

"No, I don't think you're fulfilled at all. Let me finish, Catherine, let me finish . . . I see you getting more vague, more passive. Sinking into yourself. It's not even a matter of what you do or don't do, you just seem diminished. You don't impress me with the tremendous feeling of life, or whatever it was you used to have. Your bursting vitality."

"Vitality? Did I really have some, Muriel? Funny . . . I always thought I was barely managing to get through. I was faking it. Pretending to know who I was, and what I wanted to do, and what everything meant, if anything . . ."

Muriel, in her perspicacious, scholarly way, had made a great discovery about Rick. The semi-invalided fellow was not suffering from a recrudescence of his childhood polio; no, that was impossible, as it was impossible to be infected with the virus a second time. What Rick had was a progressive impairment of his neuromuscular function, consequent upon the earlier infection. This syndrome, which was widely recognized, was now known as "PPMR, or PPRM, something like that. I don't remember exactly what it stands for. But something."

"Actually," Rick corrected her, when Catherine informed him of Muriel's diagnosis, "it's PPMA. And it stands for progressive post-poliomyelitis muscular atrophy. It's not so well known — not at all. What seems to happen is that the motor neurons that survived the childhood disease are called on to do extra work, to direct many more muscle fibers than usual, and after working overtime for years, they begin to burn out. Usually, it's in the patient's thirties or forties. And there's no known cure. No effective treatment."

Using two canes, Rick had hobbled down to the veranda, where the two sisters were sitting together, drinking margaritas. He remained standing, since getting up from a chair gave him trouble these days.

"But Rick, why in the world wouldn't you tell me? If you already knew this, why not let me know?" Catherine asked. "Don't I have some rights? Shouldn't I be told such things?"

"Yes, Catherine. You have rights, plenty of rights. My function is just to waste away from the damned thing; yours, to hear all about it. Even before I do, if possible."

Serawan Goldfisch, Rick's internist (who was coming to seem ever more inept), had figured out what was going on only two weeks before. The powerful, frightening anti-viral medicines that Rick had been taking had thus been completely beside the point.

"Goldfisch has a chair at UC Med Center, for Christ's sake — a distinguished professorship, believe it or not. And still he didn't know. He read about it by chance, in a medical journal, he says. Probably while waiting at the dentist's office."

"It's probably the same journal I read," Muriel put in. "As soon as I heard you were sick, I ran to my computer. I accessed everything there is on polio. I knew what you had in about four minutes, as I recall."

"Muriel, I'll be bringing you all my medical business from now on. You take Blue Cross, don't you?"

"Don't you want a margarita, Rick?" she inquired. "I made them myself, you know. From my own special recipe."

"I remember your margaritas fondly, Muriel. Very fondly. Unfortunately, I'm not allowed to drink anymore. When they don't know what you've got, they begin by making your life as miserable as possible. Hoping, I guess, to jolt you into a cure."

Rick had put on weight lately; since ending his course of anti-viral medicines, he had gained fifteen pounds. His doctors claimed to find this encouraging. Aside from his muscular disability, which was currently in a pronounced, rather bothersome phase, he looked much like a man in the bloom of health, with just the right amount of meat on his bones. This paradoxical air of well-being was the result of much bed rest, undoubtedly; of calm, non-goal-oriented time spent at home. Rick ascribed it to his organic diet as well, and to certain herbal remedies that he had recently begun to take.

"Come on, Catherine," he urged. "Don't look at me that way. Don't get mad. You know I would've told you eventually. I just didn't think it was important."

"Oh, I know you didn't think so, Rick. And that's what galls me. I'm just your wife — it doesn't matter what I know, or when I do. Well, you can keep it all to yourself from now on. You make me crazy sometimes, with your prideful, unostentatious suffering, which is such a sham, really. You deny yourself, then deny everyone else around you, too."

Rick would only smile at her. He could hardly take this outburst seriously, his posture seemed to imply. Muriel, however, squirmed on her canvas-covered lounge chair. She had rarely heard her sister and brother-in-law disagree before; certainly, never in such tones, never with such an air of conviction.

"I'll be a good boy from now on," he promised, "and I'll even take my medicine, if you make me. And I'll go to bed on time."

"Do whatever you want, Rick. Whatever you want."

Ben, who had been playing below the house, came marching up a moment later. A few paces behind him walked his governess, holding a hammer and a bag full of nails. Ben walked much like a rag doll, loose-jointed and stiff-limbed all at once; it was something he often did these days, it simply suited him, entertained him, and as he mounted the hill, he was shouting incoherently at the trees. The governess meanwhile waved to the group on the veranda. Karen wore a short cotton frock this evening, very green and fresh-looking, and her expression suggested that she had good news to report, happy tidings. Rick let his gaze slide over toward those who approached; and his slightly absent, vaguely indulgent smile remained constant as he shifted jerkily on his canes.

T*hat night,* Catherine drove into Cuervo. She had people to see at the health food store, and she was still upset with Rick, who had gone upstairs immediately after dinner. Muriel, at the last moment, decided to accompany her sister. After completing Catherine's business at the store, the women walked along the quiet Cuervo road, not really sure where they were going, nor why they were out in the chilly air.

"There's the bar," Catherine said as they rounded a curve. "Do you want another margarita or something?"

"Not especially. Do you?"

But they continued on anyway; they approached the low, disreputable-looking building along the road. Half a dozen cars and pickups were parked out front, and even now other vehicles approached, arriving in a sort of caravan. One of the cars, pulling into the unpaved lot in front of the bar, raised twin plumes of dust by skidding; at which the car behind it, and the pickup behind that, began honking in tribute.

"It must be a party," Muriel said. "How nice for them."

"Oh, let's not go in," Catherine replied with real distaste. "Sometimes they have fights. It's a stupid, unhappy place. I've been here before."

Even so, they stood out in the road in front of the bar; the dust slowly settled, and the bar patrons trooped inside. The moist October night fell upon them, strangely close and quiet, dense, and as no cars passed in either direction, they, catching the spell of darkness, became still and quiet themselves. But after a few minutes Muriel made a complaining sound. Catherine reached out in the dark and pushed her.

"Be quiet. I'm waiting," she hissed.

"Waiting for what?"

"I don't know. I'll tell you when it comes."

She had not been waiting for anything, consciously; but as she made this cryptic comment, she did begin to anticipate something. She could almost remember it: only a moment from long ago, possibly from their childhood. Maybe they had stood out in the darkness, just like this, on some equally cold, dismal night, in attitudes approximately the same; and possibly they had been waiting then, too, for something that never arrived. A car, traveling slightly too fast, swooped along the curve of the road, and the two sisters, as if by prior agreement, began to walk forward again, the car's tires beginning to squeal. Their steps led them inevitably to the entrance of the bar.

"I guess we have to go in now. I guess it was foreordained."

"Only for a minute," said Catherine.

She had been inside only once. She particularly remembered the thick tobacco smoke of this bar (which was named Brauch's Town 'n' Country Tavern), and she remembered also the unfriendliness of the patrons, who had looked upon her and Rick, on their one night here, with a rather remarkable hostility. But in those days, more than four years ago, Rick and she were not known in the town, and they had probably been taken for people from "over the hill," therefore somehow hateful. The room of the bar proper was paneled in knotty pine, and over the bar itself were signs for Corona beer, Budweiser, Coors Light, and others. At just this moment the room was empty; not even a bartender awaited them.

Catherine looked to left and right, wondering where the people had gone; she heard a vague scraping of chairs. Then laughter, followed by a vamp of chords played on a guitar, came from some other room.

Soon the bartender returned. He was a young man, wearing his wet, gleaming hair tied in a ponytail. He began polishing the bartop with a heavy cloth. Catherine suddenly felt the utter falseness of this scene, its extreme typicality (which for her amounted to the same thing): it was a room looking exactly like a bar, with a flashing jukebox, leatherette stools, a gleaming mirror festooned with neon logos, and then this grinning, indifferent young man at the center of it, complete even to thick cloth for polishing. Someone was playing rather deliberately at running a bar, she felt. At that moment people began to filter in from other rooms, all of them perfectly cast for roles as bar regulars: the rough, lumberjack-looking Cuervo men in their flannel shirts and beards, and their usual women, all appropriately rough too, a bit dissipated-looking, actually, with their lower ends encased tightly in blue jeans. Some wore heels, some cowgirl boots.

As if choreographed, everyone returned casually to his own place now, to this or that barstool, this or that table. The movements of the small crowd, weaving in and out among the tables, seemed both desultory and cunningly prearranged, like some insolent ballet.

"Can I *help* you, ladies?" the bartender asked with excess of causeless irony.

"Yes. Two beers, please," Catherine answered, disliking the challenge.

Conversations resumed. One of the lumberjack men threw back his head and laughed, ostentatiously making a sound from a cartoon, "Har har-de-har."

Catherine and Muriel, in a corner, remained observantly silent. Muriel had a particularly vigilant look, as if she, the social scientist, had here stumbled upon an odd subculture, one whose peculiar rites she must necessarily study. The gleaming yellow light of the room seemed thick with a kind of self-consciousness, an actorish archness, and after a while the source of this odd contagion, in the form of three strangely dressed musicians, entered from a back area.

Catherine had never seen them before. But she immediately

took them for local heroes, mountain-town paragons. Just from the way the people gave way, looking on them with a knowing, snidely amused respect, it was clear that they were a local cause, everyone's tongue-in-cheek darlings. The leader (there could be no doubt which was the leader) was tall and thin, a severely homely man of about forty; he carried two guitars. Dressed in an old, big-shouldered suit of filamentous wool, he moved forward with comical determination, followed by a much younger man sporting a half-grown Vandyke, hauling a double bass. Then came a stumpy, disgruntled-looking banjo player. He also wore an old, unpressed suit, one made of wash-and-wear polyester, possibly from the sixties. These three remarkable individuals, to the hoots and catcalls of the sparse throng, now arranged four chairs in a corner and sat down to play.

They were well practiced, and Catherine took pleasure in the offhand, plinky-plunky sound they made. The banjoist played mandolin, too, and the skinny leader alternated between steel and six-string guitars, achieving on the former a certain whining, insinuating tone that made her shiver, it was so personal, so impudent. This sadly ugly man — but she stopped feeling sorry for him immediately, as he continued to play with exceeding confidence — had a sallow, hatchet-blade face, with the mouth always twisted up to one side, as if he were sucking his teeth. " 'Bimbo on a Bamboo Isle,' " he announced with a meaning leer, and the bar audience applauded enthusiastically, even before the first note was struck.

His voice was resentful, sour; Catherine hated it, or rather, hated the attitude it expressed. However, she admired his skill and was strangely disappointed when he stopped — she had not quite heard him out, not quite caught his sense. His fans instantly demanded more vocals, more funny tunes, and he responded eventually with arcane jazz numbers, among them "Pig Meat Shuffle," "Three Little Words," and "Grass Shack Interlude." On a song called "Billets-Doux" he improvised a

lyric in phony French; the objects of his disdain, in extended
passages of convincing gibberish, seemed to include the
French themselves, romantic love songs, musical culture in
general, and his own solos on six-string guitar. When the
audience, which had swelled by another dozen, achieved a
delicious vicarious sarcasm, he suddenly shut his mouth de-
cisively. He would play only instrumentals henceforth, he
made it clear — no matter how much they pleaded, how
insistently they requested this or that tune.

"Well, I don't know exactly what it means," Muriel mur-
mured, "but it's sophisticated, don't you think? Highly accomplished?"

"Sophisticated? Is that what it is? Is that why my teeth are
constantly on edge?"

As it happened, this was an introduction. Fifteen minutes
later, when the audience had grown even larger, everyone
moved on to a back room, which had a dance floor and a
small stage. Catherine wanted to hear more, and she persuaded Muriel to stay. Thus far they had been left alone, but
in the other room they jostled with the other people, the
dance floor being small, crowded in by many tables. A man
wearing red suspenders quickly attached himself to Muriel;
he somehow got hold of her hands and began hopping to the
music, making her move along with him. At the same time, a
surge in the crowd carried Catherine several yards away, to a
distant corner of the floor. She found herself standing among
a group of seven or eight, men and women alike, all holding
beer bottles.

"Yeah!" a beefy man shouted near her ear. "Yeah!" he
repeated again and again, his thick, sunburned throat avidly
thrusting forward.

The music was amplified now, and it had a different character. It sounded less personal, less full of causeless, fleering
animosity, less rude. At the same time it gained hugely in
color and fluency, and one of the novelty tunes that the three

played, called "Tico Tico," was so full of a pungent Latin *sabor* that Catherine could hardly credit the change. Then a violinist joined them, another ill-suited masculine figure. He stood on the extreme right of the stage with his back half turned to the audience. When this new player insinuated his rough, resonating voice — rough like a cat's tongue, she thought — Catherine felt an immediate answer in her own chest, a torturing sort of gladness. From his almost scratchy tone, produced with only subtle movements of shoulders and bow arm, came an amazing series of effects, none of them actually rough or scratchy at all: flashes of aural color, odd sound-visions, and, from time to time, corresponding catchings in the heart, unexpected urgencies.

The torture she felt was of something impending: some glorious, non-specific revelation, a kind of crisis. It was as if his violin were always leading her on, pointing the way to an ecstatic resolution. This climax, however, never quite occurred.

Muriel eventually got away from her dancing partner. She came up from behind, quietly taking Catherine's hand. Glancing into her sister's face, Catherine felt a surge of tenderness, and she saw this face as if for the first time, how sweetly, oddly beautiful it was, it truly was. The room was dark but for a rosy glow from somewhere, and a bit of this glow had concentrated in Muriel's fair brow, rendering her ordinary look of vigilant, half-disapproving acuity as something strange, intimately touching. The whole story of her life seemed to quiver there, in her rapt expression.

"He's very good, isn't he?" Muriel asked a moment later, after the song ended. She seemed oddly unaware of her transfiguration.

"Oh, yes," Catherine replied. "Very good." She wanted to say more, but for some reason felt helpless to communicate the precise commotion she felt.

Twenty minutes later, having pushed to the front of the

throng, she finally saw the man up close. Under the influence of his music — "Them There Eyes," followed by "Satin Doll," plus an Irish air — she found an amazing spectrum of qualities in his stark, clear-cut profile, the dominant feature being an infernal concentration, as if he were continually saying to the audience, "Take that. And then that, too." But he also seemed relaxed, vaguely self-amused, sardonic. He played his Irish air, "Farewell to Erin," so that it dripped with a plangent, lachrymose beauty; at the same time, with tongue a little in cheek. Her heart stirred unexpectedly, beholding what she took to be evidence of vulnerability and shyness. He could never turn all the way around, never quite face the audience directly, or even his fellow musicians.

"I think if I could play like that," Muriel said an hour later, as they were driving home, "I'd finally be happy. I'd ask no more of life."

"Well, but you couldn't just fiddle all the time, could you?" Catherine replied chirpily, for some reason feeling a need to make light, to deny. But in her heart, she agreed completely with her sister; and in the rest of her she felt a sweet gladness, as if they were coming back from some unexpected, exquisite feast.

A *few days later* she saw the man again. He was without his instrument now, and the romance of his appearance, which had depended on the spell he cast with his music, was largely gone. Having delivered her son to school one morning, Catherine was talking to the vice principal, a Mrs. Breitenbach, when the fiddle player and a little girl came in. The girl, about eight years old, was fuming. She stamped her foot and shrugged the man's hand from her shoulder, refusing to go any farther into the school than through the front door.

"I won't because I don't *want* to," she said, in precisely the tone one would have expected.

But she was a beautiful little girl. She was dressed in a clean, hastily ironed red dress, her glossy hair held back with plastic barrettes. Catherine, who thought she knew all the children at school, had never seen her before.

"All right. If that's what you want to do," the man replied calmly, a bit distantly.

He entered the principal's office by himself. The girl cowered in the hallway, too shy to look at Catherine or anyone else.

A minute later he returned. He was followed out by old Mr. Dodds, the fussy, always hurried school principal, he of the much-stained red cardigan. The father stood stalwart and rather self-possessed as Dodds, with overpracticed friendliness, addressed himself to the little girl. Then later, as the man was saying goodbye, he placed his hand on his daughter's shoulder, and she shivered as if with disgust.

At this point Catherine also said goodbye to Mrs. Breitenbach, and she trailed the violinist out of the school.

He never actually looked her way. But now he asked, casually, if she might be headed into town. His truck was in the garage, he explained. He had had to walk up from town this morning, a distance of a mile or more, with his daughter complaining at every step. She had only recently returned to him — for the last year she had lived with her mother.

"She isn't used to it yet," he explained. "And neither am I."

Catherine needed to stop at the town store in any case. The man waited by her car, and when she came out, he took her bag of groceries.

"My name's Henry Bascomb," he said. "I should have introduced myself before."

He lived on the Cuervo road, he added. His house was two miles below the ridge, the highest point in the canyon. Catherine's route back to her farm would take her up to this ridge, then south three miles along a narrow road.

As she drove, Bascomb sat on the far end of the seat seeming ill at ease, with his large, squarish hands attached to his kneecaps. Neither spoke. She planned to say that she had heard him play, and that she had enjoyed herself, but his silence and his apparent self-absorption put her off. When she chanced to look over, he had an amused, silly expression on his face, as if recalling some recent contretemps, something of a deliciously piquant nature.

A few miles farther along, she suddenly declared: "Your daughter looks to be about eight years old. That means she'll be in the third grade. Am I right?"

After a moment he replied, "That's about right. That's about it, I guess."

"I have a boy in second grade myself. The third grade teacher's very good, by the way. Mrs. Bowers."

"She might be in the third grade," he continued, "or maybe the fourth. I don't really know."

This seemed annoyingly vague of him: how could he not know such a thing, his own daughter's grade? She lapsed into silence then, feeling irritated. However, when she glanced over again, his odd expression seemed evidence of discomfort, of an unhappy self-consciousness, nothing more; and she felt herself growing more kindly disposed.

"I live out on the ridge," she declared eventually. "We have a farm there. Every morning I drive my kid to school, or someone does it for me, and we could pick up your daughter if you wanted."

"Well — that's very nice of you," he responded quickly. "Very nice. But I'll have my truck back soon. I can do it myself then."

He shifted uneasily on her car seat. They were driving through a grove of redwoods at that moment, an especially dark, remote stretch of the canyon road, entirely quiet and still. Often there were bad accidents here, as people drove off the unbanked roadbed, then down to the creek.

"Very nice of you," he repeated. "Very kind." But something made her wonder a bit at his tone — it seemed poised between gratitude, or at least politeness, and a kind of ironic suspicion.

"By the way, my name is Mansure. I'm Catherine Mansure."

"Yes — I already know who you are," he replied, a bit cryptically.

He said nothing more. He merely sat, staring straight ahead. And somehow she was made to feel that this fact of who she was spoke volumes: it was as if there were something disagreeable, something entirely disreputable about it. Only an admirable discretion, it seemed, kept him from commenting further on her questionable identity.

"Well," he finally said, "we've met once before. It was up at your place — on your farm. You were hiring people to work on your fire trails. It was in the spring, I think, three or four years ago."

"Oh? I don't remember."

"I never did come work for you, though. Something else came up. I sent my cousin instead."

Now he mentioned a name, presumably the cousin's. She had hired crews every year for the past several, so it was certainly possible that they had met before; however, she couldn't recall. Even his cousin's name didn't ring a bell.

They drove on, Catherine now somehow disconcerted by what he said. She felt put off, offended in some obscure way. His hands still rested absurdly on his kneecaps. She could feel his nervousness, the upset she caused in him, but there was a kind of pride in his shyness, too, as if he were determined not to make any effort to overcome it, no matter what. He was one of these genuine Cuervo men, she understood then: one of these unforthcoming, passively unpleasant ones, these men who were determined not to charm. They lived in the woods, most of them, eking out a rough existence cutting firewood or working construction jobs; and most of them drank and had messy relations with their women. In America, it seemed, there was still room for this outmoded type, enough room to trace a stupid, pridefully ornery path with one's life, if one wanted.

Only by chance did she happen to recall, just as she was about to drop him off, what else he was able to do with those large, squarish, inexpressive hands. His house was completely invisible, lost in the foliage above the road. On a lonely, greenly desolate stretch he asked her to pull over; his driveway could hardly be seen through the looming trees.

"This is it. It's up there somewhere."

"Oh, by the way. I heard you play music the other night. And you were very good, I thought. Surprisingly good."

"Oh? You were there?"

"Yes, you and the others. You and your funny little band."

Something in her voice puzzled him, it seemed. He looked at her directly, curiously. Her tone had been a bit dry, she supposed, with more meaning than she intended. Perhaps she had said it wrong.

"Actually," she corrected herself, "you were wonderful. Just wonderful. I was glad to be there, happy to be hearing you. We just stumbled on it by chance. My sister happened to be in town that night, and we had nothing else to do . . . but there was a special feeling in the room, I thought, a funny mood. Everybody seemed to be glowing with it — I don't know how else to say it, they just seemed electrified. It lasted the whole time you played."

"Did it? A special feeling?"

She had pulled her car off the road by now. They had come to a stop, here at his place. He opened the door on the passenger side, but rather than get out he continued to sit, with one foot placed on the ground.

"So — you were there," he mused. The idea seemed to tantalize him. "I'm glad you were. I felt something special in the room, too. But I wish I'd known you were there. I would have played something just for you."

"You would? But you did play something just for me . . . you played a lot of things, beautiful things. For me and for everybody else. I think everybody felt that you were playing just for them."

Having brought the conversation around to this unexceptionable expression of rather banal sentiment, she felt foolish. The man smiled at her oddly, though not unkindly. Possibly he found what she said amusing, or maybe he was simply enjoying another of his thoughts, his piquant memories. Then with a vague wave of his hand, he lurched out of her car.

As Catherine pulled back onto the roadway she looked behind; the man had already disappeared, swallowed up in the gloomy trees.

Two weeks after Halloween, Rick reached a crisis. He had been "holding steady," as he said, neither getting weaker nor improving, although he continued to give the impression of someone in robust, pink-cheeked health; but then one morning he was actually too weak to get out of bed, even to go to the bathroom. He called for Catherine, but since she was out of the house (it was one of the mornings when she drove Ben to school), Rachel, a nursery worker who helped in the kitchen, came running up, and she found him lying in wet sheets, angrily thrashing from side to side. When she had quieted him, he announced in a weak voice that he couldn't breathe; she then called the medical service in Palo Alto, and by the time they sent someone (Catherine had also returned by now), he was nearly hysterical, covered in sweat and mostly incoherent.

The medical technicians administered oxygen out of a portable unit. Then Rick relaxed, with the mask still on his face, and soon his respiration returned to normal.

The physician who arrived later, a Dr. Weiner, took Catherine aside and asked her a number of questions. He had heard of Serawan Goldfisch, Rick's internist in San Francisco. There could be no doubt of Goldfisch's competence, of his rightful eminence. However:

"This is a condition with a strong psychological component. Your husband needs all the help he can get. Has he been to see a therapist?"

"No — not that I'm aware of."

"And not before? Not ever?"

"No, I don't think so. It's almost a point of pride with him. Not to have ever gone."

The doctor nodded, as if he now understood everything. "I could recommend someone," he said, "or you could call the service. They'll probably give you someone who works at Stanford. But I think you should consider hiring a nurse, too. Someone he can call at any moment, around the clock."

"Well, you see, I'm almost always home. I just happened to be out this morning. Then there's his great-aunt, who lives in the house. And the girls who work downstairs."

"It's a question of support," the doctor persisted, "of continual physical reassurance. Right now he's terrified, because he feels he's losing control. Think of it: if you can't get up just to go to the bathroom, what happens next? Maybe you wake up one morning and you can't breathe. Or swallow. You dwell on these things, and pretty soon you've worked yourself into a state."

"I'll tell him what you said, Doctor. Or maybe if you tell him yourself, it might have more meaning."

Rick predictably thought that Dr. Weiner was "full of it." However, there might be something to the idea of hiring a nurse, he admitted. He felt uneasy whenever Catherine left the house; if he knew he could get hold of Rachel or Karen whenever he wanted, he would be reassured. Rachel worked in the kitchen half of her hours, and already there was something custodial, almost nurse-like, in her relation to Rick. She was a great believer in herbal concoctions, Ayurvedic medicine, Shiatsu massage, and the like, and she had been quietly pressing her point of view. She was proud to have acted the heroine in the recent crisis. Catherine praised her for calling the doctors promptly; and without much trouble, it was arranged that she would work in the house most of her hours for a while.

Rick considered himself quite knowledgeable when it came

to psychotherapy; his aversion to it applied solely to his own case. For almost everyone else it was, if not really necessary, then certainly appropriate given many sets of circumstances. When Bob Stein, for example, decided he needed to see an analyst some years ago (and a fourteen-karat, four-times-a-week Freudian at that), Rick had been enthusiastically supportive. But in his own case he saw drawbacks. He was proud of never having been so troubled as to need "help." Weiner's suggestion, however, had an unexpected and paradoxical effect. In the midst of all the usual refusals, the bluff and scornful dismissals, there were vague comments about the likelihood of there being a psychological dimension, another side to what had recently befallen him. No, he was not unaware of the psychological aspect; he could see clearly enough, for instance, the raw irony of his situation, of a man so used to being in superb control, suddenly unable to manage dominion over his own bladder. Nor was he blind to the whole question of his childhood, his strange upbringing, its relevance here. One could make a good case that by getting sick, he had returned unconsciously to a condition of childish weakness and dependency, to precisely that condition which it had been his life's work to escape.

"Not only that — returned by means of almost the same device, almost the same disease, by a kind of re-enactment of my childhood collapse. The muscular failure, the lying in bed for months on end . . . a good shrink could make real hay out of this. But as Dick Ferguson once said" — Ferguson was a psychologist friend, often quoted in such circumstances — "you go to a shrink for one reason and one reason only: to save yourself from incipient madness. Anything else is just an indulgence, a waste of money."

"If you mean you have to be on the very brink of insanity, Rick, before you go, why, that's just absurd," Catherine replied. "People see psychologists for a million different reasons. When their lives just feel wrong, for instance. When they can't figure things out anymore."

"Catherine, I won't be fooled, not at this late date. I'm not about to make a new career of pondering my presumptive infantile wounds ... in the end, it always turns out that Daddy didn't show you enough affection, and Mommy showed you a lot but the wrong kind, so nothing that happens later in life is your fault. If you believe that, you really are on the road to being crazy."

"You had a serious episode back there, Rick — you can't deny that. Dr. Weiner called it a classic panic response. Things are going on with you, deep emotional things. You know it, and you can even talk about it pretty clearly, but that doesn't mean you can help yourself."

"I know it would be the real capstone of this experience, Catherine, if you could only get me to humiliate myself a little bit more. Get me to give up in this final, definitive way. But I won't do that. No, I simply won't."

"But what does that mean, Rick — 'humiliate' yourself? That I *want* you to? What in the world are you trying to say?"

This was not the first time Rick had said something of the kind, something implying that Catherine was enjoying his suffering, that she secretly rejoiced in seeing him brought low. She protested vociferously, as always, and he soon apologized, claiming that he felt so frustrated, so truly desperate, that things simply came out of him sometimes.

"I'm sorry. Really sorry. That wasn't fair ... but I can't go to see someone now, Catherine, I just can't. Don't you understand — if I can't make sense of this myself, if I can't conduct my own illness, so to speak, then I have nothing. Leave me that, at least."

About a week after Rick's crisis, Catherine got a phone call from Henry Bascomb. He needed her help, he said. Could she drive his daughter to school that day? Something had happened to him; in point of fact, he had fallen in the woods, sprained his back. He couldn't manage the truck today.

It was a morning when Karen, the governess, was supposed to drive Ben to school; but Catherine went herself instead. She dimly remembered where Bascomb's driveway was. Ben sat quietly, attentively beside her as they drove through a nearly solid wall of foliage, which parted around their car like theater curtains forced from the front. The driveway went deep into the woods, then rose sharply for at least a hundred yards. The house itself, like many in the canyon, had a gloomy, derelict aspect; Catherine would have thought it uninhabited if she didn't know better.

Ben strained forward against his seatbelt. He blinked rapidly several times, somehow not believing.

"It looks just like the house in *The Seven Sisters of Whmmm*," he said, "where all the witches live. The good witches and the bad."

"Well, do you want to go out and get her, Ben?"

"No. I don't think so."

Catherine got out of the car herself, and Bascomb and his daughter appeared at their door just then. The girl came forward jauntily, carrying a lunch bag and wearing a knapsack, and her freshness seemed odd, coming from such a dwelling. Bascomb stood uncomfortably in the doorway, with his hands pressed against either jamb. He said nothing to his daughter as she departed, and it seemed to Catherine that his attention was entirely elsewhere — probably focused on his sore back.

"I'll bring her home this afternoon," she called out.

"That's all right. I've already arranged with someone else."

"You look . . . in pain. Do you need to go see a doctor today? Would you like a lift somewhere?"

He said nothing in return, and at first she thought he hadn't heard. But some minute change in his expression led her to understand that he had, and moreover, that her suggestion, her instinctive offer of help, had disturbed him in some way.

"Thank you very much," he said slowly. "Thank you. But no — I'll be all right. It's not that bad. Go on, Mary Elizabeth. Get in the car now."

His daughter stopped upon reaching the door. Inside Catherine's station wagon, still strapped into his seat, Ben sat staring straight ahead as the little girl gazed curiously in at him.

She had been mean to him once before (Catherine learned later), had hurt him on the playground, and he hated her. On the drive to school she talked about her mother, who was named Terry, and who also lived in the canyon now but would be moving back to Lake Tahoe next summer. She would be taking Mary Elizabeth with her.

"We have a big house up there. It belongs to Jerry, my mom's boyfriend. And we have a boat, and you come in through a private gate with a lock. Tahoe's all right in the summer, but in the winter there's just too much snow. Way too much."

"Well — not if you like skiing," Catherine said brightly, turning to look at Ben. "Isn't that right, honey? Wouldn't you agree, Ben?"

Her son made no reply. No sign — nothing.

"And how about you, Mary Elizabeth? Do you like to ski?"

"Not so much. But I'm pretty good for my age."

Ben continued to stare straight ahead. In the rear-view mirror the girl's eyes came to rest on the back of his head, attracted no doubt by his uncommon silence, his perfect stillness; these dark eyes fixed him with a look of momentary, bird-like interest, then abruptly flitted off.

When Ben came home from school that day, Catherine heard all about Mary Elizabeth: that she was hated by everyone, that she had thrown a rock and hit somebody in the mouth, cracking a front tooth. Since no one wanted to play with her, she often played with the littler kids at recess, and she always bullied them. The rock incident happened some time ago, when she first showed up at the school. "Well, she was probably just nervous," Catherine said. "It was a new situation for her. Think how you felt on your first day, Ben — think how afraid you were."

"Yeah, Mom, I was afraid. But I didn't hit a kid in the mouth with a rock."

For the next four or five days, Catherine ferried the girl to school. Bascomb walked her down to the road each morning, so that Catherine could avoid negotiating his driveway. His back continued to bother him. He walked deliberately, standing fearfully erect, using a home-made cane. Then one evening he called her at home to report that he felt better now. He could drive his daughter to school himself tomorrow.

"But I want to thank you," he said carefully. "That was generous of you. I appreciate it."

"Well, it was really nothing. Any time. Any time."

They talked about the schoolbus scandal then — the county in which the canyon was located, like all the other counties in the state, was required to transport public school students, any who lived more than a few miles away. But an ongoing, ever-deepening financial crisis had led to the schoolbus service being dropped. There had been some grumbling on the local bulletin boards, but so far the families affected, recognizing budgetary realities, had not complained officially.

"The canyon always gets the short end of the stick," Bascomb observed. "It's an old county tradition. Going way, way back."

"Oh — are you an old Cuervo hand?" she asked. "Born and raised here, and all that?"

They talked for a few minutes along these lines. Catherine felt that the man had consciously decided to make himself known to her, slightly better known, somewhat against his own instincts. Then something he said made her feel that, in addition, he was slyly amused, facetiously pleased to be having such an exchange with her; it was something in his tone, some broad, not unpleasant undercurrent of irony. He was laughing at no one but himself, she understood — but he was definitely laughing. Eventually they exhausted all possible topics, all conventional and ordinary matters of discourse, and they had to hang up.

"Catherine," she heard as she put the receiver down, "who were you talking to?"

"It was no one, Rick," she called upstairs. "Just another parent. Someone from the school."

"Well, would you come up here, then? I need you."

"All right. I'm coming."

In late November the year seemed as if it would never end, never complete the old, seasonal turn. The rainy season should have started by now, but the thin, throat-drying weather kept on, a sort of ghoul's summer, after the usual Indian summer. Everything in the woods looked sick and dry, without color or spirit. The air itself seemed soiled — full of a yellowish, irritating dust. Roaming down toward the pond one morning, Catherine felt the lack of rain with every step. She kept thinking of fire: the idea of it was everywhere, brooding over the woods.

At the lookout place, the vista now oppressed her. Far below her the pond looked shrunken, oddly discolored; the vivid, living green of it was gone. The air above seemed dirtied, clotted. She was suddenly disheartened — there seemed no point in going any farther if the natural world itself, whose purity she had taken for granted here, had passionately treasured, was degraded. She sat on the edge of the brushy cliff with her legs dangling down.

"So this is how I feel," she said to herself, "this is how it is. Well . . . the outer world, and the inner. And I've been feeling this way for a long time. Impossibly long. I'm just like Rick that way — just as bad as Rick."

But she wasn't just like Rick. Rick denied himself, she believed, consciously suppressed his feelings in order to surmount them deliberately. This was how he became himself, achieved the high and exemplary level of himself. While she, in her avoidance of impossible, difficult things, took a yet more devious path. In some sense she admitted everything into herself, absolutely everything; but she refused to accept some things consciously, declined to comprehend them. As a result, she felt unaware of her own life.

There was a secret of her life with Rick: that they did not agree, they did not really coexist. On matters of importance she often found it impossible to yield to him, simply could not make herself; while he, of course, never considered the possibility. No one else really knew this truth about them: that she passionately, flintily resisted him, largely with her will, and at some unreckoned, undoubtedly serious cost to herself. The reality of their transaction was this continuous, enervating conflict of wills, with never a satisfying issue.

She rose to her feet. She was eager to be pushing on — walking again, changing place. But the soiled tapestry of the lake basin down below — the browns, blacks, and dry grays of it, with here and there a note of deadly, blackened green — oppressed her. She was just like this tapestry, she felt; the quenching of all livelier colors, and the introduction of tones of decay, of ruin, was her condition exactly. She could see the external sign: the very weave of her inner life.

"Yes, I'm ruined," she said to herself a little dramatically. "My life is certainly wrong, false. Why go on living it, then — why bother? And who is this person who wants to live in this unreal way — half dead, sickly, and out of touch? Was I always like this? But I thought I used to know how to live — I used to know what things meant, once."

The tone of these ruminations — earnest, tending toward the tragic — was somehow a comfort to her. If her analysis immediately struck such a note, then it had to be partly false (she believed), since it failed to include the answering, more even-tempered appraisal ("You are sitting on top of a wild ridge, in your late youth and health, and looking down on a spread of glorious forest, meanwhile trying to convince yourself that you're sick of your life"). There was something foolish, not to mention schoolgirlish, about such a line of thought, and this idea was a comfort to her.

"I may be tired," she mused. "I may be exhausted in spirit, what with all this trouble with Rick. I may even be at some crucial turning point in my life, which will only become clear later. But I am not entirely without resources, thank God. I know I won't always feel this disgusted, this wintry. But oh — that lake looks so bleak. So sad. It's like the very end of something. And I'm . . . like that lake."

She began to walk. She simply had to, to feel herself again. Soon she located the old path, the one that led steeply down the brushy cliff. Half an hour later she found herself in the basin itself, in the area of thickest undergrowth. Here the path had a way of petering out, and her usual signposts, particular trees and bushes, looked completely strange in their blasted, dried-out condition. If she kept on walking, regardless, trusting to her general sense of direction, she felt all right; but whenever she stopped the foliage, colorless and stiff, drew attention to itself, seemed to mock her with its quietness.

Eventually she saw a break in the forest wall. And through this break the pond, not two hundred yards farther on. She continued to walk.

At this deepest part of the basin, the air was cold and more moist. A false-feeling, yellowish light slanted in from the south, lending the morning a feeling of evening, of depletion. On the far side of the pond the clearing showed itself, and then — someone just walked casually across it. Catherine disbelieved, at first, what she had undoubtedly seen; she argued against it with herself. But no, there he was, unmistakably. Another male figure — another bold, shameless trespasser. Then after a moment he vanished again, into the rushes.

She thought of the stranger of last spring. He, too, had worn dusty work clothes, and he had also seemed at home here, casually occupied with something or other. Seeing this second figure recalled her feelings of that other time, the rude and harsh surprise of it; and she realized that she had remained disturbed, alarmed in her heart.

Now with insouciant poise, as if insisting on his very factuality, the man emerged from the shrubbery again. He walked briskly to the pond's edge. He took off a dusty hat, tossed it to the ground; then rolling up one sleeve, he knelt by the water, plunging an arm in up to the shoulder. After a moment he disappeared into the rushes again.

Catherine now began to move. She would throw him out, punish this intrusion, erase this memory. But at a certain point she began to think more clearly about what she was doing: just grimly sneaking up on a stranger, here in the wild woods. They were miles from any help, and she would be at his mercy if he turned against her. But even so, she moved forward. Arriving at the pond she found no sign of his presence, just a slight disturbance at the water's edge, where he had knelt. The pond, like an implicated witness putting on a straight face, gazed back at her placidly, with a blank, entirely unrippled surface.

She waited. She imagined him watching her from the rushes: he would be enjoying his hiddenness again, his secret view of her. But after a moment she called out in a clear, reasonably calm voice:

"You might as well come out of there . . . I saw you. I already saw you. You're not fooling anyone anymore, so just come out."

No reply. The absence of even a breeze, and the stillness over the pond, seemed to reinforce this perfect silence, this breathless reticence.

"I won't come in after you. I won't chase you down through the bushes, if that's what you want . . . but you have to understand, this is private property. You can't just come up here any time you want. This isn't your land."

A voice declared: "I don't come up here any time I want."

Nothing more. It was as if the pond itself had spoken, or the wall of tall, broken-headed bullrushes, as they bent toward her limberly.

"I've seen you here before," she continued, "haven't I? You were the one who watched us — spied on us. But this is private property. This lake belongs to me. To my husband and his family, and to me."

Complete silence. It was as if the reeds, as they bent their heads to her, were the symbols of his shame; or was there something mocking, falsely chastened, in their dipping submission? "If it belongs to your husband," came the voice after a long pause, "then I'd better just give up, I guess. I'd better come out right now, in that case."

The weeds moved slightly. But he appeared from behind her — he had sneaked around. And as she had somehow imagined, his hat was humbly in his hand.

It was Henry Bascomb. It was Bascomb the violin player — the sometime father, the lonely woodsman. She was deeply surprised for a moment, and then not very. He stood out strangely from the background of dark foliage. The physical details of his appearance were all-present, powerfully vivid to her: for a moment they were almost too much to assimilate.

"Yes — it's me," he said dryly. "You've got me dead to rights this time ... I guess the game's up. It's really over now."

The yellow light, slanting in from her left, gave his head a gleaming, tawny cast. She wondered that she had never noticed before the peculiar richness of his hair, its complex, bursting thickness. Just in the time since she saw him last, he had grown a sparse beard, and this weedy growth gave him a wolfish look. But his eyes were simple in expression — boyishly mild. Looking at him this closely, with the tacit excuse that she was surprised, that she had to stare in order to identify him, she reached the astonishing conclusion that he was quite beautiful — she had known him for a while, for several weeks at least, and this fact had never been borne in on her before, never quite registered.

"What should we do now," he wondered, "call the police?

The county sheriffs? But I have to eat first. I was just about to have my lunch. I'm hungry."

He offered to share this lunch. But she was still too confused — she declined. Nevertheless, she followed him a short distance into the rushes. There was a path here, a corridor down through the overshadowing plants, and they followed it.

After a few yards they came to a small, almost circular clearing. Here the rushes gave way to chaparral. Overhead the growth was densely interwoven, giving the spot something of the feeling of a covert, a nest.

On the floor of the clearing rested a knapsack. There were also a pair of gloves and some clippers, along with other gardening materials.

"What are you growing in here?" she asked. "Blackberries? Oh, wait a minute . . . now I see. You're one of these cultivators. These marijuana growers. One of these dangerous local criminals. Yes — now I understand."

He said nothing; he would neither confirm nor deny the charge. But in the meantime, let them get on with something important: let them get comfortable, and eat. The knapsack contained lengths of flexible plastic tubing, plus a brown sweater, which he spread out on the ground. He offered her some cheese, a hunk of bread, and two bruised pears. Then a large bar of chocolate.

"No, I'm not hungry. I'm shocked, that's all — deeply shocked."

"You don't want anything?"

But he continued to urge her to eat. In the end, she took a bite of one of the pears.

"That's why the pond's gotten so low," she observed after a while. "Because you've been watering your crop out of it. Isn't that right?"

"Actually . . . the pond always gets low this time of year. Especially without much rain."

He devoured a half pound of cheese. Then the hunk of bread, the remaining pear, and part of the chocolate. She noticed that his hands were rough and swollen — he had been working without gloves in the thickets, punishing his hands, mistreating them. His fingers looked almost bloated.

As she sat, slowly eating her bruised pear, he seemed to grow amused. He would say nothing, but their situation intrigued him — did it not amuse her, too? He ceded her the brown sweater, and he spread out nearby, his legs stretched out to one side. Again, she had a feeling of not quite being able to take him in, of being astonished, overwhelmed by his physical vividness. The small, nest-like clearing just fit him, seemed at last the proper setting in which to take his measure — him with his rough clothes, roughened hands, and hidden gaze. He was like a forest creature, she thought, something encountered in its burrow, where, by the intensity of its habituation, its customary presentness, it threw off precise details, meaningful impressions.

"If I was to grow a few plants," he mused, "I wouldn't do it here. I'd grow them down below, down in the next meadow. It's less obvious there, and it gets more sun. But you could drain water out of the pond, run it down through a drip system . . . that is, if you were interested in that kind of thing."

"I see. I see," she replied.

"Have a small garden or two. Make a fence to keep out the wood rats and deer. Just something modest, enough to get by on. And you could live that way — yes, you probably could."

She nodded. "Yes, it sounds very reasonable."

But she liked him for saying it in this way, without apologies. It was better than denying it, certainly. And there was something almost intimate about the way he casually spoke to her, the way he simply confessed. He put himself in her hands without thinking much about it, apparently.

"I don't mind," she said. "It really doesn't matter to me. As long as it's small, and very quiet. Someone can do whatever he wants down here, in that case."

"Yes — always very quiet."

He took a bite of his chocolate.

They lapsed into silence at this point. She felt slightly uncomfortable, and he began smiling to himself in that peculiar way he had. All his standoffish behavior of the weeks before, his discomfort in her presence, his attitude of a man with something on his mind — all this suddenly made sense. He had been poaching on their land, after all, secretly taking advantage. Probably this had gone on for years, and he had been laughing up his sleeve all the while. There was a feeling of superiority about it, no doubt — of putting one over on the landlords.

But his smile did not exclude her, in the end; and when he happened to catch her eye, his expression became soft, almost grave. Something about him moved toward her. And when she saw this, or rather, felt it, something answered in her, seemed to rise in her own chest. It was a feeling that came from far away, vertiginous and surprising, like a bird swooping.

"I saw you that day," he confessed, still with his strange, intent expression. "Yes — I was watching you. It was more than I could take, seeing you, looking from the bushes. You and your friends. You were swimming in the lake."

What was she supposed to say to this? But she had a feeling — it was in her throat now, as well as her chest, a pressure, a sort of hope. She shook her head, putting her hand out instinctively. And he, mistaking her, also put his hand out. He would have touched her, but she drew her hand back.

"Have you thought about that day? Well, I have. I'd been thinking about you for years. Ever since I saw you, since I first met you. I'd been hoping something like that would happen. Dreaming about it, knowing it never would . . . but when you came out of the lake, came into the bushes here, I knew I had to wait. I wanted you to find me, I think. I probably let you." She shook her head. "No — I don't think I understand. I don't know what you're saying."

He touched her hand as she looked at him, but she pulled away. But he kept watching intently, seeming to move toward her, with warmth and curiosity. Then she touched the back of his hand, using only the back of hers, and only for an instant. And afterward she stood up. She said that she had to leave. She had to go back to the pond.

He watched her go. He seemed only curious as she hurried up the path lined with rushes. A few minutes later, he also emerged from this path. He found her standing beyond the rushes, very close to the water. She seemed wounded to him; he saw that a weight had gathered about her.

"Not here," he said. "Not now. But soon. Soon."

"No, I don't think so," she answered. She shook her head. He touched her. She allowed him to turn her around, to kiss her chastely. Something about the feel of his breath — the rich, unexpected taste of him — made her stand closer, less broken than before. He kissed her, and as she yielded he held her carefully in his arms. But she soon pushed him away. She held him back stiffly. She looked at him almost angrily.

"No — I don't want you to," she said. "Don't do it."

They stood this way, at odds, not embracing, for a long moment. Then with a softening of her expression, making a sound between them like a sweet, soft curse, she brought him in against her.

But they soon broke apart. She said that she had to go now — had to go back to her house. He asked if he could walk her up through the forest. She said no. She had become deliberate in all her movements; without speaking, she disappeared into the undergrowth, stooping, turning with care, as if listening to her own limbs moving.

Rick *wanted* to go away. He had been talking about Mexico — they would leave Ben home, under Karen's care, with Gerda to help out. Rick ignored the question of his own physical condition: whether or not he was able to travel at all. This was his last gesture in the direction of the old, indomitable autonomy, the old Rick showing himself one last time.

Catherine, understanding the gesture, said nothing. She prepared herself to go away, or possibly not to go. Some days he could hardly walk, but then, for about a week in mid-December, he felt much better, almost like himself again, and the trip was definitely on. They would fly to Mexico City, where Rick's uncle Gower owned an apartment. Then on to Oaxaca or wherever they wanted.

"Mexico D.F. is the only great city in the world," Rick suddenly announced, "it makes New York look like a tacky village. You can never belong to another city if you've ever lived in *la capital* for a time, although, of course, it's nothing like it was in the fifties, when I was there. My old schoolboy friend Hernán Goldmann still writes for *El Diario*, I think. We can look him up and all my other old friends, too."

"All right, Rick, but we can't go till after Christmas," Catherine replied. "Is that understood?"

"No, why not? Is it because of Ben? Oh, one Christmas without his parents isn't going to ruin his whole life. Believe me."

"I know it won't, Rick. But it'll ruin *my* Christmas."

Rick contemplated, then made the great concession. "All right — after Christmas then. But I'm talking about a real trip now, Catherine. Months. Lots of moving around. And no doctors. No more of this screaming insanity."

Rick, in an amazing turnabout, had begun to see a psychologist, the one recommended by Dr. Weiner. The psychologist worked and taught at Stanford, and he had been "pretty helpful so far," according to Rick. They met twice a week at an office on the Stanford campus.

"He's about my age," Rick explained. "Went to UCLA, never been married, big scuba diver. Travels all over the world visiting coral reefs. We have a few things in common, and I immediately understood his game plan: pretend to be my pal, my good buddy, just a companion on this trip to enlightenment together. All right — I like to play-act, too. Last Friday, we spent the whole fifty minutes talking about Belize, the rancho Uncle Regis owns on the Caribbean coast there. You can take a motor launch out from his dock and be on the second-longest coral reef in the world in fifteen minutes.

"Bill said we should go down there together. He likes me to call him Bill, by the way. Then as I was driving home, I thought about what happened, how I'd just spent a hundred forty dollars so he could talk about scuba diving. But the funny thing is, I felt wonderful afterwards — more relaxed than I have for months. I began to see unexpected subtleties in his presentation: how, just by introducing the idea of escape, he'd given me hope, how the very thought of release summons up the energy you need to get away. In a sense, he's finessing the whole idea of medical incapacity. Since no one really knows how much of this is physical, how much mental, just act as if everything was within your powers. A question of right attitude, nothing more."

"Well," Catherine replied, "that's very Californian of him, wouldn't you say? To think that someone can do just about anything. Overcome any obstacle, if he only believes he can."

"Oh, don't be cynical, Catherine. You're not the one with

the crutches, remember. Any port in a storm, I say. If it takes believing in some vapid happy-think, so be it. I'll do whatever it takes. I'm surprised to find out how proud I'm really *not* — that I'll try anything, almost anything to get results. It's all very well to take a strict-constructionist view when you have two good legs to stand on, but just wait till your body starts to fail. Wait till you're pissing in a plastic bag."

Rick wasn't pissing in a plastic bag yet; but he had never recovered from that episode last November, the one when he couldn't get out of bed. The trend was still downward in many ways. Dr. Weiner, who to some extent had replaced Goldfisch as supervisor of Rick's case, had referred him to a new team of neurologists, two of them important researchers/practitioners at the Stanford Medical School. These new nerve men were devising a whole new course of treatment for Rick. In addition, he saw a physical therapist twice a week and an inhalation therapist on an occasional basis.

"There's the world of medicine," Rick observed, "and there's the world of hope. The two rarely, if ever, intersect. When I'm with the specialists, I become stupidly passive; I hardly care anymore. But away from them I start to wake up. I see how maybe I can save myself."

"Rick, whatever you do, I'm behind you," Catherine sought to reassure him. "I don't mean to sound cynical about things. I just think you should give the specialists a fair chance — they may actually know something."

"But they don't, they really don't. They're the best in the world, and they still don't have a solution. Their whole approach is wrong. Powerful medicines and invasive procedures, the whole stupid bag of cruel, dehumanizing Western medical tricks. It's like every malpractice case you've ever heard of, the experts inflicting brilliant stroke after brilliant stroke while the baffled patient only goes downhill faster . . ."

Passionately angry at his doctors, enjoying a brief remission, Rick boldly launched their expedition to Mexico. But only three days out of the country he collapsed, had to be taken to a Mexican hospital, and was soon sent home. Catherine chatted to him brightly on the flight back to California, but she was just as depressed as he was. It seemed like an end to everything: the final, crushing rebuke to his hopes for recovery.

In February, he took a number of sedatives and other prescription drugs and fell into a coma. It lasted eighteen hours. He maintained afterward that he had not actually been trying to kill himself — only to get a good night's sleep, relief from this awful distress.

≈ ≈ ≈

Rick was an invalid now. He rarely left the house, used a wheelchair on occasion, and steadily lost weight. All his doctors' appointments were crammed into two days a week, usually Wednesday and Friday. Catherine escorted him on these medical pilgrimages, but one week she was sick with a cold, and Rachel went in her place. Thereafter, the kitchen girl–cum–nurse always asked to go, and Catherine often let her.

Rachel had undergone a remarkable transformation. In the months of Rick's illness she had become more outspoken, less irritatingly servile; Catherine accepted her help with few misgivings, only sometimes wishing that she was less underfoot.

"I always wanted to be a nurse," she once confided to Catherine. "When my mother had her gall bladder out I stayed in the hospital with her, and it started then, I think. I was ten. All the years I was using drugs, I knew there was something else, something to get back to. I lived in the Meadow Ashram for a while, and Baba recognized me and said that I had a 'healing breast.' He taught me Ayurvedic practices."

"Yes — Rick says he likes your herbs and things. But who is this Baba? Is he a teacher from India?"

"He's from Bombay, yes. He took a vow of silence in 1976, and he only writes on a chalkboard. He's a beautiful man, the most beautiful I've known. A *sadhu,* an enlightened being. Oh, but he loves to play. He's full of tricks. I fell in love with him. I was his *sanyasin* — it means a sort of student . . ."

Catherine learned that the Meadow Ashram was located on a large forested property northeast of Santa Cruz. This Baba had about thirty disciples, and he had recently celebrated his sixty-eighth birthday. Rachel would probably go back there someday.

"I may go on to nursing school, though. When I met Gerda I had the same feeling — that this was a master, a perfect soul, and I could learn from her. You know you were meant to meet this person on your path. I didn't even mind that she was mean to me all the time."

"Oh — is she still mean to you?"

"She just says that she doesn't love me, and it makes her sick when I tell her all the time that I do. But I have to honor her perfection — her beauty. She calls me 'stupid girl' and says that she can see right through me. But that's what I want, for her to see through me."

Gerda had accepted Rachel as a worker a year ago. Rachel wasn't the first: there had been a considerable run of acolytes over the years, aspiring daughter-candidates who somehow found their way to the farm, there to attach themselves to the crusty old matriarch. Gerda employed them in the nursery at low wages, abused them liberally, and claimed to be repelled by their promiscuous affection for her, which she had done nothing to earn. She had a certain vanity, however, and might have been disappointed if there was no one following her about.

"When you say that she's perfect," Catherine asked, "do you mean she's perfect in spirit? Or a perfect master of something . . . of what, native plants?"

"The plants are just her symbols. She manipulates things,

brings out their meaning, that's all. She has a correct way about everything she does — she hates mistakes. Now I love that in her. The Germans are a beautiful type of people, I think. I have German blood too, on my father's side."

Catherine decided to increase Rachel's wages. Now she was earning three times what she had made before, mostly for helping with Rick.

Catherine *had never* felt this way before. She felt hollowed out — utterly useless, hopeless. She achieved a sense of reality only when caring for her son; soon, though, the feelings of sickliness and worthlessness affected even that aspect of her life, and she became afraid. She worked, taught her late-winter gardening class, cared for Rick, and this round of once-sufficient effort mocked her with its emptiness, its howling falseness. She awaited the inevitable crash — there had to be some terrible outcome, a disastrous end to this failed way of being.

She thought of the marijuana grower, Bascomb, and felt a mild shame sometimes. In her current condition, she might very well have done something foolish, simply in order to feel, to come awake. He had not contacted her after that morning in the woods. And she was grateful for that, mostly grateful. When she thought of him, she allowed herself only to puzzle at what had bloomed between them so quickly — it was further proof of her desperation, her self-estrangement.

When her mother was Catherine's current age, she had a breakdown; and Catherine began to wonder whether this wasn't an inherited disposition, although the circumstances of her life, the ongoing trauma of Rick, were enough to depress her, certainly. Yet she wasn't really concerned for Rick. The problem of Rick affected her less and less. She had an acute but distant sense of his disaster — she felt the failure of his body in no corresponding part of her own. She never doubted that he would beat this thing, work out some accommodation with his disability. After all, it was his nature to surmount: to survive challenges, to find a way to win.

His suicide attempt — which was certainly what it was — hardly touched her. When she saw him in a coma, when Dr. Weiner explained that this was not yet a "profound vegetative state" but that it might become such a thing, she barely winced. The condition of not-feeling was already so established in her that any disaster, the worst imaginable outcome, would find her already prepared.

Rick began to rally, and she felt distantly glad about that. He had been wrong about his psychologist, who in fact did not wish to be his buddy, but who led him instead on a fairly rigorous, conventional examination of his family background, with corollary questionings of his "denial of sensitivity" and "suppressed female side." An analysis of his character that would have amused him only months before, that he would have dismissed for any number of pathetically obvious reasons, struck him as plausible or, at the least, efficacious, given his dire situation. He became almost talkative about his deeper personal feelings, as when he said:

"When I wrote about my mother, in *Escambeche*, I wasn't in touch with my rage. Children always experience the death of a parent as abandonment, you know, and they blame themselves. But I was so austere, so controlled when I wrote that absurd book . . . Everything that the critics liked about it was a lie. The *real* book I needed to write never got on the page, never got close."

Or, on another occasion:

"Uncle Gower raised me, but he wasn't like a real father to me. My *real* father was a passionate, spendthrift ne'er-do-well who fell in love with a sexy Spanish girl, then spent the rest of his life in bed with her. Their years together were one long alcoholic tryst in the afternoon, a complete denial of responsibility. The only thing that kept it from being sordid was the money."

Catherine knew that Rick was getting better when he spoke this way; the gears were engaging, he had taken hold. Soon he

would have it all in perspective, and for Rick that was sufficient: a complete, penetrating understanding was always the
first step. But she was as unaffected by this new forthrightness
as by his suicide attempt, or by the spectacle of his body
giving out. She just didn't feel it in herself — certainly not in
her own heart. It was strange to hear him speak of the "denial
of sensitivity" when she herself felt radically desensitized,
almost bloodless, heartless. On her worst days, the world
itself seemed unreal to her; and in a spirit of self-punishment,
to mortify herself further, no doubt, she let this condition
become almost ordinary with her.

≈ ≈ ≈

Bob Stein had been out of touch for half a year. He never
responded to her critique of his manuscript, which was now
nearing publication. She felt that she ought to talk to someone, but Bob was wrong, for this and other reasons; at the
same time, Maryanne was often in New York, where her
stepfather was dying. That left only Rick. She had to talk to
Rick.

"I've been so depressed lately, Rick . . . nothing feels right
to me. I wake up anxious, and I only make it through the day
by turning off to things. I think I'm going crazy."

"Yes, I know. I know, Catherine."

"You do? But then what's the matter with me? What's
happening?"

"It's just depression, Catherine — common, garden-variety
depression. You're blue because you've been spending all
your time with a cripple, and you hate it. You pity me, you
feel disgust for me, and it's getting you down. You're afraid
you'll be stuck with me forever. Well, it doesn't have to be like
that. You're free — you're completely free. You don't have to
hold my hand anymore. I have my resources . . . the question
is, do you have any of your own?"

She was taken aback. This curt, rather cool declaration

made her feel that he had been thinking along these lines for weeks — storing up, pondering, preparing a definitive statement on the subject. His eyes were cold, with an undeep, invulnerable expression. Yet he also seemed amused somehow. She could imagine him thinking: There, I've said the worst now, uttered the unutterable. And look — it didn't even hurt. The world hasn't come to an end, has it?

"Rick, you don't understand me," she replied. "I'm not thinking of leaving you — I've never thought that, not once. There's something wrong with me, that's all. I just feel empty, withered and hopeless. It started last fall. It came on suddenly, or maybe I just became aware of it then. And I have to do something about it, Rick. But I don't know what."

"Catherine, you just have an echo sickness, that's all. Weiner said something about it once. His chronic cases often have family complications, where the spouse or even the children develop parallel psychogenic symptoms. You're just too close to me. You have to start to separate, emerge on your own. You've always been dependent on me in psychic ways. Start taking life on your own terms — you'll soon feel better, believe me."

Dr. Klepper, Rick's psychologist, had asked him about Catherine; to some extent, he had anticipated her problems, Rick said. As Rick had dropped his "armor of not-feeling," Catherine could be expected to put it on. Their marriage — any marriage, for that matter — was a dynamic unity, something created from disparate elements, strengths and weaknesses blended, combined. The common goal was to present a unified image, an "integral duality," for the world at large to recognize. But in their marriage, Catherine had been for many years the exclusive repository of all sensation and sensibility, while Rick's tendency to self-control had become exaggerated, developed to a point of dangerous overelaboration.

"I have to learn to feel again," he said simply. "The danger is that I'll suffocate if I don't. I'm already half paralyzed, as you can see. Anxiety is more or less a diaphragm disorder, a loss of elasticity in the chest muscles. When we deny what we feel, we make ourselves physically as well as emotionally rigid. I've been crushed by this extra burden ... it's literally been squeezing the life out of me."

"Well, Rick, it sounds like I've been doing something pretty terrible to you. I guess I'm the bad guy, after all. Who ever asked you to be strong for me, anyway? I don't remember it. And I'm not so sure I'm the only one around here who's having feelings — you have plenty yourself, it's just that they're all angry, resentful. And what's this 'image' we've been trying to project? Is *that* what we've been doing with our marriage, putting out an image?"

"Don't make it sound crude, Catherine," he replied icily. "Don't make a joke of it. I'm not saying I buy everything Klepper says, but there's a core of truth to it. Look at me, just take a good look. You don't become a helpless cripple for no reason at all ... and in the prime of life, when you've got everything to live for. Just look at me, will you."

Catherine asked Dr. Klepper, through Rick, if he thought she should come in for a few of the sessions. But Klepper sent back a surprisingly formal and adamant note: he was Rick's doctor, Rick's alone, and the therapy that they were pursuing reflected that fact. If Catherine was eager to see someone, he could recommend several excellent therapists in the area; indeed, it would be his pleasure to do so.

Catherine rarely went walking in the woods anymore, and never down toward the pond. The rains that hadn't come in November had not come later, either; February, often the wettest month, was entirely dry, and there was a feeling of ongoing disaster in the lifeless forest. In January she sowed the seeds for her second cold-season garden. But two weeks later, when the starts had begun to come up, she felt funny about watering, with a drought so clearly in the offing. She gave her starts to friends.

Normally the rains soaked California from December through March, heavily; but there had been but a single normal winter out of the last eight or nine. Gerda could remember other protracted dry spells, but she, like Catherine, found something sickly about the current state of affairs — the strained, exhausted condition of the forested land. Pagini, an old friend, a retired artichoke farmer out on the coast, maintained that the back of the weather had now been broken: fourteen years of drought out of the last eighteen, as he reckoned them, creeks all drying up, springs disappearing. A well that his grandfather Nicolo dug in the middle of the last century had gone completely dry. The climate was certainly changing.

"Pagini always complains," Gerda said. "He always sees a disaster. But he may be right. And I have seen his well — the old stagecoach well, the famous one. Where they would water the horses driving through."

"I expect a disaster, too," Catherine replied, thinking of many things. "It all smells so odd this year. The trees started blooming too early. I hate these premature blooms, the plants that know they're dying, and they put out blossoms, it's just grotesque. The acacias have a particularly poisonous smell this year . . . it catches in your throat, almost makes you gag."

"Pagini thinks he knows everything," Gerda continued. "No wonder his wife and his children left him. He's like me: he's been left alone, almost all alone. But you look unhappy, Catherine . . . do you feel all right? Rick takes his sickness and he puts it on you, on your own back. I see it every day. I think maybe you should go away."

"Yes, maybe I will go away, Gerda — and sometime soon. But today I'll go see your old friend Pagini. I have to buy a load of mulch from him anyway."

Catherine took Gerda's pickup, thinking to drive to the coast. Her route took her north along the ridge road, then west through the redwood stands along Cuervo Creek. She had heard nothing from Bascomb in more than three months; she had almost stopped thinking of him, and this allowed her to consider stopping at his house, just to say hello. However, she soon decided against it on general principles.

But as she drove the stretch of road, feeling no excitement, no strong inclination one way or another, she began to reconsider. Near the place where his driveway entered the road, she pulled the truck onto the shoulder.

"It's not like I'm coming to see my lover," she said, musing in the truck seat. "It doesn't feel that way, not at all. Too bad."

After a while, as if not quite conscious of what she did, she drove the truck inside the wall of hanging foliage. She parked it in Bascomb's woods.

Walking up his driveway, she heard the blows of a hammer, or possibly an ax, coming from above. Otherwise the dell was perfectly silent — the redwoods curtained it effectively from the road, making a sharp separation, a seal. The ax blows came at long, uneven intervals, as if someone were pausing after each strike, examining the effect produced, and only then proceeding. In the moments between, the silence of the glen reasserted itself, rushing in like bright water.

Where the driveway, after a steep and curving climb, emerged from the redwoods, she saw the roof of his old house. It sat in a small, sunny clearing. But surely she was wrong to believe that people lived here, that anyone could have an ordinary, daily life inside this structure, this off-kilter bit of wreckage. The cabin had no particular style, came from no recognizable period of local history; clearly it had been built from the cheapest materials available, many years ago, then left to weather unprotected. But it had a charm, as weathering wreckages sometimes do. Before the house spread a large yard, which might once have been a vegetable garden. As she approached across this area, she imagined the house concentrating its feeble, fragmented attention upon her: the darkened windows and the sagging, off-plumb façade itself seemed turned to confront her, like an aged face.

The hammering had ended. He was not here working on his roof, nor anywhere else about his property; possibly he was farther up, cutting firewood. And in the absence of the hammer or ax blows, she heard the steady breathing of the house, a sort of regular, confiding ebb and flow, like a pressure against her chest. She mounted the steps. The blows resumed suddenly — they were still far off, still well up the hill.

She tapped at his door. A feeling of sadness came over her then, as no one came, no one answered; after dithering down on the road, wondering whether to visit him at all, she had hoped, at the last, to find him home. So she knocked again, more firmly. Still no one responded, and she sat down on the porch steps in a strip of sunlight.

It was after noon. He might be the one who was hammering up in the woods; then again, maybe not. But she wouldn't wait for him here. It had begun to feel uncomfortable. Still, the sunlight on her legs made her stretch out, and something pleased her about being here in the broad strip of sun, shamelessly indolent, possibly up to no good. She did wait for him for a while. But then she tried the door again. And finding it open, she stepped quickly inside.

The house seemed to breathe at her. It seemed to confront her, to inquire into her motives; and she had to inquire into them herself. But no — she could justify this intrusion in no way, on no realistic grounds. Still, she moved forward. The front rooms were surprisingly tidy. Belying the exterior, which suggested decay if not chaos within, the rooms showed signs of a comfortable, orderly life, many books and magazines, an old stereo, colorful rugs, overstuffed furniture. Several well-framed watercolors were mounted on the walls. The walls themselves looked freshly plastered and painted.

One of the watercolors, showing a rainbow trout in the hands of a crouching fisherman, whose head and legs were cropped by the frame, caught her attention. She admired it for a moment. Meanwhile, the house remained conscious of her, continued to confront her; its passive, peevish expirations of silence continued to daunt her slightly.

After five minutes she returned to the front porch. She had glanced only briefly into his bedroom.

She walked back down the drive. She was vaguely ashamed of what she had done now — the whole thing seemed foolish, to have come at all, hoping to see him. Certainly he would have misinterpreted the gesture, and what then? But at the bottom of the driveway, standing close to the truck, was Bascomb himself. The way he silently emerged from behind some trees, without quite turning to face her, struck her as peculiar.

"Hello," she said, almost alarmed. "I was at your house for a moment. You weren't there. Here you are, after all."

He said nothing, barely nodded. He was wearing his workman's outfit again, and nothing he carried explained his presence here; he had no tools, no axes or hammers. He was simply here, standing in his woods.

"I wanted to say hello," she continued. "Have you been all right? It's been a long time, at least a couple of months."

"Since November," he replied, in almost a cold voice.

He only waited. And she, too, now waited — she tried to understand him meanwhile, to interpret his sudden appearance, his stark, unforthcoming presence before her. His expression was dark and inward. Then, seeming to master himself with some difficulty, he looked up at her. And she began to feel something, almost to understand.

"I've been waiting for you," he said. "Down here. But where were you all that time — since last November?"

"Since last November? Oh, well . . ."

She stood calmly above him. She was on the slope of the driveway, several yards up. But now she walked quickly down to his level. He moved closer to her. He touched her hand.

"You almost killed me," he said, very calmly, clearly. "Did you know? Staying away from me all that time. I almost died, waiting here for you."

"Waiting here? Oh, don't say things like that. That's not possible. It can't be true."

"No? It isn't possible?"

He took her hand. And now she drew back, shook her head; she wouldn't smile, although he was smiling.

"You aren't well," he said. "I can see it. But why didn't you come to me before this? Why did you wait so long?"

"I don't know . . ."

Something about him moved her. It was his frankness, after all; his simple urgency, which was somehow tinged with sadness, with an unself-conscious misery. Which she, supposedly, had caused to arise in him. In response to which, something again failed in her — some reserve of dignity, of not-caring, which she had been counting on, had always counted on. But he felt this about her; he felt the change in her. It caused him to stand closer to her.

"You almost killed me," he breathed out. "I would have died for you. I almost did die, thinking you might not come again."

He pulled her against him, half embracing her. They stood together under the redwoods, not speaking.

≈ ≈ ≈

They walked up to his house. He wouldn't stop touching her, even on the gravelly slope of the driveway; and when she slipped and almost fell, he caught her, practically lifting her off her feet. He would have carried her to the house in his arms if she let him.

"Don't, now put me down," she ordered him.

He said nothing. He had an intent, comfortable look.

The rooms she had visited only a few minutes before awaited them now in a different mood. They went directly to his bedroom. He refused not to touch her; she could hardly get her clothes off, for his hands and chest interfering. He seemed afraid to break contact with her, as if, having found her, having embraced her now, he would not be denied this intimacy ever again. They settled onto his bed. A rush of thoughts carried her away, lessened her consciousness of what was happening; and she wanted to be carried away. Then he said a few words, whispered against her throat. As he found and entered her, he made other sounds, tender and raw, which, though she could not understand, filled her with curiosity and pleasure. She felt a corresponding need to kiss him — to taste his intimate mouth.

"There," she said, "kill me if you want. If I almost killed you, then kill me too." These strange words, which she had never spoken before, had never even considered speaking, sounded only slightly wrong in her ears.

They moved together. Something was odd about the time, each instant felt too fully packed, was wobbly with sensation. Then he came inside her, in complete stillness, without a sound, half of him seeming to run into her prodigiously; and afterward, she had a swift, offhand, imploding sort of orgasm, not from his movements but just from his presence within her, her awareness of him.

"Oh, my," she said, sounding to herself like a startled schoolmarm, with hand thrown up to forehead.

He lay listlessly against her, his arms disarranged. Slowly he came back, and his first movement was in her direction; he put his face into her throat, against the warmth and softness of her there. She almost fell asleep, and when she awoke fully he was making love to her again, lying with his head between her breasts, his arms circled under her hips. It was an innocent sort of lovemaking, she discovered — just a close embrace, as if he only needed to be near, pressed against the center of her. But his capture of her hips became exciting, and she felt top-heavy again, unbalanced with sensation. From the inside of her ankles all the way up to her throat she felt warm, brightly quick, and she pulled him up from her chest.

"Go inside me again," she ordered. "There, that's right, just like that. Just like that."

"Oh, is that good?"

She had a feeling of full, engulfing, enduring comfort — as if she were padded around, her heart held gently, tenderly and finally cradled. She moved against him more loosely, more confidingly than before.

≈ ≈ ≈

"But what about your wife? Doesn't she hope to get back with you?"

They were lying in bed together, later.

"Oh, no. God, no."

"You mean you don't see her anymore? You don't even sleep with her anymore?"

"Don't *even* sleep with her? What's that supposed to mean?"

She had heard a few things about this Bascomb. Everyone knew everyone in the little canyon town — at least, everyone thought he did.

"Someone I know says that you . . . that she and you are still together. Attached in some way."

"Yes? Yes?"

"Well. And that you aren't divorced yet. Hasn't it been a long time, anyway?"

"Yes, it's been a long time. But let's just keep my wife out of this, shall we? Let's keep her out of bed with us."

"All right. If you say so."

She was hungry. Bascomb went to the kitchen and made her a sandwich. He brought it back to the bedroom on a plate, with a glass of red wine. He was naked, placidly, unthinkingly so; his white chest, each breast slightly prominent, a small, perfect thing in itself, struck her as both beautiful and unremarkable.

He sat at her feet while she ate. Her knees were bent up, and he felt between her legs, his hand reveling in her wetness. She made him stop. Then he sat back from her, looking vaguely satisfied, pleased with himself.

"So — did you have a good time, then?" she asked a little bitingly.

"Yes, I did. I did. Why — didn't you?"

"I think I did. But now I don't feel so good."

His expression changed slowly. Everything else about him was quick, gave an impression of directness, frankness; but his look altered slowly sometimes, in overobvious stages.

"Don't feel bad. No — we're only at the start," he said, fairly cooing the words. "It has to feel strange to you, because we hardly know each other. You hardly know me — what I think, what I feel about you. But you will. I know you will."

She shook her head doubtfully.

"Here, give me that plate. I don't want you to feel bad," he said, and he climbed up next to her. "I want you to stay here with me all day. Can you? Will you do that? And then let's make love again. Come on, let's do the same thing, all over again."

"The same thing? The very same thing?"

Then he kissed her breasts, each in turn. There was an impudence in the way he peeled the blanket from her suddenly, as if he knew that she would protest, that she wasn't in a mood to be exposed, but there was a forthrightness, too, an innocent, boyish sort of avidness. When she crossed her arms to hide her breasts, he gently pried them apart. Then he kissed her just between the breasts, just above her heart.

"Just look at you. A rosy-red woman . . . a beautiful, astonishing woman. I can't quite believe you. Come on," and he put a hand between her knees. "Let's make love again. Let's just do it, be lovers again. Fuck each other well again —"

"Oh — don't say it like that. Don't say it."

"No? You don't like that? Well, let's lie together, then . . . is that better? I'll lie with you, and you with me. And we'll see what happens. I love your legs, all golden inside here. You're so much more beautiful than I thought. Much more beautiful. God — just look at this cunt of yours. Such a beautiful, winning place you have . . . I want to reek of you. I already do, but I want to even more."

"Oh, would you stop?"

But he wouldn't; he continued in this same deadpan, too sincere way, fairly drooling over her, ostentatiously adoring her. And as he spoke, his cock came up against her knee, jerking, tapping like a blind man's cane. She laughed to feel it there again.

"Go on. Just lie back and think of England," he commanded. "Think of the Republican Party, if you'd rather . . . you make me so happy. There, isn't that good? Isn't that just how it should be? Isn't it sweet, my dear, isn't it fine?"

His expression underwent another of its slow, falling changes; intention and consciousness seemed to drop away, and she watched out of wide-open eyes, not wanting to miss a single stage of this strange process. She hoped to see the very moment when he yielded — when the tenderness all leaked out of him, in a sort of hemorrhage. But her own eyes had to close, after a while; she only saw enough to soothe her, to make her dream. Then her body became full, it stood in for all of her, and she felt his tenderness act on her directly, even in her muscles and bones. They seemed to triumph over the afternoon.

It was only while driving back to the farm in Gerda's pickup that she realized overpoweringly what she had done. It was a cold, jolting realization, an awful thrill that she had, as if her mind had suddenly shaken itself free, out of another level of awareness.

"I did that . . . yes, I did. I did it. I can still feel him in me, so I know I did . . . my God. Well, it can't be helped. Nothing can be helped now."

She was still herself, however. She was still driving the familiar road in the dry, unliving weather. And again she felt as if her mind had been jolted free, forced into another dimension; even though this new dimension, this new consciousness, was much like the old. It contained no new ideas, no fresh understanding.

"No — I'm not really surprised," she said to herself. "It's not the sort of thing I would do, not at all . . . but I *did* do it. And in my mind, a long time ago. I only just now caught up with myself, I think. Maybe it started that time at the lake, that very first time when he looked at me. It had already happened, even then. And all this misery, feeling depressed last fall, crazy and worthless, it wasn't for Rick, nothing on account of Rick, really. I was sad and depressed just for myself. Well — but something is over now, really finished."

Although she was physically calm, she felt as if a dynamo were racing inside her, not her heart, which was only beating softly, but some other, more essential engine of her being. She looked at herself in the rear-view mirror. In her nervousness she smiled, which only made her dislike herself. But her face had more interest for her now, it attracted her strangely. Then at the farm, Gerda met her dauntingly in front of the house. The old woman was armed with a short rake and a canvas satchel, somehow like the accoutrements of a mythological figure. She commented dryly that Catherine had not, after all, brought back a single spadeful of mulch.

"Oh — I didn't go out to Pagini's. I just went to town. I went to Ben's school."

"I see. I see."

Was it possible — was there already a sign, some outward manifestation of disorder, and was the canny old woman, as sensitive and suspicious as Catherine knew her to be, responding to it?

"I just went to town," she repeated. "And then I had to go to the Starry Plough. That's all I did."

"Yes, yes, I understand, Catherine. But you took my truck. And you said you would return it by three o'clock. And I believed you, unfortunately."

Feeling like a figure in a trite melodrama, some woeful tale of sin, she rushed into the house. But she couldn't find Ben. He had already returned from school, she knew, but he wasn't here, and no one seemed to know where he had gone. She looked for him out back, then down by her gardens, and by a process of elimination she found him up at the quarry, where he sometimes went to paint or play with Karen. The governess and the boy had brought an easel along today, and they had set it up, though they weren't painting. Karen lay by herself in a patch of sun at the head of the quarry, in the willowy spring grass. As Catherine approached, the girl stirred herself and looked up, a bit in confusion.

"Are we late? Does he have to be somewhere this afternoon?"

"No. I just wanted to see him. Where is he, anyway?"

Ben was off by himself in the woods. He had walked

around the quarry, a distance of about a quarter mile, then gone uphill into the madrone forest. He often walked up here with Karen or by himself.

"Karen, I don't know if it's such a good thing. He could fall in the quarry. He could hurt himself. I don't want him playing down there alone, I think I told you that."

"No, he doesn't go down by himself. He knows he's not allowed. I'm sure he's all right . . . he'll be back any minute. I told him not to go far."

The girl, sensing Catherine's anxiety, got to her feet. She smoothed the back of her skirt softly, thoughtfully.

A minute later, Ben emerged from the woods. They could see him across the quarry: he made a short, herky-jerky figure as he marched along, just stiffly, mechanically marched. He stopped at the edge of the pit. A pool had formed in one of the excavations, and he liked to throw stones down.

Catherine felt a surge of longing, a painful need to hold him, to caress him; as the "fallen woman," the figure in her melodrama, she might have been expected to feel this way, although the expectation had nothing to say about the intensity of the sensation. But at the same time, a mood of dissociation, an inexplicable strangeness, came over her, and it seemed to her that she had nothing, really nothing, in common with this stone-tossing, clockwork boy, her jerkily animated forest-child. She called out his name and waved to him; and after throwing a few more stones, he started back around.

Karen looked at Catherine. Then she looked at Ben. A prickly oak leaf had gotten caught in her hair, and Catherine pulled it out for her.

"I'm sorry. I shouldn't have let him go off, I guess. I won't do it anymore," the girl promised. "I'll go up there with him."

"No, that's all right. He knows the paths anyway. He just looks so small today. Don't you think so? Just look at him there. Look at him." And as they stood gazing across the quarry, marveling at her son, Catherine took the younger woman's hand in her own.

This surprised the girl. She peered at Catherine again, and then at their hands; this contact, this unself-conscious connection, seemed to baffle her. Then, as if it had decided something, as if it were physically forcing something from her, she said: "I was going to tell you, Mrs. Mansure ... I meant to tell you before. Well ... but I don't think I can work for you much longer. I have to be with my family more, you see. My mother's having her operation" — they had talked about this before, it was a hysterectomy — "and I should be with her then. It's in June. I could still come up a day or two a week, if you want me. But I think you want someone living in."

Catherine was surprised. "Oh, Karen, you can work here as much as you want, you know that. Or as little as you want. It's okay with me. Take time off if you have to, do whatever you need to. So — it's this June. That's not far off, is it? Tell me if there's anything I can do for her. Are you sure you want to live at home again? Is your father back there now?"

"Yes. Everybody's back now."

Karen's father, a native of the canyon, had himself been in a hospital lately. He was an alcoholic, a contentious, unregenerate drunkard in fact, and his depredations upon the family — seven children, one long-suffering wife — were well known. The girl's move to Longfields had been in part an escape from this — a happy escape so far.

"But don't you think you should stay? Don't you? You could go home any time you want, for as long as you want. But still keep your place up here. Because you may need it."

"Well, I don't know ..."

The girl averted her eyes, as if embarrassed. Ben emerged from the bush then, and he walked stolidly forward, to stand between them. Catherine looked at the girl for a moment longer, then succumbing to painful necessity, she grabbed her son, pulled him roughly against her breast, to kiss him, to caress his forehead and his dark, glossy hair. The boy squirmed in her arms. Then she let him step back without quite letting him go.

"Did you go for a walk, Ben? Where did you go — up to the ridge? Up to the very top?"

"Mom, cut it *out* . . ."

She had to let him go. And he immediately jumped back, a little wildly. After cocking a fist as if to punch her, he abruptly lost all animation. This made him seem to become smaller.

"Mom, I saw the place where we found the coyote pup. Remember? There's lots of blood now. Just lots of blood."

"Well, that's to be expected, Ben. That's what happens up in the woods. It's wild up there. If we'd taken him home, he never would've had a chance. He had to get back with his family. We had to leave him."

"No. If I ever find another one, I'm gonna take it home. I don't care what you say."

Standing stiff, very straight, like a hingeless puppet, he moved closer despite his defiant words; when his shoulder was almost touching his mother's hip, he reached up and calmly took her hand. Then moments later, they set off down toward the farm. Karen walked behind them on the narrow path.

"Mom, does a coyote have puppies? Or should they actually be called cubs?"

"I don't know, Ben. Baby foxes are called kits, I think. So maybe it's not either puppies or cubs."

"A coyote is the difference between a fox and a wolf. Sort of like that."

Catherine nodded. "I see what you mean."

Karen suddenly remembered the easel, left at the quarry, and she turned back to get it. Catherine and Ben waited for her on the path.

"Mom, Karen cried today. She said she had a stomachache. Then she lay down, and she was still crying."

"Well, I'm sorry to hear that, Ben. Is she feeling better now?"

"I guess so."

The young woman returned. No stomachache now — she skipped along in her full, pleated green skirt. Something awoke in Catherine, and she saw the girl's beauty, really saw it, for the first time — felt her freshness and youth, recognized it as if in her own body. This beauty, this remarkable manifestation, produced a strange response in Catherine, something combining envy, remorse, attraction, and identification all at once — because she, too, was newly young and beautiful today, dangerously fresh. "Oh, Karen," she said without thinking, "you're so lovely today. So fine and alive. You're grown up now. You've become a woman now — a beautiful, graceful woman."

"Oh!" the girl cried out, frankly amazed.

Catherine took the easel from her. She did this studiously, with deliberate, almost ostentatious care — as if to imply that nothing must impede this beauty, as if her own role were to relieve the bearer of any burden, any appurtenance disturbing her natural carriage.

Karen blinked her eyes. She looked almost wild, frightened for a moment. Then her eyes became soft, and they filled with tears.

"You always say such nice things to me. Why? Why are you so kind? I don't want to leave you . . . why are you good to me, anyway?"

It was a strange, unnerving question. Catherine was taken aback. "Well, there's no reason. It's just that I like you, I guess. We all do. Ben does, and I do, and Rick . . . I guess you remind me of myself, too, a little. Some way that I was, or wish I had been, when I was your age. Well, come on," and

she put her arm around the girl's waist, bringing them together. Their hips touched.

They continued down along the path. Ben walked between
them now, and from time to time he looked up into their
faces. His expression was like that of a small bird, Catherine
thought, a puzzled and curious hatchling, which hears a distant call in the forest, something it can't yet identify.

The next day, Wednesday, Rick went to Palo Alto for his medical appointments. Catherine stayed behind. Late in the afternoon she heard the car in the circular driveway, and she went out to greet her returning husband. Rachel was helping him at the passenger door. He stood up slowly, haltingly, despite her aid and the support of his cane; he moved much like an old man these days.

"New wonder drugs," he said sarcastically, showing Catherine a plastic bottle with a label. "They've found something else to poison me with. Wouldn't you know it."

"Did you see Klepper, too?"

"I saw everyone, absolutely everyone. I've been probed, massaged, analyzed, and x-rayed. Get me a drink please, Catherine — just get me a drink."

He couldn't drink anymore. But he still liked to order her to "get me one," whenever his patience ran out, whenever his ordeal became too much, exhausted his capacity to offer comment.

They brought him into the house. Rachel on the right of him, wearing a nursy smile, and Catherine on the left. When she put her arm around his waist she drew back inwardly, not from him so much as from herself, from her own perfidious normal-appearingness; and she had a sharp, devastating intuition of the ordinary intimacies to be shared, the months or even years of them, stretching on into a poisoned future. At the door of the library she tripped on a woven rug, and Rick spoke sharply to her.

"I'm not a sack of fertilizer, Catherine. You can't just fling me around, you know."

"I'm sorry, Rick. Sorry."

Again he begged her to bring him a drink, in earnest this time. He had collapsed in a corner of the vanilla-colored couch. Rachel went out soundlessly and returned with a glass of Calistoga water.

"No, that's not what I meant. Not at all."

"Maybe you could have some wine at dinner," said the attentive kitchen girl. She looked to Catherine. "Would that be all right?"

"Yes, well, I guess so."

Rick fumed for a while about this and that. He became very cranky late in the day, and his awareness of his own moods hardly mattered — he preferred to give vent to things, he was tired of being brave, of enduring. He had decided that the most idiotic of his doctors was precisely the one who pretended to be most commonsensical — Weiner, young Dr. Weiner, the general practitioner, the one who kept counseling him to wait, to be patient.

"Time heals all wounds, he says. In the meantime, I hate his dull, fat face, I can't stand his droning, measured way of putting things, like he's learned it all out of a book. The whole medical service there is corrupt, entirely corrupt. If you're well insured they pull out all the stops. This week it's something new and different — rheumatoid arthritis. Maybe it's not the old polio thing at all."

"Rick, are you serious? Can they be serious?"

"Who knows? Really — who knows? It's like that old engraving, by Hogarth or somebody, with the ghoulish quacks all gathered around the rich man's bed. They're just vultures, that's all, they're scum. And Weiner, who doesn't even try to control them, who doesn't have the guts for it, keeps telling me to take it easy. 'Have faith.' "

"Allopathic medicine is just a cesspool," Rachel commented placidly, as if this were an old chestnut. " 'Do no harm.' Yeah — but all they ever do is harm."

After dinner, Catherine left the house by herself. After turning on the drip lines at one of her gardens, she took the path that led below the barns, and soon she was among the cabins. There were four of them: sturdy, high-gabled dwellings, built more than thirty years before. She knocked on Karen's door. The young governess seemed startled to see her — it was growing dark outdoors, and she was already dressed for bed, in a cotton nightgown and wool socks. Catherine came in and they sat together on the bed.

"I wondered if you were all right. If you'd been thinking about going home anymore."

"Oh, I'm all right," the girl replied. "I'm just a little sad, that's all. I don't see how I can get around it."

"Well, try not to be sad. There's probably a way."

The cabin was tightly built, with board-and-batten walls of unfinished fir. It reminded Catherine of ski huts in the Sierras. The bathroom was in a separate structure, as was a laundry room. The girl had brought most of her clothes up from the family home in Cuervo over the last few months; just a few weeks before, one of her brothers had trucked up an old, heavily shellacked pine dresser with painted designs, which now sat in a corner supporting a plaster lamp.

"Don't be sad, Karen. And tell me all about it. There has to be some way to keep you here. Has to."

"Well, I don't think so, really. It's been good for me, wonderful, to be living here, working for you. But I think I have to go back now."

She had a quiet, unapologetic willfulness; the more they talked, the plainer it became to Catherine that she had made up her mind, had reached her decision thoughtfully. While her mother recovered from her recent operation (there was a long history of medical interventions, this only the latest and most severe), Karen would keep house for her, try to keep her fractious father sober, and though she would be acting in the old capacity, as a sort of brood hen to her younger brothers and sisters, she would not be overcome, she promised; she would remember to escape again.

"I talked to Rick," Catherine said. "He wants to help you any way he can. If it's only a question of hiring someone, a nurse to be with your mother or something, he's happy to pay for it. A housekeeper, a nurse — whatever you might need."

The young woman nodded, although this idea seemed to puzzle her. A stranger, a complete stranger, to be introduced into the chronic disorder of her family: no, it couldn't work, it would be terrible. The shameful, incurable disaster of it all — this could be shared with no one else, certainly not with some stranger.

"He wants to help you, as I said. If you ever decide you want to go to college, for example, he can help you with that. Financially or in any other way. But I think he already told you that. Didn't he?"

"Yes, he did. He did."

The girl adopted a softer tone; she dropped her eyes. "He said that to me once, yes, that he wanted to help me. He's been so good to me. So generous. Just like you — you've both been good to me." And she smiled sweetly, with her eyes still downcast — large, cool green eyes, Catherine noticed, lovely and unalarmed.

She now proceeded to read the governess the usual lecture of encouragement: about how bright she was, how capable, that someone of her abilities, had she only been born and raised somewhere else, would have gone to college, on to some career. The backward, isolated canyon was a curse sometimes, despite its quiet and its rustic beauty; it acted to retard the ambitions of its children. The young woman never once lifted her gaze, and at a certain point she actually shivered with discomfort — but whether from embarrassment, unease at hearing her praises sung, or for some other reason, Catherine couldn't tell.

In the middle of this little pep talk, this stock recitation,

Catherine suddenly felt a thrill entirely at odds with the subject under discussion, and she realized what had brought her here — the true urge behind it. The girl's slender neck, meekly bent as she inclined her head submissively, awoke a feeling of reckless warmth in Catherine, a strange displaced affection, and she declared:

"I was like you once, Karen . . . yes, I was a lot like you. I remember it so well. I tried to please everyone, and often I succeeded, but deep down I was false. I wasn't really like that — not at all. I didn't care about anyone else, not in the way I'd heard you were supposed to care. I didn't understand the concept. How were you supposed to care about somebody, anyway? I didn't get it. And I was always asking what things meant, seeing a kind of emptiness behind it all. I think I was looking for some more authentic feelings — something like that. Some powerful, unquestionable emotion, a perfect feeling of some kind . . ."

The girl, mildly startled by this new tone, this air of urgency and intimacy, lifted her frank green gaze. But her expression was entirely blank: her inner state, whatever it might have been at that moment, registered hardly at all, and she appeared in the end rather cunning, as self-possessed people often do.

"I tried to fall in love," Catherine went on. "It seemed the right thing for me at the time. And I was away at school, and it was all part of growing up, I guess . . . right off the bat, I found someone who could give me those 'strong feelings,' whatever they were. Feelings that I couldn't pick apart. Not necessarily the *right* feelings, mind you, but something strong, really something. And it was a great relief to me, you know. I could let life just sort of happen to me after that."

The governess, with a look of guarded perplexity, seemed to gather herself at this point; her expression was slightly disapproving, as if this kind of talk went against her instinct and she had learned to fear its outcome. But Catherine touched her hand reassuringly, then continued in a musing, almost eager tone:

"I went to see that friend of mine, you know. The one we were talking about — the one I was asking you about. And I walked up to his house, because he lives way up in the trees, far above the road, where the woods are really dark. It's very remote-feeling . . . you're afraid somehow, you almost think it's enchanted. Well, but he wasn't home. I knocked and knocked, and then I heard someone up in the forest, chopping wood or something. You know how that can sound sometimes — the slow, steady strokes of the ax, the muffled, sleepy sound of it . . ."

She felt the young girl drawing back, arming herself, establishing distance. Still, she needed to speak; she had a truth to tell. Then as she spoke Bascomb's name, declared it aloud, she felt an uncanny excitement; his foursquare, ungainly name, which she didn't know if she liked, thrilled her, recalled the sensations of the previous afternoon. The ax blows, which had lulled her, actually seemed to hypnotize her; when she had first heard him play, down at the bar in Cuervo, the rasp of his fiddle had had a similar, transformative, half-hypnotizing effect. The girl listened to Catherine's words in evident perplexity — she seemed unable to imagine the need of this, the point of them. But then her expression relaxed. It became truly distant, truly composed, even as it relaxed. They had talked about Bascomb only once or twice before.

"He still lives with his daughter," Catherine was saying, "but otherwise, completely alone. He doesn't see his wife anymore, he made that very clear. But he seems coarse to me sometimes. You think he's sneering at you, sneering at everything, and then he'll do something sincere. Something that touches you. He's a strange sort of man, I think. I don't know if he's better or worse than the others, but he's not completely obvious . . ."

She was saying too much, speaking out of turn. Even so,

the pleasure she felt was real, somehow it was its own justification. The very innocence of the girl, who in the woods the previous day had seemed poised between maidenhood and something else, impelled her to speak, to lay instinctive claim to the judgment that womanly innocence would give of her.

"He looks a lot like someone I used to know, someone out of my past. Not that I really *do* know him, not at all . . . but he seems that familiar. I've only met one other man in my life who affected me that way. It was years ago, when I was living in Guatemala . . . there was a man who worked on our farm, the man who managed all the Indians. I didn't like him for what he did, but there was something about him. The first time I ever heard him speak — in Spanish, I think — I felt I already knew him, just because of how he sounded, the feeling you got from his voice. It made you think you understood him, no matter what he said . . . and the whole time I was there, I was quietly but madly obsessed with him. Half in love with him, I think, just because of his voice. And I had just gotten married, you know . . . and I remember thinking: What's the point of this? Why am I even made this way? Why should I be feeling this — it's ludicrous, it's destructive, that's all. But when you have that feeling, you don't doubt it. But why — why are people made this way? What's the reason, why this capacity for feeling, for being against yourself, for ruining everything?"

Now the girl nodded — it was as if she had finally heard something that made sense, something recognizable. Then in the same instant, she stifled a small yawn, and Catherine was brought up short. This polite, half-furtive yawn, easy enough to explain in terms of the hour, the stresses and strains of the day, utterly deflated Catherine's need to confess, her joy in speaking her mind. For a moment she considered the possibility that this yawn, this ordinary, entirely explicable response to her going on so, was less than involuntary, and the remarkable self-possession of the younger woman impressed itself upon her yet again. And at the same time, she became aware of a stolid, implacable quality to the silence between them, as if the air of the room itself had become disapproving.

A moment later she rose up, saying, "I left the water on at one of my gardens." And then with wishes for a good night, promises that they would meet again tomorrow, she went away.

Ben *was* a good chess player, and out of the blue he received six chess books on his birthday at the end of May. The books came from Bob Stein, who could hardly play, but who had been impressed with the boy's interest the year before. Ben often came home from school these days and went straight to his father's computer, which he booted up and programmed with "ChessMaster 2000." He had already beaten the machine at level four (out of a possible ten).

As often with Bob, this sending of a gift was a prelude; a few days later he called and proposed himself as a house guest, for a weekend early in June. Catherine said yes, uneasily.

"I feel more than a year older," he said to her over the phone. "Seven or eight at least. You were so right about that book. It's been trouble, nothing but trouble. My editor left and my publisher tried to back out of the deal. Then after making me feel worthless, they're finally bringing it out in a haphazard way, and if this one fails, it's the stake through the heart of my ludicrous career. I saw Maryanne last week, by the way. She's talking about getting married, believe it or not . . ."

When Bob arrived that weekend, still driving his old blue Volvo, he looked tired and troubled. He explained that he was at the end of his tether now, both physically and spiritually. This had been the worst winter of his life, a time of obsessing about everything, of coming to terms with his failure on every front. He was utterly unable to write. Two of the courses he taught at the University Extension had been canceled for reasons having to do with administrative politics, and he would soon run completely out of money. "But I mean completely this time — absolutely rock-bottom." He had no girlfriends, not even much interest anymore. "It's a terrible time to be a Don Juan. The whole culture's gone anti-sex, violently so. Except where there's a commercial tie-in, of course ... in Berkeley, you can't even look at a girl on the street — you feel the Behavior Police lurking 'round the corner, waiting to pounce and punish. Every natural action violates some grim new code, it seems to me. If I see an attractive woman, I'm oppressing her if I dare chat her up — insulting womanhood, you know. Probably spreading disease, too."

They went upstairs, intending to see Rick, but he was taking his mid-morning nap. Rachel, the kitchen girl, actually closed the bedroom door as they approached down the hall, shutting Catherine out of her own room. "He's just exhausted," she explained without a hint of apology. "He's been reading and writing in bed for hours" — as if Catherine hadn't known, weren't aware of what her own husband was doing.

"All right, Rachel. We'll talk to him later, I guess. But don't ever shut doors in my face, please. It puts me in a foul mood."

"I'm sorry. I wasn't thinking."

Bob seemed relieved. He had been dreading this encounter with Rick, in some ways; they hadn't spoken to each other in a year, since his last visit to Longfields. The news of Rick's ongoing physical decline had somehow leaked up to Berkeley, where current rumor had it that he was suffering from AIDS or multiple sclerosis, or possibly both. Catherine explained the medical situation in detail, dispelling all likely rumors. Bob nodded, shook his head mournfully, and occasionally threw up his hands in exasperation listening to the outlandish story of medical false starts and bonehead moves. He had a similar story of his own, as it happened: a cousin of his had recently come down with similar neurological symptoms, which had been completely misunderstood for months, totally misdiagnosed.

"They're calling it Epstein-Barr now — the chronic fatigue

thing," Bob said. "But in the meantime she lost her job, her boyfriend, and her apartment, and for a while they had her on weird brain chemicals, the kind they only give to epileptics. But you know what Rick's illness sounds like — it could be Lyme disease, the one you get from ticks. You live in a real jungle here, Catherine, almost a wilderness. It must be teeming with ticks and other diseased beasties."

"No, Bob — I've never heard of Lyme disease around here. I don't think it's gotten to this part of the state yet."

"Well, you could be wrong, Cath. It's already gotten to Berkeley — it's in Tilden Park, six blocks from my house. It's the revenge of the natural order. As we degenerate humans encroach ever further, destroy more of what little remains of the wild, diseases inevitably get passed on. Giardia and Lyme disease, Rocky Mountain spotted fever. Things that used to be restricted to animal populations. AIDS used to be an infection in green monkeys, you know — that's if you don't buy the theory that the CIA introduced it, purposely put it in a batch of hepatitis vaccine that they sent to central Africa, in the seventies. There's a professor at Cal making a big career now correlating the early outbreaks with proximity to World Health Organization vaccination centers . . . myself, I prefer the green monkey idea, it's more horrifying. This human existence that we find so hard to support, that's a trial under the best of circumstances, turns out to be incredibly fragile, too, a matter of vicious microbes held only temporarily in check, plagues of the future and the past just waiting to break out . . ."

When Rick did appear, later in the afternoon, Bob had already had a number of drinks. He greeted the semi-invalid almost tearfully. Rick endured the earnest, ungainly embrace Bob offered without bringing his own arms and hands into play — they were occupied with his two canes, in any case — but he seemed touched by the effusions of sympathy that followed, and then the two men, perhaps startled by their own display of feeling, lapsed into an uncharacteristic silence.

Catherine saw Rick as she imagined Bob now saw him: as a cripple, a degraded version of the graceful, powerful masculine figure he had presented as recently as ten months ago. Likewise she imagined Rick to be experiencing a new, yet more terrible kind of mortification, as this old friend who knew him so well, who had admired and resented him during his years of formidable accomplishment, had to struggle for minutes to compose himself.

"I'll get you a drink, Rick," she eventually interposed. And then she poured him a small scotch, his first taste of whisky in nearly a year. He nodded gratefully.

"Life is strange," he said a moment later, blinking and seeming bemused. Then he smirked at his own use of the bromide, and turning to Bob he inquired, "Or would you say just stupid, Bob? Fundamentally second rate?"

"Well, I don't know, Rick. I'm not sure what I'd say. Unfinished — that's for sure. Not well enough thought through. These crude things that happen to people, and then we're supposed to supply all the commentary, you know, the meaning. But there's always a sketchy sort of feeling. You wish the author'd taken more time, dug a little deeper for material."

"I keep thinking of a population of lab rats," Rick replied, in a half-bantering voice. "And in the 390th generation, one happens to break his hind leg, and he can't quite make it to the drip feeder anymore. So he starves to death. Then the 391st generation comes along, followed quickly by the 392nd, and so on. And no one makes a fuss. No one cares — nothing, nobody cares at all. The life-stream just flows on stupidly, unstoppably."

"Oh my, Rick," Catherine observed, "that sounds very detached. Very Buddhist or something. But you aren't quite dead yet, I think. And you're still making it to the drip feeder, I notice."

"Don't try to cheer me up. Please, Catherine, spare me

your healthy attitude toward my suffering. I don't know why people always assume that they can patronize you just because you're sick and crippled ... here, fill her up again. That's a good girl."

Catherine dutifully replenished his drink. Whether because he had anticipated a strong reaction, or because he was really experiencing one, Rick suddenly subsided onto the couch, seeming to lose all starch in only an instant. He grinned wickedly at Bob Stein.

"It's really good to see you, Bob. Really good. But I suppose it's special for you, too, after writing about me for so long. To see me so reduced, I mean. Wasting away, just as you'd always predicted ... they'll be saying you have prophetic powers. Was it in your first book, Bob, or was it the third that my 'character' broke his neck in a car accident? I can never keep them all straight, you know — the indignities you inflict on me, I mean. I know my wife always leaves me in your books, too. So, if Catherine takes up with a lover soon, we'll have played out your entire scenario. And what a triumph that will be."

After a moment Bob replied, "There's no feeling of triumph, Rick, none at all. And I wasn't ever writing about you — not in the way you think. But I do feel strange about it, I have to admit. And I feel very, very sad for you — you have to believe that."

"Thank you, Bob. That's touching. You know, I always thought it took a special kind of guts to write about me the way you did. To say such ugly things about me, then come down here and pretend to be my friend. But do you really think you have the gift of second sight, Bob — that you can foretell things, that you saw the inevitable fate of someone of my regrettable personality type? Or did your books actually influence fate — how about *that* as an idea? Can a work of fiction, of the imagination so-called, actually change the living model — can it rewrite reality so to speak? I'm beginning to think so, you know. Fiction as a sort of program, something we run on life's mainframe computer, and reality has to conform to it, surrender to its greater integration, its more far-reaching consistency. Not completely, but little by little. Well — but that's how we judge the great books, don't we? They're the ones that make the world look different afterwards, make it act that way later on. Not that there's anything great about your stuff, of course. Don't get me wrong, Bob, I don't mean to imply such a thing."

Rick knocked over a cane at this point; it clattered unpleasantly to the floor, making a vibratory sound. Bob, a little pathetically, bent over and picked it up for him.

"Just put it here, Bob. Next to my useless legs. And don't worry — I won't beat you with it, I promise."

"Rick, I wasn't writing about you. You must know that. Or about Catherine, either. Some people just stimulate you, they evoke something in you, bring up archetypes or something. You want to understand the process better, that's all . . . it's like the people you dream about, even though you don't know them anymore, don't see them anymore. Friends from childhood, unimportant acquaintances. You write about them because you want to understand the hold they have on you — this subliminal claim on your soul. They represent some hidden part of you, I guess."

"Very interesting, Bob, very. But someone simple, someone with a less developed artistic sense, might say that you *were* writing about me, about me and no one else. That you were doing it because you envied me, resented the hell out of my success, and for some reason needed to bring me low. You couldn't do it in real life, so you did it in your books. And you wrote about my wife because you've always had half an eye on her sweet ass yourself . . . but now that I'm broken down, not enviable anymore, you're in for a hard time, Bob. You may not be able to write at all without betrayal as a motive . . . better start looking around for another one, another promising victim. Someone fairly close to you, who you supposedly like, but a more genuinely evil person this time. I've always felt slightly over-sold in your books, you know."

This tone of controlled animus, of facetious accusation, with Bob being called to account for his fictional indiscretions, persisted throughout the afternoon and early evening. Catherine became more and more morose under its influence. But the two men, speaking more frankly than they had in years, worked up a sort of excitement between them, a pseudo-warmth well oiled by whisky and red wine (two bottles of a Heitz Cabernet at dinner). Catherine found it amazing, later on, when she considered how freely Rick had spoken about himself and his feelings: Rick, who before had considered this subject unmentionable, utterly beneath notice. In this she thought she saw the influence of Dr. Klepper, his psychologist.

"When you're my age, when you reach this point in your 'career,'" Bob said after dinner, as they retreated to the courtyard veranda, "you realize you're really up against it, and you don't argue with your imagination anymore. You just take what it gives you, gratefully, humbly. If that means writing the same book over and over, so be it. You just do it, you do whatever it takes. I stand speechless in front of my imagination now ... I know what's embarrassing in my books, where I've told tales out of school and so forth, and I'm ashamed, believe me. But I don't feel false anymore. I'm just transcribing my tape, that's all. Speaking my inner mind. And as ignoble and tiresome as that might be, as the books may be, they're all I have to give the world, in the end."

"Bob," Rick replied, "I haven't read your new book. I'm sorry to confess it. But Catherine tells me it's not very good. More of the same. More of the same old nonsense. Now we'll *all* have to stand speechless before it, I guess ... what I don't like, though, is this tone of victimization, of martyrdom almost, as if someone else was forcing you to write. Where does that come from, pray tell? Because deep down, you must feel you have a right and a license to say these stupid things — moreover, that the world has a responsibility to listen to them. And that, it seems to me, is presumption enough. Don't ask for my sympathy, on top of all the rest . . ."

Bob could only assent to this. He had drunk too much, or perhaps he was just tired. But Rick had hit a vein of interest and energy in himself, and he continued to hold forth for some time, well past his normal hour for rest.

≈ ≈ ≈

Next morning, while they walked down to her gardens together, Bob asked Catherine if she had been "seeing" someone. She denied the idea immediately, almost angrily. He apologized for being so blunt, so presumptuous, saying in his defense that encountering Rick in this condition had disturbed him profoundly: "The only time I ever felt like this before, and it wasn't this bad, mind you, was when my own grandfather lay dying. A pillar of your universe suddenly starts to give way. Something you've counted on unconsciously, steered your life by unthinkingly . . .

"You were so quiet last night, Cath. You hardly said two words. And I could feel something new between you and Rick — something sad, resigned. I'm worried about you, too, you know. But it would kill him. It really would. He loves you desperately, you know, in his own peculiar way. You can't pretend that he doesn't."

Catherine thought that this was quite amazing — this paean to Rick's love for her, coming from Bob Stein, of all people. "I'm not pretending anything, Bob," she said, still nursing her bit of anger, hiding behind it. "And please, don't start giving me marital advice, not at this late date. I'll do whatever I can for Rick, for as long as I can, you know that. If he needs me, I'll always be there to help. That can't ever change."

S*he had seen* Henry Bascomb three times now — twice at his house, then once in the woods, at the western edge of her property. To her surprise he wrote her a letter that arrived the Monday after Bob Stein's visit. It read:

"Catherine — I go to the lake every day now. I always hope I'll meet you. This morning, I walked up through the woods where we were, and I found the bed of clover flowers that we lay on, and I lay down on it again. I could almost feel you there. The clover bed looks surprised, I think, and the trees are quiet because we did something in front of them that they don't understand. I lay down on it again. I could smell the earth, and I was afraid, thinking that I wouldn't see you again, that you would feel wrong about what had happened. That you would turn against me. In a way, you're too fine for me — finer, much better than you know. And after I'm with you, I always feel a little afraid, that maybe I wasn't meant to feel this way. Maybe I wasn't meant for this happiness.

"I lay down in the flowers again anyhow. And after a while, I felt much better. The spell of the place came over me. The trees and earth seem different now, and even the air is disturbed, I think, it cools you, it thrills you. I think that if a stranger was to come walking up there, entering the woods in the same place we did, he would immediately know that something odd had happened. He might even know that someone had been making love there, some large animals, maybe a deer and his doe. Or maybe some of the coyotes that live thereabouts. He would never be able to imagine what I saw, though: a naked, rosy, red-haired woman, real and glowing, golden-limbed, lying down in the white flowers.

Shaking her hair loose, shaking her head and turning to look at me. Shamelessly, purely offering herself . . ."

After describing a problem he had been having lately — something to do with his marijuana gardens, which required him to drain water out of her pond again — he continued:

"Even if we can't go on this way, if you have to end with me, for a hundred good reasons, I won't blame you. I don't think I ever could. But for me, something important has happened. Something I always expected, that I had stopped waiting for, even so, but that I still hoped for. When I understand it sometimes, I lose all sense of myself (usually it's when we're making love, and I get crazy with wanting you, wild from it; my arms for holding you, my chest to warm you and my cock for fucking you aren't enough, not nearly), I forget where I am, I go somewhere else entirely, and the beauty of it almost drowns me. It almost finishes me right then, brings me under and destroys me. What I feel is something only rapture can see, only passion can show it to me. Otherwise, it's wholly mysterious . . ."

With this letter in hand, Catherine walked down to one of the tool barns. Here she felt secluded enough to read it through a few more times. Her nervousness at having received such a letter, and at home, dissipated eventually, to be replaced by feelings occasioned by his alarming seriousness — or maybe it was only the strangeness of his expressions: what exactly was this "rapture" he spoke of, and did she really have to be the one who "finished" him, who "brought him under"? But as she read on, a peculiar excitement arose in her, not exactly equivalent but corresponding to his own, and she knew that she wanted to be with him. He seemed to present a different aspect entirely, almost a different face, as he spoke to her through this letter, and her need to see him took the form of simple curiosity, as if she wanted only to piece him back together, fit this new facet with all the others.

As it happened, she couldn't get away till that Friday. She wrote him a note arranging the time and place, and asking him not to contact her at the farm anymore, at least not for a while.

≈ ≈ ≈

She saw him at first from a distance, as he trudged up a path in the forest. The ravine where she had proposed to meet was a remote spot, several miles south of the farm; she had found it only two years ago, after studying the topographic maps. A steep hillside had split in two following some movement in the earth, and the deep cleft resulting was full of moisture, fringed with great bay trees that gave a greenish, cooling shade. Bascomb looked small when he first appeared, walking up from the distant canyon floor. She lost sight of him in the trees; then, coming down a little from her position, she saw him again.

His neck was bent and he looked tired, climbing laboriously upward. His thick, waywardly waving hair swung slowly side to side, wings of it falling free. She walked down farther, and then they paused, still some yards apart, on the mossy floor of a small plateau where moisture seeped from the cleft hill.

Bascomb took something out of his knapsack. It was a bouquet of sorrel flowers and wild irises that he had picked; he placed it in the pool of a tiny spring. Catherine walked over after a moment, as if to admire the bouquet and nothing more.

They said hello, quietly. He asked her to forgive him for sending her a letter. "It was a bunch of drivel anyway," he said. "I don't know what I was trying to get across. I never can write what I feel. I just can't do it."

"No, it wasn't drivel," she corrected, "and I liked to have it, I liked getting it. But I'm worried about my husband now.

He's very sick, you know. I can be unfaithful to him, I guess I'm that sort of woman, but I don't want him to have to think of this, too."

Bascomb nodded after a moment. "They say he's crippled now. And that he'll die, sooner or later."

"No, he won't die. Who told you that? Who said that?"

"People I know. Some people in town. They say they know him pretty well, too. And you."

He hadn't touched her yet. Nor had he even turned to look at her directly. It was as if, each time they met, he had to recapitulate the whole process, the entire nervous, uncertain movement toward intimacy, with all his shyness, and their mutual resistance, still to be played out. A thrill of longing passed through her even so. Possibly it was provoked by this perverse, resentful standoffishness; and she hoped that the sharpness of her feeling, as she had it just at that moment, would be clear to him.

But he didn't seem to understand. He stepped back, crouching near the little bouquet. He had tied the flower stems together with some blades of grass, and the flowers as they floated in the pool came unbound. He fetched two wild irises, dripping wet, from the spring.

"They said that he was dying. And that you never loved him, either. That you wanted to leave him a long time ago, and you only came back because of the money. That's what they said."

"They did? Is that what they told you?"

He seemed indifferent to this matter, in the end. Nothing could have concerned him less, he wanted to imply, even though he himself had raised the issue. Now he took one of the flowers and placed it in her hand. Then he kissed her throat — kissed her peckingly, where her shirt collar was left unbuttoned. She felt his warm mouth despite the haste. And his breath was warm and sweet, redolent of flowers.

"I picked these just for you. Because they remind me of

you. All the plants in the forest remind me of you, sometimes."

"Do they? Even the thistles, and the poison berries?"

He made a bed for her on the cool, moist moss. He lined it with his own clothes, taking time to pad it out, to secure her comfort. The light was cool in the grotto, and his shoulders glowed almost greenly. Then after a while she too undressed. When he stood completely naked before her, with his stout, youthful-seeming cock half twisted up, colored lavender and a sort of cream, she felt almost sorry for him, as if the paleness of his shoulders, the smoothness of his placid chest, were talismans of a fatal, hopeless vulnerability. Then she kissed him at the waist. There was something exotic about the taste of him, his skin reminded her of the forest itself, the flowers. It made her think not of other men, not even of him, but of other times, other locales, a foreign country she might have visited in her youth. Then, when she had him precisely in her mouth, she continued to think of this other place, this other time, of satisfactions she might have had there in her other life. She would have been bold then, she imagined: the idea of happiness, of raw, heedless satisfaction, would have accorded better with her own nature.

Feeling something like a tremor in him, which ran along his whole frame and up his spine, she had a satisfaction of her own, a short, preliminary, answering vibration. Bascomb drew quickly back.

He shuddered, waiting to calm down. She remained before him on her knees. And after a while he also knelt down, pressing his face to her breasts, one cheek and then the other. He slowly stroked her thighs. When they kissed he became completely still; that yielding, hopeless thing was in him again, a physical suggestion of helplessness, of despair.

"What is it? Are you there?" she wondered. "Where are you, Bascomb?"

"Not yet," he said. "No."

He came forward on his knees. He pulled her straight against him, but regretfully, it seemed, almost sadly. She was aware of the forest all around them — he made her think of that, made her picture it, by his stoic, distanced calmness. Then he lifted her up and on, pulling her against him a little roughly. Somehow this only made her think of the woods, too: of the moment they were in, of the place, of the shaded quiet afternoon. Lying back in the moss, she smelled the forest shade in his skin; and the limbs of the trees above were like his bones, kindly arching, gaining a leverage.

≈ ≈ ≈

They dressed slowly, pausing from time to time as if they forgot what they were about. The trees looking down (if trees do look down) saw a man and a woman turning away from each other, picking up their clothes casually, she with one sock on, he with pants but no shirt.

"What was that?" she asked. "What was that about? Where did you go?"

He looked at her, seeming puzzled.

"You weren't here," she said. "I didn't feel you with me. I don't think I can do it this way, it frightens me. I don't know you well enough yet. I may never know you."

He found his shirt and pulled it on slowly. Then he helped her with the buttons of her blouse; his smile seemed fixed, but he buttoned her tenderly, and a warmth moved out from his hands.

"I need to feel you," she said, almost pleading. "You can't just go off somewhere. Tell me — tell me what you think of. Tell me what happens when you go off like that."

"What happens? Well ... I don't know. I'm thinking of you, actually ... picturing you, feeling you completely. But maybe I don't believe it yet. I'm a little afraid still. I feel a lot with you — maybe too much. I don't understand it yet."

"You have to try to be with me — have to. That's the only way I can do this. Try to let me know you."

"All right. Whatever you say."

He turned away. It was time to put on his shoes — that was all, he simply had to turn away. And she was baffled. She felt cut off at just her moment of wanting to understand, of trying to speak to him. This kind of physical intimacy was always a mistake, then, she decided; it always outstripped everything else, it created imbalances. First they needed to know each other — but by other means, in other ways. And only then might they move on to this, to these powerful intimacies. It was wrong to begin this way. They might even hurt each other, playing with this power, which seemed unfocused, ungrounded.

"I have to know you better," she pleaded. "And you have to know me. And then you won't feel strange. Or afraid, if that's what it is."

"All right. But even so . . . I think I will always feel afraid. I need to be afraid, a little. It's appropriate — don't you think?"

"No. I don't understand that," she said, smoothing back her hair, shaking her head as she looked at him.

So *far* Catherine had assumed she was "only" having an affair, misbehaving, straying, in some moderate, discreet way. It was something she had never done before, in twelve years of marriage, despite occasional strong attractions; and the outrageous impropriety of it, considering Rick's current condition, almost seemed to excuse it. If she was indeed the kind of person who could do such a thing, then it hardly mattered how she acted; she was worth less, made of lesser stuff, than she had always pretended.

The ordinary line of excuse — that she was lonely, needed to be comforted physically — had no meaning for her. She knew that she did not act out of physical need. For that matter, she had never acted that way, the whole idea was strange to her, glaringly incomplete; the emotional aspects of a situation had always bulked so large for her, constituted so much of her experience of it, that to speak of a separable physical component hardly made sense. She had always felt her way through life, giving and taking sustenance, living on an emotional level, mainly; the physical was something she'd had to learn, almost against her natural inclination. In the ideal situation, the feelings simply flowed for her — from heart to heart, from mind to mind.

Consider, then, her profound disturbance when certain physical acts and caresses that she shared with Henry Bascomb set off virtual detonations in her body: sudden blank convulsions, with all of her physical being, her very blood, seeming to rush out and then back in. She had known of this before, of course; she had even had it before, partly and more remotely. But there was a frightening force and completeness, an absoluteness to it now. She became aware, through these experiences, of a separate existence inside her body — of secret whims and capacities, a desire for a kind of finality, even a kind of extinction.

But she did not act out of physical need. Not that — not that at all. Every time she saw Bascomb, each time they overcame, a little more easily, their resistance to each other, she experienced her body with shock and joy, and she went away from him with a whole sensation, every part of her awakened, her body not so much used, stimulated, sated, as brought to a new consciousness of itself. So when she left him, to spend days and sometimes weeks apart, she did not long for him, not really; what she longed for was that awakened, intensified state, that feeling of being suddenly, consciously whole.

Even so, she remained a little distant. She was aloof from him sometimes. She never refused him, and she took extraordinary steps to be with him; but still she held back, despite her protestations of their need to know each other. What she denied him was a final, really personal interest in him as himself, as this particular, individual man, one with overpowering, possibly fatal claims on her feelings. She would learn all there was to know of him; she would encourage him to speak about himself, to become fully intimate with her. But in the end, she refused to cultivate a fanatical, hopelessly-in-love sort of interest.

"You're very cool," he said once, "very calm about all this. Sometimes I think you don't really like me. Do you? Do you really?"

"Like you? Why, can't you tell?"

"Oh, I can tell about some things. I can tell some of the things you like. But I can't tell that. You don't really show it."

"Well — is it so important? Do I have to like you, on top of everything?"

He told her about his family. None of what he said surprised her; she had heard much of it before, in a simplified, uninformed version, from Karen Oldfield. His mother had long been dead, and his father lived by himself in San Francisco. His father was a violinist, a teacher; he had played for years in the symphony orchestra. His mother had also been a violinist, originally one of his father's students, and Bascomb had loved her in a complete, unthinking way, and he still felt her loss keenly — he spoke of her sweetly, always with a subdued look, as if the loss of her were something that would always make him feel boyish, partly forlorn. She had been his main defense against the father, who was demanding and invasive (and at one time exceedingly ambitious for his son). Bascomb had started his music lessons at age four; he studied briefly with his mother, then with his father for a period of seven years. The father and son had never really recovered from this period of instruction.

"He thought he could make me a performer," Bascomb said. "Or he *seemed* to want to do that. But really, he wanted to ruin me, spoil me for music. When a woman has a beautiful daughter, you know, at first she takes great pride in her, as a reflection of her own beauty. But then the mother sees how she'll be outdone someday, devastatingly overshadowed. And at this point she becomes excessively interested, overly involved. You see things like that all the time. Beautiful women, with daughters who might also have been beautiful, but something got twisted as they grew up. And now they're almost funny-looking. Crude parodies of their mothers, you know."

"So . . . you might have been beautiful too?" Catherine asked, not quite persuaded by this. "Like your mother? If only your father had let you?"

"That's right. Yes — now you've got it."

Seven years of study with his father; followed by five years at a music academy in San Francisco. He played in the city's youth orchestra from the age of ten, and he once placed second in a statewide competition, at age fifteen. But he was to rise no higher than that; in fact, he began to fall. The period of his adolescence coincided with the emergence of the counterculture, the wild time, the days of sanctified youthful rebellion; this wave of great social change, this mad turbulence, picked him up, swept him out far past his father, beyond all his early, borrowed aspirations. The oceanic upswelling came to very little, in the end; but it was there to be felt, to be seized upon, especially in unhappy cases like his own. He left his father behind, drowning in disappointment (in false disappointment, Bascomb now believed). The old man actually lost conviction at this point — he apologized to his son, blaming his excessive ambition for Bascomb's defection.

"He never cast me out, though. Never rained curses down on my head, which should have told me something. He wasn't pleased when I failed, but he learned to live with it pretty quickly . . . actually, I don't blame him at all. I had a gift, but it wasn't big enough for me. I needed things to be easier than they were — I was like my mother that way. She had an instinctive feel, a greater musical gift than my father's, I think, but she was weaker. We were both lazy — we thought that to make it on the highest level required something grotesque. I was pretty grotesque myself, let me tell you, after twelve years of music schools . . ."

Though she never saw a picture of his mother, Catherine could imagine her — somehow she had gained a vivid, almost physical impression of her. A tall, sharp-featured woman, with a glowing, smoothly formed forehead, exotic in some way; Bascomb himself had elements of this, of a woman's looks, in his own face, and when he spoke of his mother, in a subdued, puzzled tone, Catherine imagined that she could see through to her, feel a remnant of the woman's presence. Similarly she imagined his father to be a small, ferrety type, a windy martinet with sense of importance wholly out of scale with reality. (There was a remnant of this, too, in Bascomb.) When she happened to meet the father, however, she found him charming, earnest, intelligently sad; he was tall and fat, a round-faced, courtly older man. He had huge shoulders and small, clever hands, and he occupied space with an apologetic force.

Bascomb had left the music academy a little early; then at age seventeen he left his parents' house for the last time, and his mother died soon thereafter. For several years he played no music at all; it was enough for him just to be living on his own, with other young people. At the end of the sixties, however, he left San Francisco for Europe, where he found work playing music in the streets. This rediscovery of his music in the foreign air of France and Denmark, Spain and West Germany, where such things seemed more ordinary, where a formal kind of emotional expression was socially endorsed, moved him to think that he could return home and begin again. But in California he found that he still spoke the language, and a native's sense of the ironies and absurdities returned, and he found that he still couldn't play. More to the point, his time was already past. His technique had failed to progress and had decayed in some ways, and his early, borrowed ambitions, once disdained, now showed themselves to be hopeless of realization. His father had a bitter, ultimate victory over him at this point (Bascomb believed). Now he would never rise even to his father's level — never surpass what he had assumed was beneath him.

"It was a shock, let me tell you. But as they say, it was good for me. This beautiful dream that I hadn't wanted, that I then decided I did want, just fell apart, and I had to walk away from it. Pretty soon I felt okay again."

He returned to Europe. He lived for a year in Grenoble, in the house of an older woman, who hired him to work as a carpenter. After working at her house he returned to California, with the woman's daughter as his companion. Then after a few months the daughter left him, headed he knew not where. His parents had always owned an old cabin in Cuervo, in the coastal mountains; Bascomb asked if he could live there for a while, and his father said yes, of course. In 1974, he injured his hand working with a chain saw; this left him unable to work or play music for almost a year. When the cuts in his palm had healed, he picked up the violin again, and for the first time in many years, almost since his first attempts to play as a boy, he was amazed by what he could do, with the sounds he could make, and his ear led him unerringly away from what he already knew. Away from all of that, toward something he had never bothered with before: music of a kind that his father, his teachers, and he, too, had always disdained. The music spoke and flowed from him; it came from him almost naturally, the snide, raw American music, something like an inborn musical language, with all the ironies intrinsically expressed, all the absurdities left in. Unimportantly, freely, it came out of him, like the copious rush of his own uncensored thoughts; and the strain between feeling and irony, an open heart and a dry, vernacular mind, was there in every note.

In 1980 he married a local woman. Her name was Terry Flynn. He had been in the canyon for seven years at that point; they lived together for the next three years, off and on, and when he spoke of this period he seemed bitterly amused, his self-disgust had a kind of consummation. Even before she moved in, he said, he had known it would be a comedy, a painful farce, but still he felt compelled, by a sort of instinct for disaster, to inflict himself upon her. At the beginning there was strong mutual attraction. She was a small, fine-featured woman, beautiful in a secretive way (so Catherine felt when she finally met the woman); her very black hair and her thick, dark little eyebrows, which arched in feathery surprise over moist, lavender eyes, made her seem like a delicious kit, something pettable and precious. She had been raised in the canyon. Like Karen Oldfield, she came from a large, disorderly family, a scene of troubles. In her parents' generation and before, only the men had seen fit to waste their lives in the local taverns; but in Terry's generation, as a token of its liberation, she could drink and use drugs with the best of them, and she lived with older men from a young age. When Bascomb met her she had already been married twice. There were two children from the first marriage; the children had been taken over by that husband's parents, and they lived out of state.

"When I met her," Bascomb explained, "she was only twenty-three. It was hard to believe she'd ever had children, and she never talked about them. She used to come over every night when we played music at the bar. She drank with all the cowboys and hard cases, night after night, getting rowdy and ornery. I guess I thought there was something interesting about that at the time . . . the way she drank made you think she was hurting herself, and that she knew she was, and you wanted to watch that. We never even lived together before we got married. We just went out, first thing, and did it — it was like a train crash."

This train crash, this ongoing disaster, was the culmination of his various attempts to immerse himself in the canyon. In the person of his wife, he embraced all that negated him, everything he might have aspired to but could never be; and the sneering, destructive answer to his genteel background that Terry represented for him was a deep wound, it had lowered him. She herself probably never knew what she saw in him. According to Bascomb, from the very start she found him absurd, pretentious, unmanly; his careful attempts to understand, to know exactly what she felt, were like insults that she stored away, to be avenged in later, outrageous attacks on his pride. His failure to wound her by the same conventional methods only repelled her — it made her ashamed of him, she said. There was never a grace period in their marriage. He was too complex for her, always finding significance, hidden motives; and she, in turn, found in him the very image of what she had suspected of the world, an intelligence that saw through, that dissected and finally disapproved of her.

"I hated her after a while," Bascomb said. "I married her because I wanted her, I guess, but it only made me colder in the end. She never needed a reason to drink, but she said that I was the reason. And she betrayed me with other men, many times. Many times. Pretty soon I didn't care what she did."

For reasons he claimed never to have understood, she wanted to remain married to him; the more widely and publicly she humiliated him in this period, the more she enjoyed him, the more she wanted him sexually. In their last year together (in the official sense, the marriage was not over even yet), she lived openly with another man, one of Bascomb's local musician friends. This arrangement — living with the other man for a while, then returning casually to Bascomb's house — satisfied her somehow, although Bascomb was indifferent by this point, cared not at all if she stayed or went. Then she discovered that she was pregnant. And he found that he did care again — cared enough to throw her out.

"Then she had this child. It's Mary Elizabeth . . . and she never said she was mine, never even bothered. Actually, I think she *is* mine, I just feel it. But I don't like her. I can't make myself be a real father to her, not completely. And then they moved out of town, although they came back last summer. I think they're getting ready to go away another time now."

"But — how can you say you don't like your own daughter?" Catherine asked. "That is, if she is your daughter."

"Well — why can't I? Who says you have to like someone else? Why can't I be free about that, too, if I want?"

"You can be, I guess. That's your right. But if she's your own daughter . . . and you said so yourself."

"She doesn't like me either. Her mother's made sure of that. So, it doesn't matter. Not to her, and not to me."

"In my experience," Catherine persisted, "no young girl

doesn't like her own father. She can't. Her need for him's too great, too absolute. And if he doesn't mistreat her, doesn't actually do things that scare or disturb her, she has to like him, even love him. Has to."

"Well, maybe so."

Bascomb was still taking care of Mary Elizabeth; the mother was living in town now, and when it suited her, she sent the girl over to Bascomb's, sometimes for weeks at a time. There was a strong element of not caring about himself, of stoic indifference to his own fate, in his response to this irregular situation, Catherine felt; he simply accepted it without protest, possibly out of guilt feelings, or possibly out of some feeling for the mother that he wouldn't acknowledge.

Bascomb *lived* on almost nothing. He paid no rent, heated his house with wood, and got by, as far as Catherine could tell, on the proceeds from his marijuana crop, which was neither so large nor so well grown as to bring a great return. He no longer traveled, and in her first few months of knowing him she never saw him buy anything for himself other than food or the occasional paperback book. He did buy her some gifts, however: a rayon blouse of an exquisite blue-green, which deepened the color of her eyes, and a hardbound copy of the Knut Hamsun novel *Pan*. But otherwise he was instinctively, unfailingly frugal. The urge to own things, to acquire materials that might make his life more colorful or interesting, seemed to have died in him completely.

Nor was there any taking of pride in this austere, rudimentary, backwoodsy existence, which for someone else might have represented an accomplishment, a rebuke to some presumed materialist ethos of the culture at large. Bascomb was scoring no points, she was fairly sure; he was making no statements. When he first moved up to the mountains, as a young man, he might have been motivated in part by a desire to live more simply, in a rustic setting, an effort that in those years, the early seventies, was sometimes construed as a political or cultural gesture. But by now, the need to oppose, to live out a counter-myth, had disappeared in him. To Catherine it seemed that there was a type of honor (though also a troubling illegality) in his lonely, furtive, pared-down existence; honor, perhaps, but not much happiness. He rarely complained—he accepted the conditions, largely self-created, of his simple life with a rueful, amused complacency.

But real joy seemed foreign to him, like some youthful indulgence now put off and vaguely disdained.

But she sensed a capacity for happiness in him nevertheless. If she had not, if he had been as bleak, through and through, as his life often seemed, she could not have stood it. And she knew that she herself made him happy. Though she still stood apart, would not quite allow herself to fall in love, she brought him undeniable pleasure. It was something strong and real.

"Even if you don't like me," he said to her once, "if you're not quite sure how you feel, I know how *I* feel. And I like it. I'm glad about it, about everything we do. I want it to go on for as long as it can."

"But what *is* it, actually? If it's supposed to go on — just what is it, can you tell me?"

"Us being together. You coming to see me, here in my house. You being yourself with me, always."

"Well, I can't help but be myself. So don't praise me for it. Please."

"Other people can help it," he replied. "They often do. They help it all the time."

But she thought she knew what he meant. When she came to see him, there in his house, she felt relieved, perfectly suited to the role she played — wonderfully well suited, in fact. His simplicity, his acceptingness, even his occasional reserve with her all had a seductive effect; and the path of her being was suddenly broad before her, and she walked it easily.

"You could be different with me," he explained. "You could be false, but you aren't. And I like that about you. I love it, in fact."

She supposed that, seeing him for these months, she might have pretended to be more in love; she might have claimed to be tortured by her situation, oppressed by its hopelessness. But she had not claimed that — hadn't even hinted at it. And he, in his strange, self-denying way, which was also somehow a sure, self-respecting way, had found reasons to appreciate this absence of complaint. The lack of outwardly passionate signs, which most other men would have demanded, or at least rued the absence of, meant almost nothing to him, it seemed. He did puzzle her sometimes; the arc of his emotions seemed to go up, but then often it twisted into dark regions, where she couldn't easily follow.

"But I *am* false," she said to him. "I *am* pretending — don't you know? I'm being false to my husband, who's sick and crippled, helpless. And I don't really feel the way I am when I'm with you. It's all a pose, all of it. I'm not really at peace, not really so easy to satisfy. I'm ruining my life, and ruining other lives, too. I can feel it."

"Yes — I know what it's like. I know."

But how did he know? she wondered. And he said it so soothingly, with his arm, carefully adjusted for her comfort, wrapped closely around her, cradling her, seeming to cherish her. His brown, square hand lifted lightly at her breast, where it wrapped around.

"I know. I know how you feel," he repeated. "And what this must mean to you. To someone like you."

And at that moment, it did seem that he knew — that his long, seemingly cherishing arm, drawing her comfortably close, was itself full of a kind of knowledge. The masculine warmth of him, the gathered presence of him, soothed her, gave her confidence; and the power of his bodily intuition was all the reassurance she needed, at that moment.

But some days later she said: "If you know me so well, what exactly *is* it you know? Who do you think I am, really? A woman who likes to sleep with you? That's all? Someone who can't get enough of making love, who gives up everything to come when you call?"

"Well ... I do know that," he replied quietly, seeming amused. "And that's important. Maybe it's even enough — just that. But I think I know who you are. I feel it whenever I hold you, when I have your body with me. I feel a goodness in you. A lovely, greedy unselfishness . . . and I feel how this consoles you. That's everything to me. And maybe, that's enough."

"That's enough? And *that* tells you who I am?"

And she smiled at him — but a little pityingly, despairingly. He was so lost, so hopelessly unaware. But even so, she didn't draw away; not for all the world would she have broken that embrace, not at that moment. His tenderness, his steady, masculine warmth was all she needed just then. She basked in it frankly.

≈ ≈ ≈

Catherine had become afraid of the nearby town, and she never went there in Bascomb's company. She was afraid of what was probably known about them. Karen Oldfield had left the farm, and she never phoned or came back to visit, and Catherine felt that they had become estranged somehow, following their evening in the girl's cabin. Karen would have carried back stories or suspicions with her; it was only to be expected after what Catherine had told her. Not that she cared so much for herself, but she had a horror of Rick's hearing about her affair from anyone else. When she thought about the steps she had taken, and ought to continue to take, to keep him from knowing, she felt ashamed, and gradually she began to feel that she deserved to be discovered. But she continued to be routinely cautious anyway. Meanwhile, she believed that this was pointless: the mean, gossipy little town already knew, probably, was already chuckling over their sad situation.

Karen had gone to live at her parents'. She had not applied to college after all. In November, Rick began to urge Catherine to visit her, to try to convince her to return to the farm, where they could certainly find work for her, and then Karen, on her own, called the farm one day and asked about the same thing, and a reunion was arranged. She could not have her old cabin back, because a workman was staying there now; but she was given temporary quarters in a larger cabin where Rachel, Rick's nurse and companion, was staying. The two young women were friendly, but not really good friends; Catherine promised that at the first opening, Karen would have a separate place again.

Ben betrayed no emotion upon seeing his old governess. He submitted stiffly to her embrace, but then, a half hour after her arrival, he took her up to his room to play Nintendo. He had mentioned her not once in the six months of her absence. Even so, he had been breathless with excitement at the prospect of her return that afternoon — his attachment to her could be measured, Catherine felt, by the very degree of his reticence, by his initial stiffness.

Ben was now eight years old, and he had entered third grade. A small, dark-haired boy who thought seriously about things, he gave the impression at times of being deeply worried; but in fact his thinking was normally of a sunny cast, brought him to sensible conclusions, ideas that he could live with comfortably. But first, he had to think them through — had to receive a myriad of impressions, then sift and order them, without undue emotional investment. Only afterward could the careful, meticulous process of reasoning begin, the moving outward. Catherine was hardly bothered by his strange self-control anymore, which was not, she knew, the desperate inner effort of one who thinks or feels inappropriate things, but on the contrary, a natural poise produced in consequence of his fervent attention to his own logical process. Like a lover of poetry who, reciting verses to himself, stands beneath a tree still and preoccupied, he sometimes came to complete physical rest while the deductions fell one from the other in his mind, in a sequence and by a method that filled him with pleasure.

Even so, he was healthy and active, ordinarily childish; he

had a number of friends, and he had recently broken a finger in a game of tetherball at school. With his friends he was rough and spontaneous, and he could be that way with Catherine, too, or with Karen, but not often with his father; the "two men" had a curious way of being together, a formal, didactic, essentially serious style. They had been conducting this studious, dignified relationship almost since Ben was old enough to talk, and Catherine watched it carefully, often wondering at it.

"When he was three years old," Rick liked to say, for the benefit of visitors, "I started putting him to bed at night with math problems. Simple subtraction, addition — you know, instead of *Where the Wild Things Are*, for the five hundredth time, a question in multiplication. Or we might talk about the concept of a negative number, say. I still remember the night I taught him square roots. We figured out the square root of four, then sixteen, then twenty-five. But then he got a serious look, and he said, 'Dad, what about the square root of two? It isn't very pretty. And it hurts my stomach to think about it.'

"And I told him that he was right — that it wasn't very pretty. I hadn't taught him complex numbers yet, mind you. Oh, he was just four, maybe five. Maybe five and a half already."

Catherine, who had heard this story many times, could not recall more than a few occasions when Rick had actually put Ben to bed. Usually the boy wanted book after book read to him — most definitely, not math problems. But maybe this adventure of the square roots had really happened. After all, she couldn't prove it hadn't.

Despite her doubts, her considerable reluctance about pushing a child to be intellectually precocious, she had to admit that Ben was bright and curious, and maybe Rick's way of being with him had had some effect. His teacher last year at the local school had given up trying to teach him math, and for the current year he was scheduled to visit the sixth grade class two days a week. Rick had brought home many interesting computer programs, and they often played chess now, with the outcome of the games legitimately in doubt.

"I beat him yesterday," Rick enjoyed reporting, "but it was hard, and it took me three hours. Then as soon as we finished he wanted to play me again. He doesn't understand what it takes out of an old man. Serious chess is brutal, it's the hardest thing I know. Except for serious writing, maybe."

Apropos of writing, Rick had recently been at work on something: a little chronicle, a kind of study of his illness. He stayed in bed and wrote for two hours or more each morning, and he seemed guardedly pleased with his progress. For the first time in their life together, he wasn't showing what he wrote to Catherine, so she had only a vague sense of it. She didn't mind; in fact, she was frankly relieved, glad not to have to endure, in this regard too, a feeling of spurious intimacy. But Rick sometimes acted as if he were getting away with something, pulling off a clever trick right in front of her eyes. Somehow he had identified her as his nemesis: she was the one who was rejoicing in his downfall, he seemed to believe; the one who stood to gain from it, who resented any signs of a returning vitality.

"I'm not much of a writer," he might say to her cryptically, "but I'm not quite finished yet, either. No — I'm not finished. There's a little more left in me, I venture to say."

"Oh — is it going well then, Rick?"

"Pretty well. Pretty well."

And he would give her a secretive, naughtily smug look, in which she read anticipation of some enormous triumph over her. Her obstructionism, her clever negativism, would be seen to count for nothing in the end.

She felt a responsibility to engage him, to bring all these undercurrents up to the surface, but she simply lacked the energy for it now. The words wouldn't form in her mouth; the urge to be a responsible, answer-seeking wife to him had been undermined, possibly vanquished. While all the other had been going on, this too had been happening, and she was horrified by the completeness of the change. So in a way, Rick's identification of her as the enemy was on the mark. But his turning against her, his decision to resent her actively, had nothing to do with any intuition about her feelings, which were now of about as much concern to him as they had ever been. In Bascomb's arms she might feel known, understood, even by his muscles and bones; while with her astute, hardened husband, she felt almost weightless, oddly insubstantial. She recognized this mode of feeling as something familiar, a product of all their years together, not just the most recent. She felt freer, in some ways, with Rick; less constrained by an understanding that gave her powerful importance, that saw her in all her remarkable particularity. But if she had a choice, she preferred to be known — the other way seemed pointless to her now.

A year ago, when she went roaming in the woods one day, she was at the point of realizing her own unhappiness, but without yet understanding an alternative to it, seeing that possibility. Now, when she met Bascomb in the forest, she had a feeling of intense reality, as if each moment were filled precisely to its limit, profuse with sensation. They had been to his marijuana gardens several times together, and sometimes they made love nearby in warm, uncomfortable places, with twigs and dry leaves and the earth getting involved. The drought was in its sixth year, and the sun of the late, rainless California fall made bizarre shadows. One of Bascomb's most salient characteristics was his feeling for covert places: he would lead her to them in silence, hoping that she would see them much as he did, have a similarly awed, wondering response. And if she did, if she seemed alive and alert to them, sometimes he made ironic comments, to mock his own nature worshiping, which he was foisting on her. But in fact he was deeply pleased, because she had seen what he wanted, had found the same meanings as he in particular arrangements of light and foliage, ground-shape and shade.

And after they made love, or only sat for a while in some lost thicket, with a feeling of ordinary mystery woven into it, he would pick her over carefully, removing leaves from her fallen, sweaty hair. Always with a peculiarly gentle, conscious touch, as if he had infinite patience for this, for her physical care and tending.

"I have to go," she might say, struggling to rouse herself, to emerge from this swoon of tenderness. "I have to get home now, I think."

"No — you don't have to go now," he would reply. "You don't have to. You're already home. You're with me."

It probably bothered him that she went away, back to Rick and the farm, but he never spoke of it. His few comments about Rick's illness, which she had described to him generally, were compassionate, as if he could easily put himself in the shoes of the other man, of one whose strength had deserted him, whose limitations had rushed in upon him. Bascomb had met Rick once before. After encountering Catherine some years ago (when she needed workers for her fire trails), he became interested to know what her husband might be like, and he contrived to speak to Rick on the street one day in town. "I said I was a local woodcutter, and that we could have an arrangement, me coming onto his land, and us sharing the wood I cut. He wasn't interested, but we talked for a while, and I remember liking him. He wasn't snotty, not like some other landowners around here. He looks like an actor, don't you think? Like someone important — someone who knows his own importance. But he doesn't ask you to kiss his ass, either. He doesn't need that."

"He may not *need* it," Catherine said, "but he wouldn't mind it if you did. When he was a professor at Cal, he used to speak in front of hundreds of people a day . . . he knows how to present himself, he's thought about that a lot. He has a confident, shallow self-awareness, very impressive at first meeting. Sort of actorish — yes, you could say that. The kind of actor who impresses, who doesn't really move you."

When Bascomb asked her about Rick, Catherine sometimes suspected his motives; she thought he might be making a show of his own openhandedness, lording it over the lord, so to speak. But in fact, he was so little concerned with his rival *qua* rival that he felt free to express interest. Rick's physical tribulations affected him immediately, almost bodily, it seemed. When he happened to see Rick one day in December, at the Cuervo store, Bascomb reported his impressions in a dismayed tone of voice:

"A girl was with him, someone who drove the car. After they parked, she tried to get him out at the other door, but it was too hard. He has to walk with canes now, I see, metal canes. She took him under the knees, then swung his legs out, like they do when they're putting a cripple in a wheelchair. But he got frustrated for some reason and made her stop. It was sad."

He went on: "I recognized him, of course. But he's gotten thinner, hasn't he? He sat there while she went in shopping. I wasn't staring at him exactly, but after a while he knew that someone was watching, and I think he almost wanted that. He likes to be watched. He's confident, as you said — very composed. And there's no attempt to hide what's been happening to him, what he's becoming now . . . Maybe he thinks it's important somehow, that the world ought to see it. That it might do the world some good."

"Yes — he's made a noble wreckage of himself, hasn't he," Catherine replied, and then she was shocked by her own lack of sympathy. "But it's his most basic instinct, you know. To be dominant and impressive. Exemplary in all ways, in all things."

"But what *can* he do, after all?" Bascomb continued. "He shouldn't feel ashamed, should he? And it's always interesting to see a man like that. A strong character, one who shows that he hates what's happened to him, that he simply rejects it. That life has no right to deal him a blow of that kind."

"No, he can't be defeated," Catherine allowed. "As long as there's someone around to see, someone to be impressed."

Bascomb preferred to take Rick at face value. They argued about this, not very seriously, Catherine insisting that he knew so little about Rick, about Rick's "strong character," that his observations had little weight. But Bascomb maintained that the external view was precisely what mattered: certain people, certain men especially, had a real existence only in the way they carried themselves in the world; they had no real talent for intimacy, not as it was ordinarily defined, by women. To ask someone of this kind to behave according to a different set of standards, to swim in the warm, rich soup of feelings that women recognized as the essence of things, the only important aspect, was absurd and unfair.

"Maybe so. Maybe so. But sometimes these people get married," Catherine observed, "and then their wives and children come up against nothingness all the time. Let them go off by themselves, I say; let them stay among their own kind. Be impressive for each other, or whoever they can find. Because they don't really need us. They don't want what *we* have."

Rick, under the influence of Dr. Klepper, had become entirely conversant in the language of feelings, however. He was always expressing this, experiencing that, raging freely against his deteriorating condition these days — so what, exactly, did she mean when she maintained that he was "unreal," that his inner life in no way corresponded to her own? She didn't know, to tell the truth. But then why was she so bitter? Had she really suffered and been deprived? And what precisely was the charge she wished to bring against him, against her lawful husband? Was he truly a monster, a kind of emotional anomaly, as Bob Stein had been insinuating all these years? If so, then he was a rather decent one: a good provider, faithful, reasonably considerate. His commitment to her and to Ben was strong, as far as she could tell, and he would surely experience the loss of her as a serious blow. Or possibly not so serious. His feelings about her were unfathomable in some peculiar way; when she wondered about them, she had a sensation of entering a realm where nothing worked quite as expected, where outward manifestations, ordinary gestures and signs, were the products of an inner process best left unexamined. Perhaps, as Bascomb said, it was better to deal with the outer man, the extrovert "behaver," who, for that matter, was probably more comfortable when taken for what he appeared to be.

Maybe married people, after so many years together, necessarily reached a point of profound befuddlement — maybe their thoroughgoing accommodation, their exhaustive familiarity with each other, led paradoxically to a kind of mystery, a deep unknowing. And then again, maybe not. Maybe this feeling of blankness she had, of not being known and not having the energy to know, was absurd and horrible. She was no longer happy being married to Rick — she knew this now absolutely. All her life-energy went in other directions; she felt as if she were already living elsewhere, becoming someone else. She had nothing left to give to him, nothing to save with him. Of course, as she reminded herself, she was in the middle of a passionate love affair — a profound, extraordinary experience for her. Her judgments might be entirely untrustworthy on that account. But she felt that she had reached an end, that there was no going back.

She reached this conclusion without notable fanfare, entirely by herself, never having discussed her marriage, per se, with Bascomb. The question remained now whether she would do anything about what she so calmly knew: announce it to Rick and to the world. The likely consequences of that were truly frightening.

Bascomb showed some concern for Rick, and sometimes she wondered whether he wasn't less concerned for her own well-being, her emotional fate. His behavior seemed designed to accord with some unspoken code, an austere, gentlemanly idea of what a man should allow himself to do and think. His policy of strict non-interference in her marriage, for instance — as if their lovemaking were not the most essential sort of interference — annoyed her. Finally she demanded to know how he felt: how she could be expected to distinguish this mannerly, honorable reticence from a simple lack of caring.

He seemed amused, and he replied that she was the one who held herself aloof. It was she who never quite knew, who never made her intentions clear. He, on the other hand, was transparent. He was in love with her; that was all. He wanted her, he would do almost anything to have her, to go on having her. Obviously, honor had little if anything to do with it.

"But you never talk about my situation," she complained. "You don't seem to care if it works for me or not. I have a son, you know. I can't be separated from my son — I don't think I could live with that."

"I know you have a son. I understand that."

"But don't say you *understand*," she went on. "Don't say you care if you can't show interest in that part of me. Because what happens between us here, in bed, doesn't really matter. It only takes me away from the other. And that's why it frightens me — it confuses me."

In a calm, deliberate voice he said, "I know you love your son. And I know that you won't spoil that — because you simply couldn't. And when we're together like this, everything has already happened for us, I think. Don't you feel that? Don't you really?"

"Feel what? I don't know what you mean."

She supposed he wanted her to say that she was so happy with him — felt so wonderfully, tenderly accepted and cared for — that the outcome of their involvement was already clear. He seemed to want her to believe in that, and maybe he even felt that way himself. But she couldn't share his confidence. Indeed, his assertion of it offended her: the solution to her problem with Rick, if there was a solution, could not possibly be contained, or guaranteed, in this comfortable feeling that they sometimes had. This lingering in afternoon beds, this exhaustive satisfaction of sex.

"Things just don't work out that way," she admonished. "They're not that simple. And don't be so sure how I feel. You have to be careful — protect yourself. You, yourself."

"Oh, I'm being careful. And I'm doing all I can to protect myself. I'm doing the only thing that can save me . . . which I finally understand. But problems *do* work out sometimes. You just need to have a right feeling, then everything flows from that. It's all there, in the first feeling."

He was hopeless, pitifully naïve, possibly even stupid, she decided. But at certain moments, she did almost share his confidence. And this talk about a "right feeling" made sense to her, sometimes. In any case, it was compelling to have a man, this particular man, say frankly that he loved her; to have him believe that their destiny, a fate they held in common, was contained in what they felt, conclusively implicated in their sturdy physical passion. She felt it as a great temptation to believe.

S*he had begun* to worry about Bascomb, transferring her womanly sympathy to him finally, and part of her aloofness was just an expression of the struggle she had, wondering whether she was not encouraging him in a useless, potentially damaging direction. His vitality increased during their months together, and she saw that she was good for him, that he liked the world more, wanted to live in it more. When she first met him, he had seemed hard and abstract; he was living alone, seriously alone, and her general impression had been of a withdrawn, well-defended individual, one of those unhappy souls who endure precisely because of the depressed level of their expectations. The only contradictory elements in this picture were his passion for her, his lively physical need, and his musical gift, which was too manifold, too colorful to be the expression of a wholly quelled personality.

Now it seemed that these contradictions were almost all he consisted of. He was fresh, open, full of a quick response to her; she loved this change in him, but she was concerned that she had begun a process that could not be sustained. How sensitive and open a man did she want, anyway? When he told her how he felt about her, with most, if not all, of the customary undertones of irony and self-mockery undetectable, why did something almost fail in her, where was the harm and the embarrassment in it? She felt unworthy of these words and feelings, she supposed; but she was also worried that a man who spoke in this way had compromised himself, sacrificed some inner force.

She reminded herself of who he was. A clever, resourceful woodsman, capable and persistent; one who had stolen a living out of her forest, quietly and defiantly, for years. Something of this woodsman still remained, but he was also the kind of man who now brought her bouquets of wild leopard lilies, and who led her for miles along a creek bottom late one afternoon, to show her a flowering winter currant bush. He crouched beneath the glorious red-stemmed plant, pulling her down beside him, close against him; and then he turned her way with a look of focused surprise, and he kissed her, kissed her deeply.

"What is it? What do you want me to feel this time?" she asked.

"Everything. Everything when I do this," he said as he unbuttoned her blouse, freeing her breast. "And this," and he took her boldly under her backside, but also tenderly, proprietarily. "I want you to feel everything. Whatever you can."

"Oh," she said, "I *do*. Whatever you say, master — whatever you want."

But she did feel certain things — maybe even "everything" — at just that moment. His attentiveness, his ecstatic presence with her, somehow was a reflection of the place; it seemed to perfect and complete the afternoon.

He had grown his year's crop of marijuana, and in late November he began to harvest. For three weeks he came out of the woods each evening with a backpack full of cut branches, which he then hung up to dry in his attic. When she visited him, she found the whole house reeking of the plant; the smell was intense, rankly delicious, insinuating, like an orchard of overripe papayas with a skunk or two wandering through it. However, the untenability of his situation suddenly came home to her, and she left the house. Six or seven days later, after he had cleaned and sorted most of the dried material, she visited him again, and the reek was less.

"I'm almost done," he promised her. "Just another week or so. Then — back to normal."

"But you could lose everything, you know . . . they could take everything. Your daughter could be taken from you. She really could. And you might go to jail . . . yes, these days you really could."

"Oh, I don't think so. That won't happen."

But he seemed vaguely disturbed, maybe even a little ashamed. Standing before her in his humble, marijuana-strewn living room, with the piles of contraband spread out over the tables, and other debris in heaps on the floor, he contrived to seem smaller and more apologetic than usual.

"They could take your own house away," she persisted. "That's what they do these days, you know. And then you'd have nothing. Absolutely nothing."

"Well — it's not so much, is it? The house, I mean. So I'm not really afraid."

"Oh, don't be that way — and don't feel sorry for yourself, please. I don't believe it, it doesn't convince . . . and anyhow, nobody's making you live this way. Nobody ever forced you into it. Just look at how you live — look at it. And it's gone on for years. I just don't understand."

He, too, seemed perplexed; she had never spoken to him this way before, and she herself now wondered where the impulse came from, what exactly it expressed. But he seemed to shrink away from her then, becoming perceptibly more remote. However, after a while he roused himself. He spoke out rather sharply.

"If it bothers you so much — well, that's too bad. I'm sorry for it, very sorry. But this is how I live. This is just how I am. I don't own much, and I'm not very important, not at all. I don't even own my own house — it's really my father's. So I haven't even managed that."

"Oh, don't," she said. "Just look at how you live, that's all I want. I don't care how much you have — don't you know that? I just worry what this means for you. Just look around you. Look! You know it's wrong, and you know it can't last. And why should it, after all? What's the point of it?"

"The point? I don't think I know what you mean."

But later that evening, when they had eaten a meal together, quickly leaving these bothersome issues behind, as if to deny that they had ever brought them up, he looked at her in a strange new way. He confessed that he sometimes thought of leaving, getting out of the canyon, looking for a fresh start somewhere. And she immediately said that she thought this was a good idea.

"Why not? What's stopping you, anyway?"

"I don't know. I suppose I'm comfortable here, in my way ... I know what to do, what I have to do to get along. I suppose I haven't thought that things could be much better for me anywhere else. That my life could change very much at this point."

And she assured him that it could — that it could only change. But her reassurance, her very interest in him, seemed to please and move him; he all but said as much. He smiled at her beautifully. And when she saw this, how quickly he responded to her concern, something turned in her — she felt him more directly, in her own heart.

"Why not?" she said again. "What's keeping you from doing anything — whatever you want?"

At *just about* the time of Bascomb's marijuana harvest, in the town of Cuervo one afternoon, Catherine saw Mary Elizabeth, his nine-year-old daughter, walking alone along the road. The girl had grown spindly and long-necked in the last year. She walked with head down, placing her feet one ahead of the other, as if following a painted line. Catherine pulled her car over.

"Mary Elizabeth — hello. Remember me?"

"Uh-hunh."

"How are you, dear? Shouldn't you be in school?"

"No. I don't go to school anymore."

"You don't? Why not?"

Catherine did not quite understand the explanation that followed. It was vague, as well as incoherently expressed. After offering Mary a ride, which she declined, Catherine continued on to the Cuervo store. But here came the girl, on foot, also toward the store; she walked in her curious, straight-line way the whole distance, with her head down. Catherine was reminded of a young sunflower, all stalk and heavy, tossing head.

"I'm not going to *this* school anymore," the girl said more clearly now, as if there had been no interruption in their conversation. "We're moving back to Lake Tahoe. Me and my mom. I think this afternoon — maybe even tonight."

"Tonight? Well — are you excited?"

"No. It's just the same place we were at before. I can ski whenever I want, though."

Like her father, the girl had large, bluish-white front teeth, slightly overbiting; hers, being entirely new, were too large for her face, which was otherwise still wholly childish, almost infantile. The bridge of her nose was copiously speckled like the hide of a fawn, with markings that would one day disappear; and her shiny, dark brown eyes looked at everything a little too long.

Catherine hadn't seen her at all lately. Her mother had taken her away, gathered her in to the maternal bosom, possibly in preparation for this move across the state. Nor had Catherine seen much of her when the girl was staying, sometimes for weeks at a stretch, with Bascomb; it had seemed better not to come to the house when she was there, to arrange her own visits to coincide with school hours.

The girl puzzled her. She seemed withdrawn yet completely relaxed, and the only time she showed her other side, her famous holy-terror side, was when she became intransigent and fractious with her father. Catherine had witnessed two such incidents now (following the time at the Cuervo school, when Bascomb first brought her in to be registered). Her wild physical response to this or that commonplace parental command evoked nothing like anger or visible irritation in the father; on the contrary, he became only distant and dry, as if slightly amused, and waited patiently for the storm to pass. Whether or not this was a "correct" way to manage a child, it struck Catherine as perverse somehow; and she found herself hoping for something stronger — some definitive, heartfelt display of paternal rage.

Bascomb became only distant and dry with her, too, when she asked him about it. Either he felt that these things hardly mattered, that his relations with his daughter were unimportant, or he was following a course of action that he preferred not to discuss — something that for him made sense, promised good results.

"I know her" was about all he would say. "I do understand her, I think. And I know what she needs." This past summer, in what Catherine took as a promising development, he had begun to teach her tunes on the violin. Their musical connection had so far not been marked by any violent outbursts, he reported.

As Catherine spoke to Mary Elizabeth, the door to the little town store opened behind them. Someone came out quietly. Catherine suspected who it was before she turned around, because the girl, looking toward the door, blinked and became disconnected to what she was saying, and a sense of unease came over Catherine, as if a cloak had been thrown over her shoulders from behind. The mother, Terry Flynn, had a sleepy, disengaged look when Catherine did turn around, and she barely acknowledged Catherine or the girl. Even so, Catherine knew she had been recognized: in that instant, she knew as well that her entire affair with Bascomb was old news, no secret whatsoever. The lazy, indifferent glance hardly bothered to appraise, as if she were a quantity already thoroughly known, and at the same time not worth real knowing.

"Take it home. Go on, go back and stay till I get back." The woman handed the girl a grocery bag. "And stay inside the house, remember."

The girl looked quickly inside the bag, then took off without another word.

Two cars passed on the quiet road, listlessly. The little town seemed empty but for the distant figure of Mary Elizabeth climbing a hill; soon she vanished behind the trunks of some redwoods, and Catherine felt the presence of the mother uneasily again, and she thought about leaving. She could think of nothing to say, nothing at all; but Terry unexpectedly began to smile, looking at Catherine in a way that insinuated an amusing connection, some piquant thought just now springing to mind. The sleepy look and the sullen, dismissive air had been replaced, although not quite convincingly.

"What if we just went and had a beer?" Terry asked. "What about that? How would that be, hmmm?"

"I don't know. I have to do some shopping first. I have to go in the store."

"That's all right. That's good. I'll wait here till you come out."

Twenty minutes later, they drove together down to Rudy's, a seedy bar-motel just west of town.

Terry knew the bartender, and she acted as if she knew Catherine, too: there was immediately a cozy, confiding tone from her, as if they often came here to hoist a few. Car troubles had kept her in town since last spring, she said; she had been trying to get away, to take a job that a friend had secured for her at a Tahoe casino. Never let a boyfriend work on your car, she summarily advised Catherine; they can't be trusted. If things go well between you, the car gets worked on, but if things screw up it sits around forever. Finally she'd had to get rid of that boyfriend. But now her car was ready. It would be delivered to her that evening.

In the emptiness of Rudy's in the early weekday afternoon, the woman's smoky, soft-loud voice called attention to itself, boomed and also rasped, sometimes hissed. Catherine decided that she liked it. It worked a soothing, almost sexy influence on her, so that she no longer wondered what she was doing here — talking so casually to this woman whom she hardly knew.

"Maybe you *do* know a little about me," Terry said then, "maybe he's said a few things. Well — they're all true. Everything he says."

"He hasn't said much. Just that the marriage didn't work, for either of you, in the long run."

"Oh, is that what he says? That's all he says?"

She looked at Catherine cleverly, insinuatingly. Meanwhile her left hand wrapped and rewrapped itself around a beer glass. But these were her totems, evidently, the drink in a glass, the lit cigarette, and she held them almost as a man would. Her slender, enticing physical delicacy, however, added another note: something almost touching, comical. She was not quite frail, but insubstantial, unweighty. Her insinuating, resonating voice came out of her by a kind of magic.

"I guess he wouldn't say much. Not our Henry — that wouldn't be his style. Henry's a gentleman, he is. One of nature's true noblemen."

"Well — is that bad? Would you rather he said a lot of ugly things about you? Would that suit you better?"

"Ugly things? About me? Well, they'd be about him, too, now wouldn't they? But I didn't say I don't like it. I'm just thinking out loud. Remembering."

Catherine allowed her to go on remembering, but in the meantime she began to feel uneasy. There was something coarse, broadly snide, about this woman, but something attractive, too, an unexpected emanation of some kind, of which the woman was wholly aware. Catherine could conceive of Bascomb being physically taken with her. She gave forth a feeling, a definite something, that mated in her own mind with the idea of him, with her most intimate image of him, in the end creating a powerful whole, some palpable, plausible sum of sexual personalities. They would have married, on that level, in a formidable and vivid way, she knew; even if the marriage, in every other sense, had turned out a disaster.

Terry looked at her then. Somehow she seemed aware of Catherine's thoughts, her most secret intuitions. The woman's appearance of a sleek, coddled pet, something precious but still half wild, whose coat it would be a lush pleasure to stroke, intensified at just that moment, and Catherine lost all heart. What was she doing here? she wondered. Did she have something to say to, or even to hear from, this woman? But Terry could sense her confusion; she was acutely awake. Her snide, triumphant projection of self seemed to augment at that moment, achieving a kind of intimidating perfection.

"Did he ever," she hissed, "when you were, you know, making love . . . did he ever do anything, say anything, really strange?"

"Strange? Say anything strange? Well — I'm not sure I know what you mean."

"Yes, well . . ."

The woman shook her head; she could not quite get herself to speak of this, whatever "this" was. Perhaps it was simply too strange.

"Never mind. It's not important, I guess. It doesn't matter."

"No? It doesn't?"

But a moment later, now on a different tack: "I was crazy about him, you know. I don't mind admitting it. I couldn't get enough of him for a while . . . because he has something, doesn't he. Some kind of sweetness. Something rich and tasty. I got to know him in the bars, drinking down there. He was playing music. Right off, I wanted him, and that's how it got started, just because of that. But then he wanted to get married. I still don't know why — it was stupid, it was ridiculous. I never understood it. I'm sorry, is this annoying you? Am I bothering you? Maybe I should just shut up about this."

"No, I don't care. But I don't see the point. *Is* there a point?"

"A point? Well . . ."

Then again: "He's a funny man, isn't he. Not like some of the others. Better in some ways. But stranger . . . he used to say that I was made for this, for fucking, you know, and that he was, too. But he couldn't just be a man about it. It had to be pretty with him, full of emotion. Lots of *meaning*. I used to say, 'Henry, you're more like a woman than I am. Just shut up about it, will you? Just shut up.' But he wouldn't."

Catherine could feel herself growing stiff, removing herself from this. And the other woman, though apparently oblivious, sensed her reaction; and she seemed to feel that she had won a victory just on these grounds. She felt encouraged by Catherine's drawing back — it inspired her to continue.

"He didn't care," she went on, "he had to talk. Tell me that he was *feeling* things, you know ... and I was supposed to feel them too. All that kind of crap — that tender, feeling stuff. More than a person *can* feel. You know, I might just like to suck on his cock sometimes, just for something to do ... but even that had meaning. It had to be more than it was — something grand. Oh, shut up, I'd say — just look at me, and if you want me, well all right. But make sure you stay here in bed with me. Don't go flying off, Henry, up to the stars."

She continued for a while in this vein — Catherine meanwhile drawing back further, becoming "dignified." Terry wanted her to see how ludicrous the man was, how worthless; but her larger urge was simply to wound, to give offense, by the simple device of using these salty words. And Catherine did take offense. She suffered on Bascomb's account; it sickened her to hear of his good body, his glowing, intimate body, in this woman's description, to think of his cock being in her mouth, and so forth. It had the effect upon her that the woman probably intended: made her feel weak, overwhelmed. Retroactively betrayed.

"He used to embarrass me. When we'd be screwing, you know, saying how does it feel, don't you like it, and don't you know how I adore you? That I love your body so much? Your tits and your sweet, hot ass ... I want to lick you all over. Well, all right, I'd say. But just shut up about it. And what it meant when two people were doing it, fucking — where did they *go*, what were they really *having?* What was the meaning of the experience? Oh, the bullshit of him! The pure crap and silliness ... but he was good, too, sometimes. He got to be a habit with me. Finally, I had to break away. And I'm cured now. I believe I really am."

Catherine said flatly, in a cold, though not a menacing, tone, "You're the one with the mouth ... you're the one who should keep quiet, who can't shut up about it. Maybe he just wanted to get rid of you — did you ever think of that? Maybe he was trying to talk you out of his life. That's all he could think of — getting rid of someone like you, a mistake like you. Why don't you shut up about him, anyway? I like it when he talks . . . I love it, in fact. You just never understood it. Because you're stupid. You're stupid, and you've got a big mouth."

The woman stared at Catherine, mildly taken aback. But after a moment she began to smile, as if this change of tone were entirely in character — just what one might have expected. And what did it matter, after all? Who cared what Catherine felt, what she had to say about anything?

"Oh, *am* I stupid? *Am* I? But what does that make you, you dizzy cunt, with your funny-headed boyfriend? What does that make you? Are you trying to move up in the world, hmmm? By fucking him all over town?"

"You go to hell," Catherine said stoutly. "And shut your mouth about him, or I'll shut it for you. I promise you — I will."

Terry sipped her beer, utterly undisturbed. She smiled. She could sit this way for hours, it seemed, maybe even for days, always with the same knowing, half-disdaining look.

Later *that week*, when she saw Bascomb at his house, Catherine mentioned that she had run into Terry. He seemed only mildly interested, possibly not interested at all. Then she gave an account of the conversation they'd had, and his only comment was that she had probably been trying to get money out of Catherine. He himself had been hearing about her car troubles for more than a year now, always with a request for a loan appended.

"She just wanted money. But she got carried away, telling you what a disappointment I was. What a complete washout as a husband and a man. So she didn't get her chance."

"Well — but why would she think I'd give her money? What for?"

"You're rich. That's all she knows. That's all she thinks about. You'd give her something just to get her out of your hair. Get her out of town finally."

"But I don't care if she stays or not. She can do whatever she wants — it's all the same to me."

"Well, she *is* gone now. That's what I hear."

It was true. Terry and Mary Elizabeth had left the canyon, finally. They hadn't even said goodbye to Bascomb — he heard about it from a mutual friend. They would be staying in Lake Tahoe all winter, possibly longer.

"You say it doesn't matter," Bascomb went on, "but how did it really make you feel when she said those things? Didn't you think she was right, sort of? Almost right?"

Catherine had to think carefully now. She wasn't afraid of offending him by telling him that she agreed with the other woman in some way; but she had to ask herself if she really did agree.

"Maybe she was right," she finally replied. "For her. But didn't you want to get rid of her? Wasn't that your purpose all along?"

"My purpose? I didn't have a purpose, not that I remember. I was in love with her, I guess I have to admit it. Sick, hatefully in love. But then I couldn't stand having her around after all that happened. But I didn't try to get rid of her. It just happened on its own."

Catherine thought that he *had* tried, however. He had consciously persisted in a behavior, a way of being, that drove her away, when, of course, he could have changed at any point in order to keep her. But on the other hand, changing was not Bascomb's way. The other side of his passivity, his not-caring about many probably important things, was a sometimes phenomenal certainty, an unaccountable stubbornness.

"You drove her away," she declared. "I can see that now. And that's why she hates you so much. Why she still says awful things about you. A woman doesn't forgive a man for that. And she never will forgive you."

"No — a man doesn't, either. But that isn't what happened, I don't think. I'm not even sure what did. Whatever it was, I'm only glad it's finished."

≈ ≈ ≈

In December, at the time of year when Rick often wanted to travel, he proposed a trip to St. Kitts, in the eastern Caribbean. His uncle Regis Mansure owned some property there, and Rick had spent his boyhood vacations sailing among the islands. Catherine reminded him of what had happened last year, when they went to Mexico; she doubted whether he was strong enough to travel even yet.

"Well, if I'm not, I'll just collapse," he said calmly. "And then they'll ship me home. That's the worst that can happen. I've arranged to have Ben let out of school a week early. I want him to see Pointe-à-Pitre and Montserrat, just like I did when I was small, and we'll go on the *Caitlin Triall*," which was Regis's largest boat. "If you don't want to come, we'll go by ourselves. Just father and son."

"Rick, when did you arrange to have him let out of school? Why didn't you ask me about it first?"

"I had Karen call the office, that's all. There's no mystery about it, Catherine. Nobody's trying to steal your precious child, don't worry."

Tickets had already been purchased. The *Caitlin Triall*, which slept twelve, had a crew and captain ready to go aboard at any time. Uncle Regis flew to St. Kitts several times a year, often in his own plane, and one of his houses was always kept in readiness. Rick could do with it what he wanted, stay there or not.

"I thought about asking Bob Stein to come. Offering to pay his way, of course. But now there's all that noise about his new book. I don't think he wants to leave the country just now. No, but *I* want to leave ... to get away from it, even hearing about it. I desperately want to."

The Poacher (as Bob's new novel was titled) had been published early in November, without much publicity. Its first printing was only 7,500 copies. Someone at Bob's publishing house must have been behind the book, however, because as soon as the first strong reviews came in, more copies went to press, ads began to appear in the *New York Times* and elsewhere, and publicity-tour plans appeared from out of nowhere. The *San Francisco Chronicle* list of Bay Area best sellers had the book pegged at number three.

"There's already been some movie interest," Rick complained, "and Bob mentioned, oh so casually, that they'd had several bids for paperback. But his agent thinks they should wait, have a regular auction with it. It's amazing, isn't it?

Once the commercial engine gets going, once the higher-ups smell real money to be made, the doors just open one after another. And then Bob finally has his apotheosis."

Catherine remembered when Rick's first book, *Escambeche*, came out; the doors had opened before it, too, one after the other. That experience, his first taste of unexpected, unmitigated success, had been profoundly important to him, even though the money meant little and his life, up to that point, had not lacked for triumphant moments. But Rick had been made more truly joyful by that experience, more purely encouraged in his impersonation, his conscious presentation, of himself, than by anything that had happened before or since, not excepting their marriage and the birth of their son. On the basis of this first publishing experience, he had anticipated a substantial career in letters, which might have taken him almost anywhere; probably, he had expected that success would follow upon success, and that he would become, down in his bones, that most remarkable thing, a *writer* (rather than, say, a scholar, an entrepreneur, a financier, or any other of the dozen or so things he seemed cut out to be).

Success had not followed upon success, however. And his attachment to the process, to the slow, uncertain accretion of ideas and pages, the production of perhaps a few good books in a lifetime, had proved faulty. There was no error involved in wanting acclaim, substantial rewards; but his enjoyment of the actual work of it, the dutiful transcribing of thoughts and feelings, had been only halfhearted at best. His corresponding reliance on other sorts of motivation had led, perhaps, to disappointment. Or as he had experienced it, the book ideas simply began to dry up, and he found he had little he wanted to say and small energy for saying it well. He eventually looked upon that period, that first experience of brilliant, untrammeled literary victory, as an anomaly, a cruel delusion — because he was not, after all, destined to be a writer, down in his bones.

"And now Bob gets the big payoff," he groused. "After all the years of bitter struggle — the big score, the transfiguration. And with what? With a dirty book about my own wife. It doesn't seem fair somehow. And he'll be quite decent about it, of course — won't rub my nose in it too much. But he'll be having his delicious little victory over me. Proving himself against me."

"Oh, Rick. If you're serious," Catherine answered him, "then I'm just sorry for you. Just read the book. You'll see there's nothing to be envious about, nothing at all. Unless he's changed it completely since I saw the manuscript, it doesn't hold a candle to the best things you've done. It's not even as good as his own early stuff. It's perverse, sexually over-charged, obsessive . . . everything that they say about it in the magazines. But sometimes that can strike a chord. A lot of people can respond to that."

" 'Strike a chord'! Oh, that's good, Catherine, very good. But tell me: have you been sleeping with Bob Stein, my dear? With my loyal old friend Bob? Or is the answer to that so obvious that I shouldn't even bother to ask?"

Catherine denied this, categorically. She shook her head, denying it over and over, and implying, at the same time, that she felt only pity for Rick if he could even think such a thing. But in the middle of her forceful response she became disoriented, and her jaw, as if of its own accord, clamped shut, biting off her words in mid-sentence. She had to turn her back to him, stifle an urge to groan, or possibly to laugh. But Rick hardly noticed. He was not so interested in this question, after all. He rose up on his metal canes, using one of them to gesture vehemently, if rather clumsily.

"He used me, that's all . . . used and exploited me for years. And the world goes and rewards him for it, of course. But maybe the story of any book, the true account of how it's conceived, how it's written, is so sordid that if one only knew, you'd never open the damned thing. All the betrayals, the deceptions involved. There *is* a kind of honest, faithful writing, though, something that simply tells the appalling truth. That doesn't mistreat or misuse. It's funny — I used to think that the real glory of a book was in its distance from actuality, its made-upness. But now that kind of stuff just makes me sick. When you stumble, when life starts to crack your bones in earnest, all you want is the truth. Something with some weight, flavor, a good round shape . . ."

Rick was still working on his own book. This was the account of his illness, considered from medical, moral, psychological, and spiritual perspectives. Bob's success, although dismaying, had not deterred him, and he was almost finished with a first draft. In a way, his recognition that he was not a real writer had been helpful, he said, because it had led him to be ruthless in his pursuit of the truth, to rely less on stylistic tricks than before. He had not shown the manuscript to Catherine yet. He had told her about it in a general way, and she had gathered that he intended the book to serve partly as a rebuke to the meretricious, merely imaginative writing that he had come to dislike so much. It would be stark, unsentimental, relentless in its examination of a life, a blasted, ill-fated life that had suddenly come apart.

"Maybe it's just a man-woman thing," he mused. "You know, that men at a certain point in their lives only want the truth. Something that you can hold in your hand, feel the weight of. Women, it seems to me, retain their hunger for romantic escape all their lives — which I don't criticize, mind you. They have enough reality already, what with childbirth, menstruation, all that sort of thing. But it's women who will buy Bob's book, I know. Women are always ready for another torrid fantasy, something about an unhappy wife, preferably, one who's perishing for lack of 'intimacy.' Hundreds and hundreds of pages of sublime fucking, no doubt. And a dream lover, someone to adore and ravish her on cue. It amuses me that Bob, with all his trouble with women, never seems to write from the man's point of view. He'd have to get honest with himself in order to do that, drop this pose of understanding them, of sympathizing. He's a sex traitor, that's all he is . . . of course, it's his bread and butter, too. That's the tack a popular writer simply has to take these days. Let a man stand up and try to speak the truth, the hard, masculine truth, and they stone him. In our thoroughly feminized world, the cultural juggernaut is immediately brought to bear, crushes him . . ."

Catherine began to form a reply to this, but she could see that Rick was in no mood to hear from her. And she herself was hardly eager to express her point of view, to begin another windy argument. She knew where Rick stood; she had heard these opinions many times before. They might speak of such issues, hash out theoretical positions all they wanted, but the real truth was that he was disappointed in her, profoundly, angrily disappointed. She had offended him by her subtle, wordless withdrawal from him, which he had finally begun to perceive. She had always before had an abundance of energy for fixing whatever was wrong between them, but now she had absolutely none. All she could make herself feel was a kind of boredom with it all — an absolute exhaustion of hope.

"We men of the sixties," Rick was going on, "we veterans of that stupid era, in the end got a terrible dose of women's hypocrisy. Because they were suddenly defined as the 'victims,' as pitiful casualties . . . and we hateful men, we guilty oppressors, bought the whole line, we conceded every point. It's become the foundation stone of everything that's happened since. But then these victims, these crushed and mangled former slaves, somehow got up and over on us, and now they have the whip hand in almost everything, in popular culture, middlebrow literature, the movies, advertising. You can never see a straightforward, undemeaning image of a man anymore . . . if we have to judge the world, the one these women have made, the first thing we notice about it is the stereotyping of men, how they're blamed for absolutely everything, routinely stigmatized. The latest bold advance is to prove that women's psychological trouble is all the fault of men. We abuse and molest them, we commit 'soul murder' on them at every opportunity. As a result, of course, no woman must ever again take responsibility for herself . . ."

Catherine listened patiently, and then impatiently, feeling not so much that it would be pointless to interrupt, but that she lacked the energy for it, the first spark of volition. She herself did not hate men; she had never been one of those who "stigmatized" them, nor was she much of an example of aggressive, accusatory modern womanhood, to her own occasional regret. And even if she had been, her quarrel with Rick was about other matters — about the fact that she had hurt him, had withdrawn from him, because she had fallen in love with someone else. He perceived her defection from him without quite understanding it. And he wanted to punish her for it, naturally — but impersonally, coldly, without sacrifice of dignity.

"The whole society begins to go bad," he continued. "When one sex is the *locus in quo* of all evil, all perversity, we get a poisonous kind of falseness. This vile fascination with child abuse — admittedly, it's a horror, a sign of utter social dysfunction, but it comes when women are grossly abandoning their own children, sacrificing whole generations of them on the altar of 'career,' of all things . . ."

If only he would take her by the throat — if only he could rant, not about this but about the other, about what was real, with his wounded, oozing heart for once exposed to view. Then she might feel differently. She might have the courage, in that case, to speak the simple truth back to him, as final and painful as that might be. But now she felt only impatience. And she waited for him to finish, then rather abruptly brought up the subject of his proposed trip to the Caribbean, which did not interest her, did not attract her. She was worried about taking Ben out of school for a whole week — he would have to make up the work.

"All right," Rick replied, "Karen can help him with that. Not that they teach him anything in that school, though . . . But she'll bring his books and things. So — you're not interested in coming, then? You don't want to have a vacation with us?"

It wasn't that, but she needed to stay at home; she had many things to do, she said. It meant spending Christmas apart from Ben, the first time ever. Rick seemed to be looking at her out of only one eye as she spoke, with his chin raised slightly, his face turned to offer her almost his full profile; it was a look she remembered from many years ago, from his lecturing days at the university, a certain mock-imperious, am-I-not-cunning look. But now it seemed only sad to her, as if he were hiding behind his own face.

"Good. I'm glad you'll be taking Karen," she said. "It'll make Ben happy. He always has a good time with her. And she'll love it down there. She'll be in paradise."

"Yes — she's never been out of the country, can you believe it? Never even been out of the state. We have to remember that she's very young, very inexperienced. She hasn't had her chance yet, not at all."

Over *the holidays* Catherine stayed close to home, for the most part, working in her drought-stricken, winterized gardens, which she was almost of a mind to plow under. It was the sixth year of less than normal rainfall, and she felt defeated in her attempt to create a new kind of growth, a decorative garden that also produced food, where native shrubs, drought-resistant and tough, grew around and among the beds of winter greens and other vegetables. She had taken her best garden site and consecrated it to this experiment, and the results discouraged her. She now wondered what she had been getting at.

"Well, these shrubs are like wolves," Gerda, the old authority, said, "growing among the lambs, among the tender green sprouts. You have two different kinds here, Catherine, the hungry killers and the sweet, soft baby lambs. You cannot grow them together."

Gerda was metaphysical in her beliefs about plants, especially native plants: she believed that they "murdered" less hardy species, often at a great distance. She had seen many examples of this. Powerful emanations, mysterious exertions of vegetative will, accomplishing strange things. Of course, some plants actually put chemical agents out into the soil to discourage competition. It was a known fact.

"But you cannot grow this, what is it, *Ribes glutinosum*," Gerda said, pointing to a small currant bush. "Not here, not in a civilized place. The vegetables all shrink away. The mizuna goes black, see what happens there? But where did you ever get this? Did I give it to you, by some chance?"

"No. I found it in the forest, Aunt Gerda. I dug it up and brought it back here myself."

It was a plant she had found with Bascomb. Not the great winter currant under which they had sat one day, trying to "feel" where they were, but a lesser individual, only about half grown. They had dug it up from a creek bank together. Bascomb helped her carry it home.

"In March," Gerda warned, "when the flowers are all pink on your *Ribes*, everything will be dead around it. In a circle three meters across. You only have to wait."

Catherine did not care. She almost desired that outcome — the plants she had brought from the forest, the winter currant and the others, taking over in a vengeful, murdering spirit. The domesticated species, which she had cultivated for so long, would wither and die out. And the garden when it reached that condition would be finished, she believed, really perfect.

"I don't care. I like that it's here," she said. "I'm sick of all this work anyway. I've been growing too much, for too long. Save me from another year of vegetables, please."

And the old woman snorted, possibly in amusement.

Gerda had become more bent, a bit more lame lately. Her right hip, injured in a hiking accident almost forty years before, required her to walk with a cane during some seasons of the year, and she had always resented this. She sometimes argued with Rick, comparing his use of the canes and her own; he had taken up his metal implements much too soon, she believed, almost as if he were eager, proud to be sick. As if he were not in fact bitter with it, passionately determined to overcome it. Rick countered that it did him no good to pretend; for him, as for everyone, there was no shame attached to becoming crippled, or rather, only the shame one felt at feeling, in certain weak moments, ashamed. But the first and most important step was to acknowledge one's disability frankly. Looking at things honestly, one could then focus all one's energies on the task of getting better.

"In my day," Gerda replied coolly, "a man hated to be known as a cripple. He disguised it if he could. Denied it. Oh, don't make it a pleasant thing, Rick, like having your hair colored brown or something. You have to hate it — really fight it."

In her response to Rick's illness, the old woman sometimes seemed vengeful, a little obtuse — because, of course, he *did* hate it, he *was* doing all he could to overcome it. But she refused to account for the physical change in him. When the California Native Plants Society, of which she was executive emeritus, held its annual convention at her home early in November, she prodded Rick to play an active role all weekend, to present himself as the natural host at Longfields, just as she was its well-known hostess. Rick's exhaustion, which was plain for Catherine to see, counted for nothing with her. Likewise, Rick's months of lying in bed upstairs, that earliest period of his illness, were an abomination in her eyes, and she was rudely skeptical of his recent rediscovery of himself as a writer. Gerda had never really liked his books — only the first one, and only mildly.

"Rick can work for the Foundation," she said to Catherine. "He doesn't need to write these books. Let others write, and let others be sick, understanding their illness down to the very bottom. Rick has a family, he has a business to follow. All the rest is just feeling sorry for himself."

"Gerda, you know that Rick isn't like that. He can't be summed up just that simply, he isn't only a businessman, not really. One of the things he likes best is to take a problem, then try to understand it completely, every aspect of it, every subtlety. In this case it just happens to be his own illness." It gave her a warm feeling, a sense of revived decency, to be defending him this way, if only for a moment.

Gerda, now in her eighty-sixth year, felt strong and capable still, despite her bad hip and a few other complaints. But she was sick at heart, angry and disappointed with life. These young people whom she had taken into her house were busily engineering their own disaster, and she was angry with them, seriously let down. She had seen signs of it from the start. She had felt their perverse need for a collapse, an end to their ordinary happiness, as if it were only a burden to them. Her grandnephew's illness, for instance, struck her as completely false, twisted both in motivation and meaning. It's only reality, if indeed it had reality, was of a spiritual or a psychological kind.

She could not suppress a feeling of triumph, however, at this unfortunate spectacle — her intuitions about his character were being borne out, one by one. He was not, after all, very different from his father, or from his hateful uncles Regis and Ferdius, whose formidable, intimidating self-confidence had been the bane of her adult existence. Just as they were cold, essentially greedy men, poisonous and soft inside their brisk exteriors, Rick was a dry and ungiving specimen, fundamentally hysterical: a more modern, slightly more agreeable example of the essential Mansure type.

This type, to which even Willy, her semi-beloved second husband, had belonged, tended toward acts of monumental self-absorption. For instance, Willy, in his forty-eighth year, became entirely and arbitrarily obsessed with making model airplanes. From the construction of extremely detailed, expensive motorized models he progressed relentlessly to ownership of a real plane; to flying lessons; to mad excursions in single-prop aircraft; to frightening mishaps, thrilling adventures, and, inevitably, the fatal accident. His end was guaranteed the day he woke up believing that heretofore he had been denying himself, taking only the conventional path in life. Thereafter, he was determined to follow his heart, wherever that queer organ might lead him.

In much the same fashion, she believed, Rick had conceived

this monstrous, gratuitous turning inward, this mysterious collapse, which could achieve nothing in the end. He had the typical Mansure conviction that anything about him mattered: that his own case was somehow instructive, that nothing could be more important.

Behind their attractive façades, such men were hardly human, she believed. And the penetration of their essential natures was the really harrowing experience of married life, after which their wives, in recognition of their own hopeless state, could only wither or console themselves frivolously. But this one, this one's wife, Catherine, had at first seemed different. She was a healthy girl, alive, truly good without being truly stupid; it was unlikely that the reality of her situation escaped her, and yet she had seemed undaunted at the start, refreshingly undismayed. However, in the last year or so there had come a change, perhaps the inevitable change. At one point, she had begun to despair; but in a paradoxical way, Rick's illness, as it gradually came on, seemed to set her free. It had nothing to do with being repulsed by him, no longer desiring him, nothing like that. Though that might seem to be the case, there was a more fundamental, long-lasting effect of his illness: the evidence of it was in the wife's unfussy, guiltless attention to his needs, quite unlike that of the ordinary, hopelessly unhappy spouse. She simply tended to him now, she saw to his physical sustenance, and that was that. Yet she had withdrawn from him; she had gone finally, completely away, and she could not be recalled.

Though Gerda admired this change in Catherine — feeling it to be the only possible adaptation preserving of self-respect — she herself was sick at heart. She realized now the extent to which she had fantasized about this little group, this adopted family. Their ability to live together had been the premise for an unacknowledged dream, a plan for a life beyond her own, here in her beautiful, lovingly cultivated forest world. But they surprised her. They were intent on living in their own way, for their own obscure purposes. Catherine, by all indications, had now taken a lover, and she remained attached to the farm only through a sense of duty, nothing more. And Rick, of course, remained unchanged. He was dry, removed — as always, fascinated with himself. The principal feature of his drama, his own preeminence in it, had not altered, and this was all that he required.

Once, seeing Catherine return to the farm after a mysterious afternoon absence, Gerda felt in her own heart the pleasure of Catherine's adventure, her affair; and she knew at that moment the futility of all her hopes, her absurd fantasy. Catherine had seemed joyfully preoccupied, almost in a dream state, her body visibly transformed by her experience; she held herself carefully, protectively, as if afraid of jarring her own limbs. And Gerda shared something of that wondrous sensation — a warm brightness seemed to emanate, out from the younger woman's breast, into her own.

She said nothing, however. And she still had said nothing many months later. She was only a little surprised by her own disappointment, which had been growing steadily, and which only proved her own foolishness, the extent of her investment in her fantasy. She had grown sentimental in her old age, she concluded; her life of tending the farm, exercising absolute control over a few patches of earth, had given her to believe in her own omnipotence.

"Listen — you have to take out those bushes," she warned Catherine. "You cannot depend on them." They were walking up from the gardens late one winter morning. "Depend only that they'll ruin the rest — that they'll grow where you don't want, kill what you have. Because they're murderers, you see. They only destroy."

"All right, Gerda. You're probably right. Maybe I'll just plow the whole damned thing under." And Catherine took the older woman under the elbow, as the path before them became steep and uncertain.

Bascomb *had gone* away to San Francisco to visit his father. As soon as he returned to the canyon, he called Catherine at the farm, and they arranged to meet. It was two days after Christmas.

"I brought my violin," he said, "but he was sick. He's had bronchitis. We've been planning on playing something together, probably the Bach double violin concerto. We used to try to play it when I was a student. He plays the first part, of course."

"Is he very sick? Is he getting better?"

"Oh, he's all right. I played him a few old tunes while he stayed in bed. He said he liked them."

Bascomb had gotten a haircut. He had dressed nicely for his father, and he was still dressed well, maybe even in the very same clothes, when Catherine came to visit. She admired and praised him.

"I missed you," he said, finally touching her. He put his hand against her cheek as if testing the warmth of it. She looked at him frankly, waiting to be embraced.

"I missed you, too." The feeling in her body surprised her. She had almost forgotten how filling it could be, how fiercely, warmly good. An ender of arguments with herself.

"Now, you have to kiss me. And touch me," she said.

That evening, he asked her to stay. They had never spent the night together in all these months. She said she wasn't sure, that she would have to call the farm, speak to Gerda. This amused him; the idea of her needing to ask permission, as if she were a schoolgirl. Then, as she stood at the phone wearing nothing but a wool blanket, which he had draped around her, he came up behind her, lifting the edge quietly, and fondled her. Just as someone came on the phone at the other end, he put his fingers inside her, holding her with his arm crossed over her breast. And she struggled to get free, while he only settled into her more deeply, clasping her warmly, capturingly.

"All right," she said, "all right. Then I'll see you tomorrow. Okay?"

As soon as she had hung up, he backed quickly away, and she came after him, kicking with her bare feet. He let her bring him down onto the living room floor. Then she rained down blows. He huddled under her on his knees.

"Don't ever *do* that," she commanded him, beating him without mercy, while he laughed.

As they lay in bed later, she asked if he would take her to San Francisco. She wanted to meet his father, she said. And he promised that he would. She had been thinking about moving recently — maybe to Berkeley, she said, or even San Francisco.

"Is that a good idea? Isn't this where you live now? And where *I* live?"

"Yes, I know," she replied, "but I can't stay here much longer. I can't stay around Rick, you see. I couldn't just go three miles away, down to your house."

"No? But why not?"

The idea she had been forming — her general plan for her separation from Rick, with all its material, as well as emotional, consequences — was founded on the belief that the canyon was too small for them both, that his anger and discomfort would be vastly greater if she remained nearby. She needed to separate from him, yes, but she wanted to do it cleanly, as far as that was possible, in order to spare him pain if she could. It seemed clear to her that it would be better to move away, at least for a while.

"But why not come live with me?" Bascomb inquired,

really perplexed. "And if he has these companions, these young girls around, then maybe he even wants you to leave. Maybe it's gone farther than you think. And maybe he doesn't care what you do, after all."

"Oh, whether or not he cares, *I* do. And I know how he'll feel about it — not because he loves me, but because everything that happens belongs to him, everything that happens here. And I can't belong to him that way anymore. I have to go away. It's all his backyard here, you know — the whole canyon. He's sort of like a spoiled prince, a jealous king, the kind who likes to banish his enemies. That's the only way he can function in a place."

Bascomb grumbled that she was remarkably concerned for Rick's tender feelings. At what point did she begin to think of herself first, or even of him?

"I'm only thinking of us," she answered. "That's all I think about, don't you know? I'm completely selfish about that. But I won't let him have my son. He can't have his way about that, no matter what. So I have to be careful. But I have an idea, I think. I know the right way to go about it."

They slept comfortably that night, Catherine feeling cushioned, nestled in the silence of the old wooden house high in redwood trees. Even Bascomb, who wasn't used to sharing his bed these days, who had gotten out of the habit, slept well, with his arms snaked about her.

When Rick came back from his trip, Catherine felt she was ready to talk to him, but the noise and bustle of his return unnerved her, and the moment passed. They had had a wonderful time. Everyone looked energetic and more fit, even Ben, who had spent eight days sailing on his great-uncle's yacht, the *Caitlin Triall*. Ben had spoken to Catherine only twice during his weeks away; when she greeted him, with convulsive hugs and near-desperate kisses, he was stiff with her, as he had been with Karen upon her return. But Catherine only laughed, her heart felt so full.

Then slowly the boy relaxed. He began to tell her about his trip, recounting it in sometimes astonishing detail but in a voice that emphasized no single event over another. He had been a sailor, he had seen sharks, he had eaten a guava. He had gone for a ride in a helicopter, and he had learned about endgames from a chess book his father had brought along.

"You can always avoid stalemate," Ben said, "but you have to exploit the weak squares. Wait — I'll show you . . ."

Rick also looked well; a bit haggard, but handsomely suntanned, which made him seem more vigorous. He had brought a laptop computer along, and while at sea, somewhere off Basse Terre, had finished his book. But he knew he had another draft to write, maybe even two. He had been in touch with his agent, who had been talking to the editor of his last book, who was now at a different publishing house. Everyone there claimed to be excited, extremely eager to see this new one.

"A book this personal, though," Rick said to Catherine, "is like a story you tell yourself, over and over, till you get it right. So I won't show them the first draft. The refinements come almost by themselves, as more stuff bubbles up out of the unconscious. I'm not talking about technical improvements, you understand. It's more like the floor just suddenly drops away, and there's this vast, terrifying depth beneath everything, which you hadn't suspected before, which you then have to explore. But I don't want them screwing around with it when it's still raw. Karen read some of it, though — the last three chapters. I found her comments very useful."

This was intended, no doubt, as a rebuke to Catherine, who had not involved herself with his new book in any way. She might be replaced as Rick's literary helpmeet just that quickly, just that easily. Though not well read, Karen was quick, an avid learner, responsive. Rick had begun to recommend books to her, and she had liked most of them.

The governess, who had also gotten a lot of sun, joined the family that evening for dinner. Her fresh complexion had changed in a beautiful way, deepened and darkened without actually burning (she had taken every precaution, worn a hat, slathered herself with creams and sunblocks, and still the glare of the Caribbean found her out). Her eyes were almost frighteningly green now. They glowed as if the luminous, quicksilver aquamarine of the tropic seas had gotten into them somehow. Her way of looking itself seemed different; as if newly aware, freshly conscious of a power to transform, to excite by her mere attention, she cast her gaze about her more expectantly, confident of a substantial, intrigued response.

To Catherine's questions about their days at sea, Karen said that she had been sick at first, but after a while it all began to make sense, the rolling deck, the swelling sea, the up-and-down horizon. "I had to understand it first, why people did it. I had to get the idea of it before I could be comfortable." But she thought that the best times had been when they anchored in little coves that Rick found on the nautical charts. They explored beaches and went swimming. She couldn't get enough of the island water, she said — the warmth and softness of it, the purity.

"Didn't you like swimming the best, Trawler?" she asked, turning to Ben. "Wasn't that the very best part?"

("Trawler," apparently, was a new name for Catherine's son. It startled her to see him respond to it. One of the crew of their sailboat, a Martiniquais, was an ardent fisherman, and he had taught Ben how to troll off the stern. Thereafter, everyone started calling him Troller — or Trawler, as the nickname sounded in the sailor's patois.)

Ben allowed that he had liked the swimming pretty much. But some of the things they saw in the water were scary. A school of barracuda swam around the boat one day, and after that he didn't want to go back in.

"Yes, we had a little problem there." Rick laughed. "He seemed to think that barracuda, being smaller than sharks, would rather eat a little boy. On the other hand, he wasn't afraid of the sharks at all. And we saw tons of them."

Catherine responded as, no doubt, she was expected to: with anguished cries, worried complaints about Rick's having put them all in danger. Rick just smiled, pleased to be recognized for the dauntless risk taker he certainly was, even with his own son. But if you swam at the right time of day, he assured her, you were in no practical danger from the sea. And Trawler had manfully gotten over his fear of the barracuda. On their last day out, they snorkeled off a spit of land called Barracuda Point. And no one had gotten eaten, had he?

When Gerda came home that night, everyone hurried to greet her. But she waved them off angrily, shaking the head of her stout maple cane. She had wasted the whole day arguing with her gynecologist, she declared. Her old doctor, who had died recently, had treated her for forty-three years, but now a "stupid ugly woman" had bought his practice. The old specialist, a Dr. Steiman, had approached her with "humor and disrespect" always, she said, speaking to her in his Yiddish-inflected German, always joking and teasing.

"He knew my insides backward and forward. But why does a woman want to be a doctor, anyway? Why does she think that she understands me just because she, too, is a woman? I come from another world, I tell her. From another time — almost another century. And she understands nothing. Her hands feel nothing. Even Steiman was better, half blind as he was."

After a while she continued: "When they have a smile for no reason, beware. They only wish to put you away, to do what's 'good' for you. I understand my own body very well, thank you. And even a doctor can have a distaste, you know. Even a doctor may not like you so much, may want to touch you in a hurry . . ."

Catherine spoke to her later, when the others had gone upstairs. And gradually she came to understand that the new practitioner, whether or not she had been insensitive, had disturbed mainly by suggesting that Gerda might need an operation. Old Steiman had diagnosed a certain growth, a pelvic mass, as a fibroid tumor; but Dr. Strick, the new one, had recommended a D and C even so, to determine the precise status of things. Gerda had had fibroids in the past. And she knew that they amounted to nothing, "absolutely nothing." Yes, and there had also been bleeding in the past.

"*I* know how I feel," she insisted. "I may be old, but still, I have all my insides. Everything is there. And I don't need this cutting and sewing, thank you very much."

"A D and C isn't bad, Gerda — they don't even put you under. I had one three years ago. And so did Maryanne, my friend, and everything was fine. It was easy."

Gerda's gynecologist had described the procedure in detail, of course; but still the old woman remained opposed, on the grounds that a "personal" approach had worked in the past, that old Steiman had been aware of her condition before he died, and that he had reassured her categorically. Catherine suggested that she go see another doctor, but Gerda ruled this out peremptorily, as if today's experience cast doubt on an entire generation of specialists.

"I have enough of them, anyway. It's like Rick, all the idiots he goes to, the charlatans. When you talk to more than one, you also become crazy, just like they are. I think they see too much death, that's all . . . without understanding, without knowing. A doctor must not fear death — he should accept it, even love it. When you come in, already you are only a case to them . . . old woman of so-and-so many years, weighing so-and-so, standing this tall. Likelihood of cancer of the breast, twenty-four percent. Cancer of the uterus, sixteen. Of the bones, so-and-so, and so on."

Catherine was sure, despite these hearty protestations, that Gerda would soon agree to the procedure. She was powerfully, aggressively rational in most respects; her enduring vitality consisted largely in this, that she fought clear of distractions, suppressed her own prejudices to a remarkable degree, and made strong, ruthless decisions about things that mattered. This was how Catherine knew her, in any case. It was this energy for deciding, which welled up out of her prodigiously, sometimes overwhelmingly, that colored her spirit, drove and sharpened her awareness.

"If you want, I'll call my own doctor," Catherine said, "my Dr. Meadows. I have to make an appointment there myself."

But Gerda only shook her head, confirmed in opposition.

≈ ≈ ≈

Catherine waited, and finally she found a moment to speak to Rick. She said that she had been thinking about going away for a while, maybe to live in the city by herself. She wanted to be separate for a time, see how that might work out.

"All right," Rick replied with a bit of a smile. "Whatever you want. Are you thinking of taking Ben with you?"

"I . . . thought I wouldn't, not at first. I can't see driving him to school every day, an hour and a half each way. I'll come to get him on the weekends."

Rick nodded.

They both became silent at this point, Catherine feeling slightly panic-stricken. They had just said the words, used the very phrases that separating couples supposedly employ, and mixed with her feeling of panic was one of giddy disbelief, as if she could not quite credit herself in this role. Rick also seemed to feel dubiously cast.

"Then he'll be staying here," he reiterated, "living here most of the time. So he can stay on at the local school. Is that the idea?"

"Yes — I guess so."

She half felt she was making a dreadful mistake where Ben was concerned, but she also felt that this was the only way, that she must seem to yield to Rick, to accept him as more than an equal partner in this and in other respects. When he was trusted, he almost never disappointed. But there had to be this kind of fealty paid — she had first to expose her throat, counting on him not to draw the sword.

"All right," he said, rising from his chair. "Then that's how we'll do it."

He looked at her skeptically. Was this all, then — was there nothing more to speak of? Would they really pretend that it was only a matter of Ben, that their marriage came down to nothing more than this?

When she remained silent he said, "If it's Karen, I'm sorry. I didn't mean to hurt you, or embarrass you. I didn't want it to happen this way, really I didn't. But I think it's more than that. It's more than Karen, isn't it?"

After a moment she replied, "Karen? Is it more than Karen? Well, yes . . ."

So this was how it was — this was what had been happening. She was hardly surprised, not really surprised at all. She had suspected for several weeks now, not really caring one way or the other.

But Rick still seemed skeptical. Did she mean to imply that this development was unimportant to her, that it meant practically nothing? After all, he had been unfaithful to her, here in their own house. It might even have been thought (not that Rick thought of it this way, of course, but still) that he had made a point of it, of being unfaithful to her here, precisely here. And how could *that* not matter?

"Well, then — if it isn't Karen?"

"Oh, Rick," she answered. "Do we really have to say it? Say it all? Maybe the right feeling just isn't there. Maybe it wasn't ever there, I don't know. But I'm such a stupid, pointlessly cheerful person — it took me years to admit it to myself, to see that something was missing. But now I do admit it. I just don't feel much anymore. I don't cherish you, Rick, I don't have a passionate interest in your life. Not the kind of interest that a wife should have, and that you deserve for her to have."

Rick smiled. This talk of what he deserved — oh no, he wouldn't grant her this. He wouldn't cede her the high ground, not just yet. For a moment, she was afraid that they would get off track, veer from the real subject; she could almost hear his parodic plays on the word "deserve," on her presumption to feel concern for him.

But he mastered himself, and in a straightforward, remote tone of voice he said, "Marriage doesn't work that way, Catherine. I'm surprised you don't know that by now. Passionate interest is all very well, but I don't expect to feel it, and I don't expect it from anyone else. Two people make a pact, that's all — they agree to live together. Then as they get older, they learn more about who they are, and still they try to accept each other. They simply go through life together, always, automatically. I guess because it's worse doing it by yourself."

She replied, "But I can't live that way, Rick. I really can't. I have to feel that someone wants to know me, all the way through. That means everything to me. When you have that, you know you weren't alive before. The only problem now is whether I like myself enough, feel I deserve that. And at the moment, I think I do . . ."

She seemed to have said something amusing — Rick chewed it over, looking as if he might break out in exasperated, half-crazed laughter at any moment.

"The dimensions," he finally said, "of what you think you 'deserve,' Catherine . . . they're impressive, wouldn't you say? *Mightily* impressive. To be known 'through and through,' 'intimately' . . . I'm not sure why women think they're so interesting, anyway. Why should a man want to get that close to a woman? Why, really, why should he want to study you, ponder you, for his whole life? What's the point of that? To be a good companion, all right . . . a dependable provider, an attentive lover. All of that might be said to be part of the bargain. But where is it written down that we should worship at your feet — that we should want to probe and mull you over endlessly, as if you were the greatest of mysteries?"

Catherine wasn't sure what all this meant. She felt suddenly that she had stumbled into another argument, possibly one that Rick had been having with himself lately, possibly in his new book. She could think of nothing to say, and he continued:

"There's no end to it, is there? Really no end. You monopolize all right feeling, you dominate the culture, control the spiritual airwaves completely. And yet you want our constant attention, too. Why, there's nothing left, really nothing at all. The answer to 'What does woman want?' is everything — more than everything, much more. But I can't give you that, Catherine. Something in me just doesn't care beyond a certain point. And I think that the world you want to make, with everything running according to *your* laws, dictated by *your* prejudices, will be an utter waste. A totalitarian sort of place, with the commissars all wearing skirts. But I can't breathe in that perverted world. I just can't. And I won't submit to your vile thought reform — won't worship at your howling, greedy femaleness, your never-ending, bottomless need."

Catherine could only shake her head. She would have turned away, left him there, but for the fact that the moment for speaking, which they had arrived at only with such difficulty, was not to be squandered. Rick stared at her strangely, his eyes gone cloudy, steamy with thought. She could feel the arguments as they massed behind, the storm of anger and eloquence that was about to break over her.

"Rick — oh, Rick," she said hastily, "Rick. I'm not asking anything of you, really I'm not. I expect very little from you. I've given up hoping, Rick, that's all it is. And I've discovered what I want. I know I can't find it with you, Rick, not anymore . . . look at me, Rick, just look. Be here for a minute, try to feel me. It isn't because I'm a woman, Rick. That's not what it is. Or because I want something enormous, impossible . . ."

And he did look at her, stormily; but even this sudden yielding of his attention, this purposeful recognition of her, had a mediated quality. It was passionless somehow, almost impersonal. And she didn't fear his anger anymore — it only depressed her, made her impatient. After a while, as he continued to gaze stormily, she began to feel the absurdity of her request. How could he ever be expected to "feel" her, how could she ask him to be directly, intimately aware of her? This was precisely what he could not do. And yet his expression, so remote, so bitter, suggested that if he *had* wanted, he could have understood her. His powers ranged that far — extended in all directions.

"I *am* looking at you, Catherine."

"Oh, Rick."

"I *am* . . . and what I see isn't what you think, not at all. It isn't someone bold, deeply authentic, someone who's taking that final, dreadful step to free herself. No, not that. It's just someone commonly selfish. Someone who's horribly spoiled. Who's never had to make her own way in life, who's never really worked. Twenty-five years of women ranting, raging stupidly at men, to convince us that they're oppressed, tragically misused, and in the end they can destroy a marriage with impunity. Even with a certain feeling of liberation, you might say. Yes — I'm looking at you, Catherine. I really am . . ."

She began to give way. She was exhausted now, but even more, her patience was at an end, she felt that she could bear no more. She said quickly, flatly, "I'm in love, Rick — that's all it is. That's all. I'm in love with another man, Rick. If you want to hate me, do it for that reason, only for that. I can see you don't care. I can tell it doesn't really matter to you, but if you have to hate me, do it for that."

He did not respond for a moment. He was still standing back from her, taking her measure in his dignified, purposeful way. She went on:

"I have a lover, Rick — that's what this is about. Someone I think I can be happy with. I want to live with him, Rick, I really do. And that's the end of it. That's all there is to it. So hate me for that, if you have to. But do it for the right reason, at least."

"Spare us the theatrics, will you, Catherine? I know all about your lover — of course I do. Did you really think I wouldn't? And I've been terribly embarrassed for you, we all have. Because it isn't very pretty, you know. It doesn't look very nice. If I were you, I think I'd keep it to myself — other people might not find it so interesting."

She felt these words, sharply and strongly. She stepped back, raising a hand between them, and half turned away. At the same time Rick drew himself more erect, using one of his metal canes. His free hand rested on the back of the vanilla-colored couch, whose soft pillow gave way unhelpfully.

"I'm sorry," she said vaguely. "I wanted to tell you myself. I see it doesn't mean much to you anyway. It doesn't really touch you. But I'm sorry, even if it doesn't matter to you."

"Let me decide about that, won't you, Catherine? Let me be in charge of my own response, at least. I know you've got me pegged — you think I'm cold, that I don't feel things. Well, that makes me easier to betray, I guess. But I have my own ideas. I even have a few feelings, Catherine, believe it or not. Maybe I'll tell you about them someday."

Catherine felt much worse after this conversation with Rick, which continued in a desultory fashion for the next two days. His strategy was to be formidable, and he revealed nothing of the feelings he had spoken of, other than his scorn for her, his profound disappointment — she had behaved poorly, not only by taking this lover, betraying himself and their marriage, but by bringing the whole matter up. Her error was in taking herself too seriously, allowing herself to become disaffected in the first place, believing that this affair, which was sordid and ought to be felt as embarrassing, nothing more, had real weight, significance. Without saying as much, he suggested that though wounded, he had been prepared to overlook it.

"Your 'friend' lives in the canyon, I know," he said at one point with cool distaste. "I guess it was a question of convenience . . . didn't he once work for us, too? Don't I remember something like that?"

"No, Rick. He never worked for us. You're mistaken."

She felt disoriented. She could not recognize her husband in this, the man she thought she knew. He was capable of great self-control, of course; and certainly he had always been capable of seeming scornful, but this Continental indifference, this sang-froid in the face of a wife's infidelity, went beyond her understanding of him. He would have wanted a divorce in the past — no question but that he would have felt insulted, refused to countenance this slur upon his primacy.

He was weaker now, because he had suffered the change of his illness. But he was not more needful of her — no, not at all. He had proved that he could substitute for her in every regard, with Karen, Rachel, others. Therefore, his unspoken prejudice in favor of saving the marriage, of living and letting live, did not make sense.

"Karen will be going with me to Los Angeles," he announced one evening, "the last five days in February, I think it is. It's for the Foundation."

And how was she supposed to respond to this? *Was* she supposed to respond? "All right," she said after a moment, "I don't mind. If that's what you want."

"Then — you have no objections? Anything's all right with you?"

Maybe it was merely a question of reciprocity; Rick had his Karen, he seemed to want to assert, while she had her friend, her embarrassing, unmentionable lover. The balance was roughly equal, the issue moot.

"I'll be taking Karen," he declared again, "so you'll have to take care of Ben by yourself." As if she had not been caring for Ben, largely by herself, ever since his birth. "Or will you still be living here then, late in February?"

"I'm not sure, Rick. I don't know when I'll find another place."

She still had the idea of moving to San Francisco; although his surprising tolerance, his scornful agreeableness, made her wonder whether that was really necessary. Maybe she wouldn't have to move away after all.

When she next saw Bascomb, he received her account patiently, without immediate comment one way or the other. He seemed to feel that this was to be expected: that she would speak to her husband finally, that she would make the affair known. Nor did he find Rick's reaction puzzling at all.

"Of course he wants you — he'll want to keep you on any terms. He thinks you'll get over this. That the storm will pass. Or maybe it's not so different from before. There wasn't much closeness before, was there?"

"No. But you don't understand. He once told me that the

only truly unforgivable act was infidelity. It showed a lack of respect — for the marriage, in the first place, and for one's spouse, for her 'pride' in herself. He would never be unfaithful, he said, because he could never care that much about passing pleasure. And he would never attack my pride. Pride being everything to him — really, the most important thing."

"But didn't he ever sleep with anyone else? What about all those business trips, going down to Guatemala, and so forth?"

"We always went together. I don't know if he's slept with other women, I really don't. I was never too concerned about it."

After a while, she could see that Bascomb, who had hoped to seem unmoved, to be impassive in the face of this great development, was actually astonished. Like someone half frozen who slowly regains animation, he held her and touched her with increasing fervor, his eyes curiously large and focused. Perhaps he had actually thought that she would never announce their affair, that she would never confer this undeniable reality upon it. He urged her toward his bedroom then. But she wouldn't go, not just yet; and he consoled himself with lifting the hair from her brow, combing it through with his hand.

"Of course he wants you . . . And he can't believe you won't stay. For practical reasons, if for none other."

"But I won't go back," she assured him. "I never will. The only passionate thing about us was the marriage itself: the terms of it were so stark, so primitive. Absolute fidelity, absolute immersion in each other on some kind of level. But then when you relax, you find there's nothing . . . a frightening nothing remains. The only thing that moved me about him was his authority: that he could insist on having me that way, so starkly, so primitively. Whether or not he *really* wanted me."

When they made love that day, Bascomb was nervous, as if

afraid to touch her too familiarly. He seemed to feel the weight of all that had happened, the great change in the terms of their affair, and to be cowed by that. Catherine caught his nervousness, and then she became sad, as her mind remained active when she most wanted it to go away. Bascomb embraced her rather than made love; he entered her only incidentally, it seemed, only as part of this long, half-nervous embrace, which was like an attempt to protect her, she felt — but from what?

But as they lay together, unhappily thoughtful, some chemistry of hearts began to work, and Catherine felt that if she was sad, if she had indeed done something fateful, at least there was honesty in the gesture; and from this simple thought, which had the form in her mind of their bodies embracing, she proceeded to see that they, unhappily enfolded, had a simple beauty together — that is, that their bodies had, and this feeling became a sensual motive. Bascomb seemed to fall away from her at that instant, pursuing some thoughts of his own. It was curious how he awoke as she, turning to him in her mind, felt a bright flow down in her hips, a stiffness turning to warmth, to iridescent quickness — thoughts becoming feelings, thoughts and feelings no longer quite separable.

They made love restrainedly, demurely, seriously. For Catherine it resolved in a sensation of being together in simple, fateful sympathy, which beautiful idea they were celebrating, for no particular reason, with their bodies.

Afterward she stood before his bookshelves — she had risen from his bed, now with a new idea. There were some novels and field guides on his shelves, and she had conceived a powerful urge to be read to. Bascomb remained in the bed.

"What do you want? There's nothing there," he said. "The good ones are all in the living room."

"I want you to read to me," she said almost petulantly. "It doesn't matter what. Almost anything will do."

He came up behind her, lightly touching her back. As she continued her search, with her arms ranging up in the shelves, he rubbed downward, as if smoothing her back and her buttocks.

"No — just stand there," he said when she began to turn around. "Just like that."

A moment later: "My, what a glorious behind you have. So generous, so fine. Did anyone ever tell you? Broad, and complete, womanly complete. Even a little too full . . . a little too much, like life. Powerful and mysterious. Life making something extravagant, for no good reason."

She looked at him over her shoulder. She wanted to laugh at this, and did laugh, briefly, but her face had begun to feel warm. She felt embarrassed, but warmly, sweetly so; and this feeling seemed to spread down her throat, even into the tops of her breasts.

"So powerful," he said, mocking himself a little, "and mysterious . . . there's something secretive about it. No, don't turn around . . . it's something to believe in, almost, something to have. When I hold you here, it's like I touch everything. I have it all, the whole world, in your one body. I understand it a little, when I touch you here."

She squirmed, making a peeved, anxious sound. But Bascomb continued to caress her in the boldest, most avid way. A little mockingly, his hand inscribed its wonder into her.

"So heavy. And so full of power. You see how we generate — how we can reproduce, just from this. Because it's generous. It's only your lovely ass, I know . . . but it's everything, round as the world, soft as a mother's breast. A little shy, with all the feeling it contains. A little ashamed of itself. But what is an ass, after all . . ."

"Oh, I'll tell you what an ass is —"

"No — just stay there. Don't move. Why do I feel this way, why, when I feel you? *You* feel something too, and I feel something else, something completely different. Even that's a kind of miracle . . . so enormous, and also small. I hold you, and it's like the world. The way it's made, the sweet completeness of it . . ."

His caresses brought her pleasure. But his words kept her on the edge of detachment — or maybe he wanted this, intended to produce this distancing, this cozy irony. Then he stopped declaiming, ceased his intimate address to her behind, though he did not cease touching her. And always intimately — somehow "meaningfully," with a kind of awed, wondering delicacy. The warmth flowing out of her throat, into her breasts, was like the warmth of his body at her side, pressing against her, looming there in a slow, red seep of feeling.

They stood up for a few minutes, Catherine bridging back against him. He pulled downward on her breasts, tenderly tearing at her. After a while they accelerated, heading, she felt, toward something known, but strange.

Bascomb *didn't* understand her need to move away, but when she began making forays into San Francisco, where she saw rental agents and answered ads, he took her more seriously, and on one occasion they went together. They looked at apartments in the Marina district in the afternoon — it was nine months before the earthquake of October 1989 — and in the evening visited Bascomb's father, Mark, who lived on a street called Coyle Terrace, in a house he had owned since 1954.

"Welcome," said the tall, heavyset older man, who wore a tie knotted askew. He patted Catherine kindly on the back as he took her coat. Bascomb stood apart, seeming vaguely amused; Catherine imagined that they often met in this way, as if dismayed to find themselves together again.

"Ah, Henry," Mr. Bascomb said, "my own dear boy. You didn't say she was beautiful. No, you didn't say."

"Dad — Father. How are you?"

"Never mind about that. We won't go into that. Where's your violin? You didn't leave it in the car, did you? Not too smart."

Bascomb went out to retrieve his instrument, which he had left in the trunk of the car.

His father had been ill all winter, Catherine knew. Now he apologized to her for the shut-in feeling of his house, for the general disarray of it. But there was no disarray: only a smart, lived-in quality, which became perceptible after a moment, a sort of intelligent disorder that she liked. Somehow it seemed as if every object, each magazine and lumpy hassock, each end table, TV tray, book, unostentatious bibelot, and bowl of salted nuts, had been placed where it might as well be, there and only there. If she had a feeling of slight oppression, with a few too many pieces of old, quietly upholstered furniture taking up space, and a polished Yamaha baby grand up to its ankles in white carpeting, this was agreeable, this spoke to her somehow.

"I like your house," she announced directly, which only made him deprecate it further, hurrying to pick up sheets of scattered newsprint.

"When my wife was alive," he explained, "we often played music together in here. I only put the carpet down after she died, because it seemed cold. Henry remembers the old days. We had chamber music in this room. His mother painted those watercolors, did you know? Maybe you've seen the ones at the cabin, the ones he has. Those are hers . . . there's a kind of woman, don't you think, who intuitively understands all the arts, who's born already knowing how to write, how to paint, how to act, to throw pots. How to play any musical instrument she wants . . . wait, here's Henry, here he comes. He'll say the same thing."

Bascomb, as he rejoined them, still seemed amused. He had fetched his violin, and he held the case almost desperately against his chest. Catherine perceived the attempt at parody: the boy coming in trepidation to see his music teacher, his censorious master. He glanced at her as if asking, Well? Didn't I tell you? Has he done anything embarrassing yet? Has he revealed himself yet?

"Bring it over here, Henry. Come on — let me see it." The son presented the instrument, and the father carefully opened the case.

In this room full of casually scattered, well-chosen objects, Bascomb appeared thin; he stood before his father with shoulders dubiously rounded, neck bent meekly. But he was not daunted, not really. When, from time to time, he looked Catherine's way, his eyes were bright, even insolent, and she took his meekness for a neat trick, a means of coping long ago devised. The father, for his part, seemed wholly aware of the ploy, not opposed to playing along, either.

"Have it cleaned, for God's sake. You're losing varnish there. Take it to LaFosse's, they know me. And don't put all-steel strings on it ever again. I tell you — you'll ruin it. You really will."

"All right. Of course."

The instrument had belonged to Bascomb's mother, and the two men now passed it back and forth with brisk care. They might almost have been handling the woman's body, Catherine thought — they seemed so conscious, so alertly present in their tender connection with it, as their hands pressed and held, measured, treasured. Catherine felt oddly moved as she watched. Would that all men might hold women, the mementos of their beloved women, with such unfinicky, forward tenderness, always wanting to know more.

"If you can't care for it properly, just give it back, give it to me. Remember, she never said you were to have it. I could take it back any time . . . maybe even tonight."

This facetious admonition was only a prelude, after all; the two men, as if by prior agreement, suddenly fell silent and sat down to play. Bascomb Senior, with remonstrative deliberateness, tuned his violin for a full minute and a half. His son hardly tuned at all; he only waited, with head bowed, till the older man signaled that all was ready, then made a few quick adjustments. Catherine occupied a broad window seat. The players sat near the center of the room with the black piano behind them, and when they began, with stunning synchrony, the music whispered and throbbed like an intimate conversation once suspended but now, with fresh feeling, resumed. They played a largo passage; as Catherine learned later, it was the second movement of the Bach double concerto, which

Bascomb had mentioned before. He played the second part. His tone was slightly more reserved, fractionally out of balance with his father's; in appearance the two men also seemed ill matched, and the way they held their instruments, very different ways, were like reproving comments each upon the other.

His father, sitting down, seemed to become more massive, almost brutal-looking. His frightened instrument disappeared into a vast, billowing chest. As he played, his head and shoulders rolled and waggled freely, and his rounded back reminded Catherine of a buffalo hump. His tone was delicious, however, kindly sweet. She could feel his own consciousness of this excessive sweetness, this precious fineness — he might have played in some other way, he seemed to imply, but no, this was what came out easiest, this was how it would be. Bascomb, by way of contrast, sat simply and comfortably erect, his shoulders hardly moving. His bow arm made subtle, unhurried gestures, which produced tones of the same character: calm, inward-looking expressions, a music only of hints. He, too, played rather sweetly, with an alert consciousness of his own tone; but his sweetness resided more in the "meaning" of his notes, it seemed to her, more in their capacity to imply, to represent.

They played the movement through twice. They then repeated one passage many times, for a purpose she couldn't discern. She had begun to be lulled and even bored, when the father, casually turning her way, surprised her by saying, "We need the piano part. You play, don't you? We should have a whole orchestra behind us. But maybe you could chop out a few chords."

"No — I couldn't. I really couldn't. I don't play anymore. I never could sight-read well anyway."

He smiled, and she felt embarrassed even to have mentioned that she used to play, since she wasn't in their league at all. Bascomb seemed puzzled: how had she failed to tell him this, that she used to play? And how had his father, of all people, come to suspect it of her — how had he intuited it?

"Would you like to look at the score, then? Oh, you would? Wait there a minute . . ."

The father brought her a copy with the piano part included. As he loomed above her, pointing out the passage just played, she felt the influence of his swelling chest, his warm, gentle massiveness, which had seemed to increase as he performed. He had a woolly, musty, big man's smell. He might even like to embrace her, she suddenly felt — not in any improper way, but in consequence of having played for her, made music for her.

"You were listening very closely. I could tell. You like it, don't you?"

"Oh, yes — I like it very much."

Now they played the first movement, announcing the themes whose reflections she'd already heard. She was glad to have the score before her, but she only pretended to follow it; Bascomb and his father, playing with more energy now, excited her attention as they alternated the phrases of the noble, almost too austere melody. The son had decided to do more than hint now: his tone took on a darker color, like a voice that by chance finds something it needs to say. Even so, his presentation partly sought to correct his father's, added irony, reserve. This impulse to correct and question served as his pretext, she felt, and he built upon it, refined it, without ever quite transcending it.

Later that evening, as they walked to a nearby restaurant, the father held her hand in a friendly possessive way she rather liked. Mr. Bascomb spoke to the Vietnamese who owned the restaurant in loud, queerly accented French, which everyone found amusing. He had been a student in France, he told

Catherine, before the war. As a callow nineteen-year-old he had even studied for a while with Nadia Boulanger, the famous mentor of Copland, Sessions, Milhaud, Virgil Thomson, and many others.

"As it happened, she was on her way to America — she spent the whole war in Baltimore. She saw me twice a week for about three months, but she never got my name straight. I wasn't a composer, you see — she knew that right off. I'm not sure what I was. Just an overgrown boy, someone with a musical urge. I was free, I was in Paris . . . you know, Henry," he said, turning toward his son, "I'm seriously put out with you, really upset. Why haven't you brought Catherine by to meet me before? Why not? I've always taken a warm interest in your female friends, haven't I?"

"No, not really."

After ordering prodigiously, the elder Bascomb declined to eat at all. His stomach was upset, he explained, chronically and perpetually in turmoil. At the age of about sixty, he had found himself unable to eat anything of interest anymore — no highly seasoned food, no rich desserts — nor could he drink coffee, tea, orange juice, whisky, or white wine. He still drank some red wine, he said, and somehow he contrived to stay just as fat as ever. His body, after a lifetime of indulgence, had turned into a sort of nonfunctional monument to itself.

"I have memories, that's all. Ecstatic, scintillating memories. For instance, once I was on a train running south of Lyon in the company of a certain young woman. Not Henry's mother — this was well before we met, well before. She was half Algerian, as I recall. Her hair was deep blue-black, richly gleaming, like a kind of prune they have thereabouts, that they grow there . . . Her mother had made a fine meal for us. We had it in a lacquered wicker basket with bottles of wine. We were drinking a red Burgundy, as I recall, a Ladoix Premier Cru, 'thirty-four or 'thirty-seven. The prunes are known as *choc de minuit*, and they stew them with garlic heads and green olives and capers and anchovies, a tapenade sort of taste . . ."

This erstwhile bon vivant — this thoroughgoing sensualist, as he seemed to want to pretend — had roughly savored life, torn into it wantonly; meanwhile, as he spoke, his eyes, with an expression of sad frankness, communicated slight confusion, and Catherine felt that on another night he might have chosen some other pose, something less brittle, less breathlessly blithe. He had retired from the symphony orchestra after many years, having risen to the position of associate concertmaster. Arthritic vertebrae in his upper spine had hastened his end, but he had no complaints, really; he had gone as far as might be expected. A retiring concertmaster, one with nearly thirty-five years of service, enjoyed a generous pension. He had also benefited financially from certain real estate investments made long ago with his wife.

"We used to own several small apartment buildings. You know, these glorious, fanciful white ones that you can still see on Russian Hill and elsewhere, concoctions of whipped cream, they look like. I sold them all to a family called Patel, Punjabis I think. They own the whole city now. Eat your soup, please — don't let it get cold. It's made with lemon grass and sugar, I can smell it. Plus red pepper paste . . ."

The father and son, seated side by side, suggested only the vaguest, most insubstantial of family resemblances. Their connection was rather in their approximation to polar opposites, it seemed to Catherine: as if they embodied two ends of a spectrum, with a full range of masculine temperament spread out between them. The father continued to expand, seeming to occupy ever more space, more time; meanwhile the son, sinking further into himself, became quieter, more densely shadowed. He was not, however, unhappy in his silence and remoteness. A kind of warmth emanated from him — Catherine understood, then, that he had brought her here, into his father's troublesome, nattering presence, for a specific purpose, consciously or not. In some way she sweetened the psychic air between them; she rendered it less portentous, more objective, as his mother had possibly done.

"I love your son," she suddenly declared, apropos of nothing. "I love him, it's as simple as that. I want to be with him. But right now I have another problem . . . I have to move away from my husband. I have to get away from him for a while. I thought I might come to the city, live here by myself for a few months. Try to see things more clearly if I can. That's not really *why* I need to come, but something like that."

Bascomb Senior blinked several times, with his head thrown back slightly. He was frankly nonplussed — yes, but even so, even given his slight distress, he was eager to hear more from her, whatever she might have to say.

"I have a son of my own, you see," she continued. "He's only eight years old. If I could find the right place, I think I could make him more comfortable . . . then this thing I'm about to do, this terrible change in his life, might not hurt him so much. I don't know, maybe I'm fooling myself. Maybe it doesn't matter. But I think you could help me. Maybe there's something you could do for me."

After a considerable pause, he replied, "If I understand you correctly . . . yes, maybe there is. Maybe I could help you find something. I don't know, but maybe I could." And he smiled, vaguely but not unkindly.

Bascomb, meanwhile, ate quietly from his bowl of soup. Laying his spoon down, wiping his lips carefully, he suddenly focused upon Catherine, peered at her strangely above his napkin. The expression of his eyes reminded her, just at that moment, of the possibly despairing look in his father's; and she felt a commotion in him, a palpable yearning, as real and specific as if he had stood up and taken her directly in his arms.

"I *will* try to help you," the older man asserted. "I'll see what I can do. I'll make a few phone calls. Then we'll see what happens. We'll see what we can do."

"Thank you. Thank you very much."

Sometime later, the father turned to the son and inquired, "Did you hear what this woman just said, Henry? This extraordinary, captivating person . . . she just told me that she's in love with you. Can that be true? Is it even possible?"

"Well — she says whatever she wants," he replied, unperturbed. "I can't stop her. And as long as she says things like that . . . no, I won't stop her. I don't want to stop her."

"Waiter — check, please," Mr. Bascomb requested airily, waving both hands, although a waiter was nowhere in sight. The three remained at the table, eating and talking, until a late hour. Mr. Bascomb ordered bottles of wine, the best he could find on the restaurant's short list, although, in the end, he could find only amusing things to say about them.

Life had changed for Bob Stein. He had become a "writer," had finally and fully taken on the part. Catherine saw this some weeks later. She attended a book-signing party at a large bookstore in San Francisco. Three hundred people congregated in the glossy, overlit central room of the outlet in Opera Plaza, and when Bob emerged from a back room, in the company of two publicists, something happened, some palpable alteration in the evening occurred, as when a TV star appears in a restaurant.

He was suddenly well known: the newspapers of the last two months had played up the local angle, his identity as a Bay Area writer, a prominent northern California figure. People who had seen his photos imagined that they knew him, and they hungrily witnessed the transformation from image into living being, which, like any transformation, was a kind of thrill. But half of them were probably writers themselves, or book people of one sort or another. They were supposed to be above this thrill; they might even have known it for a cheap, defining sensation of the age, one of the many media epiphenomena.

Bob looked soft, warm. Something about him had become finally, but unprovokingly, male. His tightly curled black hair had grown fuller, disguising the retreat of his hairline. He had always dressed well, if cheaply; but the sportcoat he wore tonight, over a silk turtleneck, was the one that possibly all male writers must one day, if only briefly, affect: a heavy, skillfully cut tweed, dark ocher in color, possibly Irish in origin. It advertised his bookishness, his fragrant, sensual maleness; it spoke of his having arrived.

On his feet — Catherine ended up just behind the lectern, with a good lateral view of him — he wore soft, low-heeled Italian loafers. In the course of his address he repeatedly rose up on the ball of one foot, the right, tensing that leg till it quivered.

"I thought that I might read from a little book of mine," he began disingenuously, "something called *The Poacher*"; and many in the audience smiled, since of course it was this that had brought them out tonight. (*The Poacher* had recently appeared on the *New York Times* best-seller list, in the number eleven position.) " 'Kathy had not considered this before,' " Bob read, " 'that you could actually hate a man, truly loathe him, down in his deepest soul, and still want to have his child. When she thought of it, she realized that she despised everything that Powys stood for as a man: his neo-authoritarian politics, for example; his brutal, bullying honesty; his impatience with social pretense of any kind. His prominent chin, which always looked as if it had just been hurriedly shaved, evoked a peculiar feeling in her, revulsion mixed with a kind of secret ache, as if something were reluctantly stirring to life . . .' "

There followed one of the early scenes of his novel, a description of a sex act performed on the grounds of a public golf course. "Katherine," Bob's confused but eager heroine, was committing adultery for the first time; and not with the right man, either, the one she was destined to end up with. Bob read quickly, with relentless irony, and his audience chuckled along: so *here* was the tone of the novel (they seemed to be feeling), here was the author's definitive voice. In manuscript, as Catherine remembered it, the story had not been quite so obviously droll; she had missed Bob's intention if, as he now seemed to imply, he had all along been writing only a burlesque.

The florid, graphic account had struck her, when she first

encountered it, as a partly successful attempt to recover an older vocabulary of emotion. Phrases like "deep in her soul," "the promptings of her heart," "the most secret part of him," had glimmered almost to life, as she recalled. She had wanted to applaud Bob Stein, tepidly, for this effort, since it had required some courage, she thought. But now she saw that she had been wrong. He had been after other, bigger game all along: something recognizably postmodern, some not unfamiliar statement about the indeterminacy of words and readings. We wised-up, ultra-sophisticated readers, he seemed to say, we clever, self-reflective culture hounds, with all our defenses and awarenesses, imagine ourselves to be immune to manipulation. But when it comes to narrative, especially anything of a sexual or ideal-romantic sort, we are as gullible as the medieval clods at a Punch and Judy show.

". . . and in the moonlight," he continued, "there on the seventh tee . . . the creamy whiteness of her breast. And the old rage awoke in him — the ancient, delirious urge to punish, to defile . . ."

Well, yes, she decided — she could see it now. The audience, with an outbreak of demure, half-stifled mirth, signaled their own profound comprehension. But here was a final position, an unassailably ironic vantage point from which to view the comic strivings of basely human characters. All assembled appreciated Bob for his clever effort, themselves for having understood.

His reading over, Bob entertained a few questions. An attractive woman dressed in a cashmere greatcoat, with red leather boots, asked if Bob had not intended, along with the obvious gloss on *Lady Chatterley's Lover* (or was it *Anna Karenina*, or *Jane Eyre*, or all of Western romantic literature, for that matter), a subtextual critique of current attitudes, male ones especially; attitudes ranging, in the just-read passage, from the blatantly misogynist ravings of Powys, who fancied himself a sort of sexual avenger, to the mealy-mouthed "sympathy" of Gilbert, Kathy's cuckolded husband? Gilbert, after all, was the only golfer in the group. As such, he was the only character who could understand the "grounds" of his betrayal; he was also the one who had foolishly tried to control, as a golf course attempts to control, raw, undisciplined nature, or in his case, the manifestations of his wife's anarchic female sexuality. It was Gilbert whom the woman in the greatcoat found most repugnant (although all the males in the book were hateful, she thought, for one reason or another): the man who claims to understand women, to hate their oppression more than his own, is the most poisonous sort of enemy — what might be termed a sexual liberal.

This question, posed with a winking longwindedness, caused Bob Stein to flex his leg over and over. He wasn't trying to present male attitudes, he said; all he had wanted was to write an entertaining, mildly amusing story. The truth was that he was bored, deeply and finally bored, with the whole question of men and women. He'd had enough of it, truly. And hadn't they all? But where did this extraordinary, obsessive need to have things work out romantically come from? What was its basis, its moral and spiritual genesis? Could it be that they had outgrown this poisonous dream, that they, as a culture, as a maturing people, had at last gone beyond?

"Speaking just for myself . . . well, I just don't care anymore. I give up. I hereby surrender. Of course, since I'm a man, it behooves me to declare a truce at this point, with male privilege still firmly established, or so you might say. But maybe you'll understand me when I add that in my life, I have nowhere else to go — I have nothing left to prove. Even if I can't figure out how to be with a woman, it doesn't much matter. Maybe it's not even possible anymore. The starving peasant in East Timor doesn't care, and he shouldn't. I say, let's move on, together if we can. Let's get history rolling again."

It was impossible to tell — even as he spoke so personally, so from-the-heart — whether he intended this to be taken with a grain of salt, in a mood consistent with his reading of his novel, or whether he was actually revealing himself. Perhaps he intended it to be taken in both ways, sincerely as well as facetiously, or even in all ways. A few minutes later, Catherine joined the others in an outburst of applause, as Bob went off to sign some books.

≈ ≈ ≈

"Yes, I've been living in the city," she told him later. "I've got my own apartment now. It's my own place. The first I've ever had."

"If I'd known you were in the audience," Bob said, opening his eyes wide in mock-alarm, "I never could've said a word. I would've been too embarrassed. You don't know what a strain it is to be up there. How weird it feels."

They had crossed Van Ness Avenue, headed for a restaurant that was located down a clean alley. One of Bob's publicists sat with them just long enough to determine the nature of Catherine's connection to her author; there being no evident threat or value in this connection, she went home.

"You go to one of these things and something just comes over you," Bob said. "You enter a different time zone — everything looks too real, too shiny. You start to read. And then this roomful of strangers, complete strangers, starts to smile and nod, to hum along, because . . . *they've read your book. They've actually read it.* Or they think they have, because they've heard about it somewhere. When the publishers sent me to Washington, first they took me to a big store in a mall, and a woman with a shaved head asked me about chapter twenty-three: 'You know: the part where you talk about vaginas, the different expressions on different vaginas, how one's like sort of friendly and another one's voluptuous, but silly, and a few look like they're trying to say something. Trying to speak to you.' And I could hardly breathe, let alone give her an answer . . . it's just too personal, in the end. Too cringe-inducing. Now tens of thousands of people think they know me — they have *ideas* about me, that I'm funny, or twisted, or maybe sexy."

"Oh — *definitely* sexy, Bob. Definitely. You've written a best seller, haven't you? And it's about love, and about sex . . . or maybe the end of love and sex, I don't know. But the room was full of women, did you notice? And there was a feeling of intense interest in there. The kind of interest that only women take, and only in a man."

Bob was not really so upset about his newfound fame. He allowed that it might prove useful, once he grew accustomed to it. His early novels were likely to be reprinted now, and his agent had called only yesterday with word of a contract offer: "A four-book contract, mind you, advances practically forever. Well into the next century." Soon he would sell, or possibly give away, his old blue Volvo. And he might not have to live out his whole life in a rented room.

"I'm not made for success, though. I have this horrible, chronic feeling of floating, of being fraudulent and unreal. Nothing gets through to me anymore. All those years of failure, of feeling comfortably disgusted with myself . . . if you're born to success, like Rick was, you know the world in those terms, intimately. It's comprehensible to you that way. But I go for weeks now without having an ordinary emotion — something that the old Bob Stein would have felt."

Inevitably, they talked about Rick. Bob had heard about the separation, mostly from Maryanne Gustafson, who had been phoning and visiting Catherine at her new apartment. It was an enormous, earth-shaking development, Bob averred, something equivalent to a shift in one of the four cardinal points. The rest of them had always navigated by her marriage, didn't she know; they had seen the world in the light of it. If Rick and Catherine could think of divorce, then nothing was safe, nothing was the same.

"Oh, Bob . . . I don't know. Somehow I think you'll survive. Haven't you been predicting this all along? Weren't you the one who wrote about the emptiness of a certain marriage, the wrongness of it? And wrote about it over and over? Well, you weren't right, as it turns out. It never actually felt empty to me, not in the sense that you meant. And it only became wrong at the very end."

"No — I never said it was empty," Bob protested, as if anxious, now, not to be known as an enemy of her marriage. "I never saw it that way, because the two of you, taken singly or together, are possibly the fullest and most definite people I know. One always felt such grand and fateful things about Rick, of course. But you — well, some people just seem to express something, they exemplify some principle. Even while they're having an ordinary, humdrum life, they're doing that other thing, too. When I first saw you, first recognized it in you, I began to see it in other women, too. It was my single great discovery. The beginning of my conscious life, you might say. Certainly, of my life as a writer."

After an embarrassed pause Catherine complained: "But what exactly do I 'exemplify,' Bob? What possible quality? Quiescent womanhood? The great receptor principle, is that it? Beautiful cowness? You've got to stop talking like this, you know . . . get back to speaking to me in plain English, in words and concepts that I can understand. And then we can be regular friends again. But wouldn't you like that? Wouldn't that be better than this?"

"All right, Catherine, all right. And by the way, I hear there's already another man. That's what everyone tells me. Funny — I always thought that *I* was supposed to be the other man. But you've gone and rejected me right off the bat. Before I had a real chance."

"Oh, no — I haven't rejected you, Bob, how could I? Life has just taken you away from me. Swept you up into the stratosphere. As you said about Rick once: now you belong to the larger world. To the ages, maybe. Or at least, to that roomful of women."

On the drive back to her apartment, Catherine felt odd, removed from herself; it was as if she had missed a step somewhere, gone off the track of her being, her personality. The city, slipping past the car windows, glowed with a possibility that she felt she couldn't understand, and she thought despairingly of Bascomb, who had refused to come with her tonight. He often refused to join her in the city these days; he would say that he didn't belong, that he simply didn't feel at home. But his presence here, at this moment, would have answered for her — it would have. She berated herself for this need she felt sometimes, this pathetic, wholehearted desire for him; the strength of it was yet a kind of bitter comfort, as if, by its intensity, it promised something, some curious satisfaction.

After *two months* in the city, Catherine began to feel the irrelevance of having made the move, but she persisted anyhow, still believing that the change in her emotional life had to be marked, given a geographic expression. There was a convention to be honored: putting oneself in isolation, as the defecting wife who contemplates her position far from the influence of her husband; who, tasting a bit of freedom, assesses her options and obligations. Maryanne Gustafson approved highly of the move. As a worker in the divorce field, she was acquainted with the best contemporary thinking about how to behave, how to minimize conflict and trauma, and so on. In her opinion this retreat to neutral ground was always a positive step, especially for the woman.

"If I were you, I'd go even farther away," she advised. "Take a trip — maybe even leave the country. The point is to clear your head and really look at what you're doing. Far away from everybody — and I mean everybody."

Catherine understood what this was about. "No — I don't want to get away from him, Maryanne. He's not my 'transitional figure,' as you put it. I love him, and I want to be with him. Whenever I can."

"I know your feelings are genuine, Catherine . . . just look what you're doing in the name of them. But I have to point out that the majority of women who leave fairly functional marriages also have boyfriends, and that these relationships almost never last. They're only a means to an end. They can be more sometimes, I'm sure — beautiful, and deeply healing, and physically passionate, of course. But they're rarely very honest. He's not anything like Rick — that's in his favor, I suppose. Otherwise, I don't quite see the point. What kind of life are you choosing with him? Really, what will it be like? A woman seeking a divorce feels enormous guilt sometimes . . . we've been trained to suffer, to be reactive, and sometimes we throw ourselves into awful situations as a result. Hoping, I guess, to bring punishment down on ourselves."

Maryanne was fierce in her advocacy of what she called an "economically rational point of view." By which she meant that Catherine had grown accustomed, whether she admitted it or not, to a certain style of living. As had Ben, her son. Moreover, Rick was not just anyone. Through his connections to his uncles and the Laurel Foundation, he was potentially one of the richest men in the state.

"The pertinent fact is that Rick owns nothing, virtually nothing — not a house, hardly even a stick of furniture. Am I right? And what he does own, he brought to the marriage. Someone might almost think he'd designed his life with an eye to the eventual divorce . . . he'll be generous, of course, up to a point, but if you base your demands on previous spending, well, you're in trouble, aren't you? Because he just doesn't spend. He doesn't own. It's some sort of holdover from the hippie days, I suppose — no cars, no boats, no condos. Pardon me, you *do* own a car. The old Ford, the old station wagon."

Catherine could live on a small amount of money, she believed; she was practically unconcerned, nearly indifferent to the financial outcome of it all. She would get a job; she had always worked, always kept busy one way or another. But Maryanne wanted her to see the larger picture. In a high proportion of divorce actions, the woman suffered reductions in social and economic status, while the man walked away in better shape than before. Would Catherine, out of ignorance, or was it passivity, add her story to this sorry statistical mass?

"Oh, I don't know, Maryanne — I'm not really thinking about that now. All I want is a year or two. Enough time to get back on my feet. And if Rick helps me do that, well, that's fine, I'd appreciate it. And then, if we can agree on how to take care of Ben, I think we'll be all right. And I'll have my own life back."

"Catherine — you just don't understand, do you? I can't believe you haven't thought about this, at least in passing. You propose to go live in a shack somewhere, with a man who has no career, no regular income, and meanwhile, to share your child with someone else. With a man who will one day own about half of San Mateo County. You're reducing yourself to insignificance, don't you see ... simply erasing yourself. I want to point this out because I see it all the time in my work. There'll come a day, never fear, when you'll be in conflict with Rick, probably over Ben, and then the sheer enormity of what he stands for will come to crush you. You'll give up without a fight, because you'll understand, at that moment, how weak you've made yourself, how negligible ..."

Maryanne wanted her to get a lawyer — in fact, she insisted on this. But not just any lawyer: a good one, a brilliant one if possible. All this talk of doing things on her own was insane, just a prelude to financial suicide. Maryanne herself would have felt torn representing either side; nor could she recommend her small, cozy firm, it simply wasn't equipped. A case of this magnitude, this complexity and sensitivity, required someone of an entirely different order.

"I know a few people, though. Sherry Corcoran, for instance. She's very good, very sharp. Rick will go with Bauer and Black, of course. They've been counsel to Laurel since the Gold Rush. But you've still got a chance, Catherine. The point is to put up a fight. Show them you're ready to mix it up, but in a *serious* way."

Catherine took down the names of three lawyers, all of them presumably belonging to that "different order." Having set her friend on the right path, Maryanne could now relax, and she spoke with relief of other things. Of Bob Stein, who had gone "completely insane" with his success, who would probably "never recover"; and of her own decision, taken just recently, to marry George, her dependable, amiable boyfriend of several years' standing.

≈ ≈ ≈

Catherine had given up the gardening class she taught, nor were her own gardens, the ones she still maintained on Gerda's property, doing well. She felt the drought personally, in her own body, and her urge to plant had died back in proportion to her sense of the ongoing catastrophe. In her eighteen years in California she had seen the beginnings of a profound change of climate, she believed; the various newspaper and magazine articles she read, purporting to prove that it was still too early, that the greenhouse effect could not yet be a factor, utterly failed to convince her. *She* felt something different — it was in the air, the earth, the cycle of the year itself.

"When I first came to California," she told Bascomb one afternoon, "I was shocked by how much it rained. Really lusty, drenching storms — and they went on for months. But now it's dry. The whole year's a dry season with just a few rainy days. At the same time, people keep pouring in here, more and more of them crowding onto this narrow, doomed shelf of land that used to feel so juicy, so rich with life. It's turning into a desert now."

Bascomb did not disagree with her, although he was less inclined to take the general view. He thought that people had always tended to see the "end of days" in local weather variations, but now they were only a little better equipped, conceptually speaking, to understand things in a global, ecological, apocalyptic way. But something was definitely happening in the woods — he sensed it, too. They no longer smelled the same, and the springs and swamps were all drying up. He had decided not to grow any marijuana this year. He would work for a tree-cutting service, one with ongoing contracts in the canyon. And after that, he didn't know.

"By next winter I might be broke. But I'm not worried — I don't think I'll starve. Maybe it's time to move on, anyhow. Finally get away from here. Maybe I've seen one redwood tree too many, as they say."

"But how *can* you?" Catherine asked. "How can you get away when you hate everywhere else so much? You're always complaining about the city, saying you don't feel at home there, don't like to visit me there. You're like a delicate forest flower that can't be transplanted. A tender, sensitive plant."

"Oh, is *that* what I'm like? Too sensitive, and too tender? And always complaining?"

She assured him that he was. He never came to see her at her apartment without showing strong displeasure; as if the city were a desperate, terrifying place, simply too much for him to bear. All the cars, the noise and turmoil on the streets, the urban grime and color of it. Too, too much.

He seemed amused. "But it's not that it's too much. It's not enough, really . . . I've lived in cities, great cities, and they were different. Paris was enough for me — more than enough. And London, too. But this isn't real. It's not a great, overwhelming sort of thing, like a city should be. More of a scale model. A prettified, simplified example, and so deeply pleased with itself, so in love with itself. It tells you how wonderful it is, over and over."

"That's not the point, though, is it — you have to take what's there. Make what you can of it. You can't stay down here in your cozy, woodsy nest forever, can you? And why would you want to, after all? Do you think that you won't have to suffer here? That you can just keep your head down, let life sort of pass you over, and there won't be consequences? But I already see you suffering — it's already going bad for you. You've cut yourself off, given up on your chance in life. And that makes you sad. It makes you seem weaker than you really are."

Bascomb continued to smile at her. He was deciding whether to take her seriously or not. This encouraging, "vitalist" sort of talk she sometimes engaged in always amused him, when it did not embarrass him. He preferred to make no response, as if to imply thereby that such foolishness, such gratuitous boosting of him, or whomever, could only be taken ironically.

"No — but I'm really serious," she insisted now. "Listen to me. You seem depressed to me, let down about something, saddened. But why should you be that way? Why should you live like this, year after year — a man like you? Asking little for himself, accepting little. I just don't understand it. The man who makes love to me, the man I'm in love with, isn't like that . . . not some quenched, defeated character, someone who can only accept. Who's happy to live in a small, defeated way. The man I know takes what he wants, and when he does, he carries me away with him."

Bascomb shook his head. She had gone too far now, apparently, exceeded all limits. "The man who makes love to you," he replied, "may not be very impressive. He hasn't gotten far in life. But he likes what he is, even so. He finds some real pleasure, here and there. But if you say I'm depressed — well, then I guess I must be. Although I don't feel particularly depressed. Nor do I feel especially defeated about anything, either."

"Oh, don't be coy with me. Don't banter, that's not what I'm asking from you . . . let me know you care. About yourself, I mean . . . that you won't let yourself be done in. If you can't do that for yourself, well, then do it for me. Because I need you to. I need it badly."

In a half-amused, half-bitter tone he replied, "But I already do most things for you. Everything I do is with the thought of you first, hoping you'll understand, that you'll see what I mean by it. But perhaps it isn't enough."

She despaired, at this point, of getting any further, of making him feel what she meant. This immunity of his, this preening indifference, disheartened her — it was unlike him, it was essentially false.

Her gardens were forlorn, and when she drove to the farm on Fridays to pick up Ben, they seemed to look at her accusingly. But it was the climate that conspired against them — she, with her foolish human conflicts, her emotional turmoil of these days, could only do so much. Surely her gardens understood.

"You should always talk to your plants," she told Ben one day as he helped her tear up her beds. And then she thought, Is *this* the wisdom that my generation will pass on, this nonsense about speaking to trees, to flowers, assuming the existence of a sensitive spirit in everything? But she continued nevertheless: "Talking to them makes them feel better. If there's something coming from you, from inside, they grow better. The scientists have proved that."

"Oh, Mom — I don't think so. They can't hear me. They don't have ears. And if I'm killing them, you think you can make that feel better?"

"It's all in the way you do it, Ben. With some kindness, paying attention. Maybe they understand that they have to die, that they get pulled out sometimes. Just think about that as you do it."

Gerda had not assumed care of Catherine's gardens; there had always been a certain separation of functions, with Catherine tending the flower beds, the orchard of pear and quince trees, and her vegetable plots, while Gerda devoted herself entirely to her nursery. The one only gardened, while the other purposely built a business, a serious small business (although Catherine's earnings from the sale of organic vegetables were sometimes substantial). From her first days at the farm, Catherine had been made to understand that the old woman was not particularly pleased, nor was she displeased, to have another cultivator on the grounds; their friendship, should it happen to develop, would have to be based on other, more remarkable similarities. The whole matter of disciples had a special meaning for Gerda. She always attracted them, and yet she raged against them, seemed oppressed by them. Before the arrival of Rachel, there had been others, all somehow stamped from the same mold: aimless modern girl-women who had heard of Gerda somewhere, made the pilgrimage to her remote estate, then begged to be hired on as assistants. Some had a prior interest in California native plants, but all had fastened on to the crusty, disciplining old matriarch with a passion.

"Yes, they think I'm their mother," the old woman explained, "or maybe their grandmother, I don't know. And they ask me about a 'woman's power' all the time — what is it. Well, I show them my power. If they don't do their work, I show them very well."

Before the advent of Rachel, there had been a Melanie, a Star, a Maya, a Geneva. Geneva still returned from time to time, all the way from Portland, Oregon, to work in the nursery for a few days. She did this in the spirit of a religious aspirant going on a retreat. Gerda had shown Catherine some poetry that this Geneva had written; most of it was addressed to or descriptive of the Goddess, a primordial female source-figure. The small, self-published pamphlet of incantatory verse was dedicated to Gerda Mansure.

"I suppose I am this Mother Earth — yes, I am her Goddess. These days, nothing is not self-conscious anymore, is it . . . even to be a woman. They have to study it first, learn it with their minds. But I tell them: Don't *think* to be a woman, simply be. It comes out of your guts, girl, from your soul."

Once, when three of her helpers were living at the farm simultaneously, Gerda became fed up with them; she declared that they were to stay away from her, they with their constant jealous bickering, for a period of ten days. "It smells of hormones in here," she said of the nursery, where all of them worked each afternoon. "Stay away, so the air can clear out."

But she tolerated these followers, these aspiring epigones, maybe even loved them in her way. In their company she became mighty, queen-like, with her thick, snowy crown of braided hair seeming to reflect their fulsome adoration. When they came to her "without any foolishness," with a modicum of restraint, she almost cooed over them, chided them more gently, allowing them momentary access to that power whose existence she professed to doubt.

"Catherine, I have said almost nothing to you," Gerda remarked to her one Friday. "I don't tell you how to live, but I do say this: you make me unhappy now. You can save your marriage, I know you can. Rick is just himself — you've always known about Rick. Well then, just accept him, I say. Live with him or not, in this house or not. But keep the marriage. Because you need it."

"But why, Gerda? What for? Rick doesn't really need me, maybe he never has. And look, he's got Karen now. She sleeps in the house, in my own bed. Oh, I don't mind . . . let them do what they want. But he's not my husband anymore. That part of my life is finally over."

Gerda could only shake her head, as if to deny that she was hearing these awful words. However, she was not, in the end, so distressed about this issue, about Catherine's marriage per se. She had other, more practical matters to consider.

"Look, Catherine — soon I will die. But when I pass on, who has it then? The farm, the house, all this nonsense? Why, it's Rick. Somehow it ends up with Rick. I don't say that he thought of this . . . that he came to me, wanting to live with me, thinking of this. But he will have it, even so. And he makes a clever maneuver then, doesn't he. Just like the others. Like all his uncles. Just as *they* wanted."

Catherine took a moment to understand. "But I don't quite see how they're a part of this. What do you mean?"

"Yes, yes — it all comes back to the uncles. As they always said, always planned. Rick doesn't want it for himself, of course. But for the family, well, that's something else. And these will all be Mansure forests once again. All back together. As the uncles wished."

Gerda could leave her land to whomever she wanted. But she would never leave it to a trust, she said, or to the state. Land was something about which she entertained certain sentimental beliefs, the first and foremost being that the land had a life of its own, a spirit, and that this quality survived only in connection with a particular human life. She, childless widow that she was, knew this for a painful fact. Barren of womb as she was — and soon to die, very soon to die — she intended to establish such a connection by whatever means necessary.

"But Gerda, I still don't understand. What has this got to do with me?"

"Just listen, then. If I give it to be a park, then everyone owns it. Everyone, and no one. But maybe little Ben would like it someday — yes, and that would be better. I like that idea much more. But Rick doesn't think of such things, they're beneath him. Still, he *knows* them. Because his uncles have taught him well. And then he comes to live here at my house. And look what happens in the end."

Catherine had never thought of these matters. As embarrassing as it was to admit, she had never once considered this, the whole idea or type of idea was foreign to her. She was ignorant in many ways, she knew; the circumstances of her life had permitted her to remain indifferent, unaware.

"But Gerda, really, you can't ask me to think of that before all else. To be most concerned about that. I can't base my decision on something like that."

"No, I know, Catherine. But don't be a child, either. Think

of who you are, and where you are. You have always lived from someone else, you know — always under someone else's house. First in your father's, I suppose, and then in mine. Under your husband. But now it could be your house. Just as this is my house. And my land."

Gerda clutched the younger woman by the elbow, as if to guide her resolutely through a door. Catherine felt challenged by this direct, imperious contact, and yet her strongest impression was of the absurdity of the moment — its wrongness, its unreality.

"I'm sorry, Gerda . . . it's strange, it just seems funny to me. It has such an air of 'fateful words,' you know. I never expected to hear such a thing. But I couldn't stay with Rick, not for that. Not even as wonderful as all this would be — to have all this. I'm just too small-minded, I guess. Too middle class. Is that what I am, hopelessly middle class? Anyhow, it's not a good deal for me. It doesn't make sense, not in my heart. And I couldn't pretend to love him — I couldn't. It just wouldn't be any good."

The old woman suddenly let go of her. "You don't understand. I don't propose you a deal, Catherine. You have to think carefully, that's all. Because this farm will pass on to someone, that is a fact. And if not to you and Rick, well then, just to Rick. So . . . go where you want. Marry and divorce as you want. I say nothing more."

"Oh Gerda — please don't be angry. Don't be offended. I don't think I want to grow up, not just yet. Allow me my one great folly, just one more. I haven't had so many in my life."

Gerda *had finally gone* to see Catherine's gynecologist, Dr. Meadows, and soon afterward submitted to the procedure her previous doctor recommended. It seemed to make a great difference that Dr. Meadows, an older man, listened to her complaints patiently, examined her carefully but not officiously, and presented his diagnosis in straightforward language, without overtones of either tragedy or chirpy optimism.

"Yes, I have a growth," she reported matter-of-factly to Catherine, "a type of cancer. But maybe it's not so bad. First an operation, he says. Then radiation treatments. And probably I'll survive. At my age you can live a long time with this, you see — the cells don't divide so quickly. The body doesn't make itself so fast, not anymore. So the cancer doesn't make itself either."

This diagnosis, and the imminence of her surgery, formed the background of her awkward discussion with Catherine about Longfields that day. Thereafter, Gerda said nothing about Catherine's marriage or divorce. However, she had one request. She told Catherine that she wished to meet Bascomb, or rather, to see him, but only from a distance. She wished to form an image of him, to take a direct impression.

"Bring him up here," she said, "but not into the house. Not inside the doors. Rick wouldn't like that. Have him come when Rick's taking his nap. Yes, let him appear on the promenade, down below the windows. On this Sunday if possible."

Catherine felt uneasy — Bascomb might not understand, he might be offended. Would it not be better for them all to meet on the patio or, if Gerda preferred, down in the pear orchard, even farther away from the house?

"No. Just do it as I tell you, please, Catherine. I'll look down from above. And if he doesn't understand what I want, well . . . then go to hell with him."

That weekend, Bascomb listened carefully to Catherine's odd proposal. And to her surprise he was not offended, not at all. The thought of appearing below the windows of the great Gerda, *la grande chatelaine*, appealed to him somehow; he would be sure to hold his hat in his hand, he said, and if she required it, he would even tug bashfully at his forelock.

"She knows," he said cryptically. "And I like her for that — I really do. I mean, she knows who she is, and who *I* am in relation to her. And that's all right. That's honest, I think. We won't be pretending then."

"Henry — you don't understand. If she brought you into the house like any other guest, she'd be doing something against Rick. It has nothing to do with condescension, nothing at all. She's free from that."

"Even so, she doesn't offer to come to *my* house, now does she? No, I have to trudge up the blasted mountain, come in by the long, winding forest path. As in days of yore. Approach the château on foot, growing ever more humble as it towers above me. Well — I understand. At least *she's* not pretending, not making out that we don't have a certain difference here. What you might call a class difference."

Catherine became annoyed with this, since it seemed to be more of his posing, his cherishing of his presumed lowness. It was absurd to say that he belonged to a lesser level — one sealed off from the upper reaches, as in some European society of centuries past.

"If anyone's pretending," she said, "you are. Whenever it gets too hard, whenever it's inconvenient, being what you really are. Someone of some sensitivity, some talent. A person who's a little remarkable . . . that can be a burden sometimes.

And then your other side comes out. The downtrodden woodsman. The shadowy, backward loner."

That Sunday, as it happened, a visit could not be arranged. But the following weekend Bascomb appeared at the farm, ready for his "viewing." He drove up rather than walked, parking down by the barns. And to Catherine's surprise he was not alone: Mary Elizabeth came with him. She had not gone away to live with her mother, it turned out; or rather, that arrangement had not proved as permanent as first promised. The young girl quickly got out of Bascomb's truck, then walked calmly around to stand beside her father.

"She's come to live with me again," Bascomb said simply. "This is Mrs. Mansure, Mary Elizabeth. You remember her."

"Uh-hunh."

She would not quite look at Catherine, however. She took hold of her father's hand, which was unusual — she had not been one to touch or hold on to him before. Then she directly asked the whereabouts of Catherine's "little boy." Was he up at the house? Did he want to play?

"Yes, I think he's up there now. Should we go look for him, all of us?"

Then they walked up, Mary at first bolting ahead on the path. The shape of the large, reticent-seeming, whitewashed house, showing all four of its stories, loomed above impressively, with its several banks of leaded windows catching a declining sun.

Bascomb did not dress as a country bumpkin, as he had threatened. He was clean-shaven and rosy of cheek, with a hint almost of style in his long-sleeved, narrow-collared black shirt, which needed only some ironing to suit him well. His gleaming, ocherish hair was combed straight back. The promising richness of it, the meet and precise way its scallops framed his high, mostly unlined forehead, gave Catherine a strange pleasure, and she kissed him full on the mouth. Mary Elizabeth noticed, but her undeep eyes gave no more hint of comprehension than would a bird's. Finally arriving at the house, they walked onto the promenade in full view of the upstairs windows. From here a flight of steps led up to a flagstone courtyard.

"Is he up there?" the girl asked, almost panting with eagerness.

"Yes, I think he is," Catherine said. "But let's let him come down. He'll notice us after a while."

Then there was absolutely nothing to do. They had only to stand there, making themselves visible. Catherine sat down on a stone bench after a moment, asking Mary to sit beside her. The girl then told her all about life at Lake Tahoe. They had gone skiing only once that winter, she said, because her mother worked so much at the casino. Sometimes she worked all day, then all night. "Then I have to get myself up in the morning. Then I have to make breakfast and go to school myself, in the snow."

While this confession continued, Bascomb stood apart, smiling to himself. He did not quite face the house, nor did he turn away from it, either; for a moment, he seemed about to sit down beside Catherine and the girl. But finally he didn't. These other poses, other attitudes he might have struck, were all implicit in the way he continued to stand calmly, placidly by himself; his head gathered in the attention of the courtyard, seemed to focus and perfect it.

"She isn't a dealer yet," Mary was explaining, "but she's getting the training. Then she can get in the union. But she wants to go to Las Vegas, because that's where the good jobs are. But Vegas isn't good for kids. It's just all honky-tonks."

After five or more minutes of this, a window swung open on the third floor of the house. Catherine and Mary immediately looked up. But it was only Ben, a window in Ben's room; they watched as a small, quick hand vanished back into the shadows. A few seconds later, a door slammed inside the house.

The little girl continued to watch the window, as if the appearance of that hand, that small, clever-seeming hand, were somehow mysterious. Then a door swung open onto the courtyard, and the boy came out. He approached directly, boldly, and Mary stood up from the bench. She watched his approach with a look of alarm, then of serious, deliberating curiosity.

When he was only a few yards off, he turned suddenly to his left, like a train abruptly shunted onto a different track. He had not intended to, but he thereby placed himself in Bascomb's path as Bascomb, roaming down along the veranda, returned to the vicinity of the bench. The man and boy almost collided, then nodded to each other. Bascomb touched the boy lightly on the shoulder, and Ben dropped his head.

"Ben — you remember Mary Elizabeth," Catherine urged. "And this is her father. This is Mr. Bascomb."

"Call me Henry, if you want to."

The man stuck out his hand to shake. He offered himself a little mockingly, exaggerating the manliness of the gesture, and the boy seemed to notice. Then Ben put his own hand out, a little too resolutely, too pluckily.

"Glad to meet you. To see you again," said Bascomb. And finally: "Good afternoon."

Ben resumed staring at the ground. He seemed to be smiling to himself, but he would only look down. The girl, the expression in her eyes now gone deeper, took a step forward. Then without a word spoken between them, the two children walked off toward the house. The girl marched behind the boy obediently, shuffling her feet mechanically, just as he did.

"Look — someone's up there at the window." Catherine made a gesture, and Bascomb turned around.

The great lady had deigned at last to show herself, to assume her prearranged position above them. Bascomb looked up briefly. Then he turned away. He shook his head, as if the absurdity of it, of his position here, had suddenly come home to him. But after a moment he pulled Catherine to her feet. He kissed her, directly on the mouth. And she kissed him back.

"Look up," she whispered. "You don't have to wave or anything . . . but just look up. Look up."

"Look up? But why? If she wants to see my face so much, let her come down here to me. I won't bite her, I promise."

But then he did turn around. And he did look up. Gerda, not waving, not quite nodding to him, nevertheless made some perceptible sign of recognition, which Bascomb silently returned. There was even something gracious, Catherine thought, in this momentary, subtle gesture. Gerda turned quickly from the window.

"I've seen her before," Bascomb said, "somewhere. She's very beautiful, isn't she. The old, white-headed queen on her balcony . . . in her castle window. But she's sick now, I think. I can tell."

"Yes — she's almost eighty-seven now," Catherine replied. "And she hasn't been well."

They wandered down from the house, headed for Catherine's dying gardens. Here they stood together, arm in arm, while the sun went unremarkably down. They kissed, holding their faces close together afterward, each seeming to savor the breath of the other. Then just before dark, they found Ben and Mary Elizabeth out in front of the house, running footraces in the circular driveway. The girl was quicker on her feet, and she had gained the upper hand generally, Catherine saw: she refused to be tricked into playing chess with Ben, saying that games like that weren't any "fun."

J*ust like that,* Bascomb's daughter had returned to him, and this time possibly for good. The mother had a new lover, and they had "plans," Bascomb heard. Terry needed to be unencumbered for a while, she said — free to travel and improvise, to move to Nevada if necessary. When Mary Elizabeth was a little older, the mother would come back for her.

"Mary doesn't seem too upset," Bascomb reported. "Maybe she doesn't like the new boyfriend much, I don't know. I guess I have to put her in school again. Fifth grade, I think it is this time."

"Oh, can't you tell — she's *very* upset," Catherine corrected him. "She's just lost her mother, don't you understand? Her mother's just abandoned her. I'm very sad for her. It's a terrible blow."

Bascomb did not argue this point. After all — Catherine might be right. But he quietly, stubbornly insisted on acting toward his daughter as before, always in his slightly remote, essentially dependable way. And he would not provoke trauma in her by assuming that it had been experienced. If Mary, for reasons of her own, insisted on seeming comfortable, largely untroubled — if she did not, for instance, start to have nightmares, wet her bed, or act depressed — then he felt inclined to take her as she was. He would let the boat go unrocked, so to speak.

"She likes your boy, by the way. Especially his two ponies. And all his computers."

"Well — I think he likes her, too," Catherine responded, although Ben had said nothing. "He used to be afraid of her. He told me last year that she used to hurt other kids, that she broke somebody's front tooth. But now I think he's more impressed than afraid. *He'd* like to be that dangerous."

Catherine's own child was also strangely, perhaps ominously, untroubled, she observed; he was outwardly not concerned at all by these momentous changes. He asked her once if she would be getting divorced from Rick. And she said that she would — yes, she probably would. And there the matter now rested. Going to visit her in San Francisco on weekends, he seemed interested, eager, because she always took him to unusual places; they had gone to fairs and museums, and on Stanyan Street they found a store selling nothing but skateboards and related paraphernalia. The "urban guerrilla" ethos of the place fascinated him, stirred something in him. He never complained about going back to Gerda's on Sunday nights, nor did he resist coming away with Catherine each Friday.

"You know, Rick," she said to her husband one week, "I very much appreciate how you've been with him. You haven't made him an issue between us, and I can tell you aren't letting him see the resentment you must feel toward me. Maybe that's not being real somehow, but I think it'll help him in the end."

"Oh, *do* you think so?" he replied quickly, rather archly.

Rick himself had been surviving quite well; in most respects he seemed to be flourishing. He had begun to make headway against his physical disability — the days of complete exhaustion, of anxiety attacks, and so on, were behind him, although he still walked with a cane sometimes. To Catherine it appeared that he had undergone, through this hateful physical trial, a final transformation by means of which he became, incontestably, the man he was always destined to be. She had never doubted his powers of resistance, the sheer cussed tenacity of his grip on life, on preeminence; but now he ascended to a different level, a yet more remarkable dominion. In countenance and even in style of dress he had come to resemble his favorite uncle, Gower, the richest and most refined of the Mansures; Gower had always favored scarves and cashmere sweaters, worn sometimes in combination with baggy, slope-shouldered imported sportcoats.

"Do you really think he'll 'survive,' " Rick went on, "come out of this even stronger? A better person somehow? With a richer personality?"

"Oh, Rick, no, I don't say that . . . I don't think so. And please, don't start with me. I know what I'm doing to him, and I'll regret it, probably for the rest of my life. But our marriage is over, Rick. We both know it is, and we have to recognize that. And I have a chance to be happy, I think . . . and to make someone else happy. As far as Ben goes, I want him to come out as unscarred as possible. And I think you want that, too."

Rick shook his head. Not in disagreement but in stunned amazement, it appeared. He simply didn't know where to begin; her thinking was so confused, her words so fatuous, so inadequate. "You think I want that, do you, Catherine? Well, how good of you. How beneficent. Your condescension is exquisite, as always . . . when did you first decide that you and you alone understood what was best for him? Was it when you coolly turned your back on us — decided that you had no more responsibility, either to him or to me, and could go off and screw the gardener, or whoever? Was that when it was? No, I don't show him resentment, Catherine. Resentment doesn't begin to describe what I feel toward you, in the first place. But I'll raise him as well as I know how, just as I've always done. Especially now, after his mother's given him a good, hard kick in the guts."

She could feel all the other things that he wanted to say; this was but a prelude, she knew. His assessment of her character had achieved a finality, she could see, taken eloquent, categorical shape. But she didn't need to hear what Rick really thought of her. She knew what *she* thought, and that was more than enough. And she knew what she would do.

"I'm sorry, Rick — truly I am. But I don't think you care about me . . . you're not even all that angry with me, not personally. Not emotionally. Let's just say that you put me aside a while ago, and it took me some time to realize. You're too strong for me, Rick, I can't make myself felt against you. It's a helpless, horrible feeling I have, and I can't live with it anymore. All right . . . but just let me go. Let me go in peace if you can. I've found someone who loves me and who wants to know me completely. Let me make my happiness, or my miserable unhappiness, whatever it turns out to be."

He was not convinced. "Your idea of love," he replied, "is just stupid. Poisonously jejune. My God . . . why should I worry how *you* feel all the time, whether you're getting *through* to me or whatever — whatever in the world that really means. If you don't have the right feelings, Catherine, well, that's your problem, after all. It's been fifteen long years . . . the truth is we had a good marriage, a decent, useful marriage for the most part. We made our adjustments, but you couldn't hold it together, could you — not when I got sick. Never mind all the rest — the way you slipped out of your responsibilities, it goes hand in glove with this spineless, sentimental idea of love, this business of *really needing* and being pathetically open all the time. I needed a wife, Catherine, that's all, and your response was to run away as fast as you could. That about says it all, I think. That was your really bold, authentic moment."

She felt sick, hearing him speak this way; something began to fail in her, but she replied nevertheless: "That's not true, Rick, and it isn't fair. It happened long before that — long before you got sick. It's that you're *too* strong, Rick, not that you're sick . . . if anything, too perfect. There's just no way in to you, not for me, at least. You're too complete, too whole, finished. I always respected that about you, in a way . . . but I found that I was dying with you. I was sicker than you were. And when I woke up, I got afraid. I knew I had to take steps . . ."

Rick began to smile. Her way of expressing herself, these trite, tired turns of phrase, appeared to amuse him. The suffocating wife, the domineering, invulnerable husband — surely these were figures out of some shopworn melodrama, with no possible relation to their reality.

"I know you pretty well, Catherine . . . after all these years, I think I do. And I know how false you are. You're a beautiful woman, Catherine, and there's something impressive about you physically, personally . . . it makes people think you know something. But in fact you're terribly weak. You depended on me so completely, so desperately, that when I collapsed you just couldn't take it. They don't talk about that anymore, do they? How women depend on their men, parasitize them, vampirize them. The needle's swung so far around that we have to pretend it never happens now, or only in the other direction . . . well, I think you've taken a fateful step, my dear. One that you'll live to regret. It's all downhill from here on, socially, personally, spiritually. Maybe even romantically — betrayal has a way of paying off in its own coin, you know. And as always, I'll be expected to support your brave, bold effort. To underwrite your adventures. I suppose I should hate you for it, but you know, I feel fortunate, actually. Every loss is a kind of gain, if you can see what I mean."

Catherine began to cry then — the tears were suddenly present on her cheeks, although she hadn't felt them threaten. They made her think of rain — a cold, unfreshening rain, not wanted and not cleansing. For a moment she couldn't speak, and Rick turned magisterially aside. He stood quite close to her, using his cane to increase his stature.

"I feel fortunate, too," she said finally, "and not quite destroyed — not quite. I guess I should hate you if you say things like that to me . . . but I've never been good at hating. I just feel an emptiness for you, Rick. My heart's just played out, exhausted. Funny — when there used to be so much in it for you. Almost everything."

"Nothing that *I* would want to build on ever again," he replied, sounding not quite as magnificent as he probably hoped.

Late *that April,* Catherine's sister, Muriel, arrived in San Francisco for a professional conference. Catherine had been dreading this visit. She had kept Muriel apprised of major developments, and Muriel, who had been all but predicting the collapse of Catherine's marriage for years, affected to be surprised, deeply disturbed. But after a few days together Catherine saw that her sister, who could seem exceedingly dry over the phone, was not really opposed to the step she was taking, nor was Muriel in favor of it. She was simply sympathetic: whatever Catherine wanted to do, that was all right with her.

"I'm sorry, Catherine. I really can't think of anything except this damned paper I have to deliver — two papers, actually. The first should go over well, it's more of the twin stuff. But the second's in trouble. Even I can see it's a bit abstract. Maybe you'd like to read it, tell me what you think."

Catherine pretended to be eager to do so. After all, she had read all her sister's books. Building on her earlier research, Muriel had devised a theory of suicide, with particular reference to its incidence among identical twins: she had found, not surprisingly, that certain families were afflicted with suicide as with a genetic anomaly, and that she could predict, with near mathematical certainty, its incidence down through the generations. A twin was seven times more likely to commit suicide if the brother or sister had already done so; and among twins separated at birth, growing up apart, the likelihood was actually greater.

"The most famous case is the Gurney brothers, given up for adoption and raised one in Oregon, one in Idaho. They killed themselves within hours of each other at age forty-three. Each was a farmer. Each had three kids, and each was married to a woman with Indian blood named Frances. That's just one case, of course — but when you abstract the data, you get even more astounding results . . ."

Struggling to understand her sister's statistical manipulations, Catherine saw from the start that she would glean nothing, appreciate nothing; not a single word or idea would speak to her human concern. A great mystery, an enduring enigma, had here been baldly finessed. Stories like that of the Gurneys had been bled of any anecdotal appeal. The implication was that this most personal of decisions — whether to blow one's brains out or not — was a function of mere mechanistic fate.

"I guess it reads well, Muriel," she said. "I don't pretend to understand the math, though . . . I would've gone about it differently, I think. Are there any exceptional cases — any identical twins who didn't kill themselves, or, if one did, the other lived on happily? To a ripe old age? I'd be more interested in that. Sometimes it seems like you take troubling issues, ideas that get to you, on a really deep level, and instead of saying what you feel, you throw Gaussian equations at them. Randomization medians, that sort of thing. It's as if you think you triumph over them that way. Besides, the underlying message is always that we don't control our lives, that conscious choice is an illusion. Yet you rely on your consciousness more than anything, don't you? Sometimes I'm sure you must be joking, writing a parody of some kind."

Muriel took this in good part; and after the third day of her conference, when both her papers had been presented successfully, she turned her attention to Catherine's situation. Everyone was probably feeling sorry for Rick, she imagined, yet Catherine was the one who had given her all to the marriage, who had sacrificed and compromised. She had fought an undeclared, subterranean war of wills with this formidable opponent, Muriel noted, knowing he could never be defeated. "It's no secret — I never understood Rick for you," she confessed. "Rick as a great figure, an impressive image — yes, all right. But not as someone you might actually want to live with. Rick's talent isn't for living, is it? It's for something beyond the rest of us, different from mere living ... to tell the truth, I could never see sleeping with him. Or maybe just once, for the 'experience' of it, you know. But there's something almost too smooth about him. Featureless, iconic."

"Rick's doing well now, really well," Catherine replied. She felt a little uneasy, talking about him in this way, in this tone. "He'll never be the same man physically, but it probably doesn't matter to him ... I think he's actually happier. He's been living with our governess, you know, the beautiful young Karen. They may even get married. Someone said that she's a younger, simpler, less substantial version of me, but I don't think she's all that easy to comprehend: she'll show him a complication or two before she's through. And she's done quite well for herself, wouldn't you say? Really very well."

That same week, Catherine heard from Bob Stein, who had gotten his hands on the galleys of Rick's new book. Having read it straight through, he wondered what to do with it now — just return it (his source was an old friend, the West Coast rep of Rick's publisher)? Pointedly failing to offer to send it on to Catherine, he made her begin to feel curious about it, almost for the first time; and she did ask him to send it over.

She immediately understood his motive, the method behind his putative reluctance. Here was a *real* betrayal, she saw — nothing like Bob's comic, mythopoeic appropriations of her for his novels. Rick had written in a spirit of contemptuous, unapologetic spitefulness; it was quite unlike anything to be found even in Bob's most ironic passages. Catherine was no-where mentioned by name. Known only as "the man's wife," "the invalid's wife," she functioned as the story's categorical dark force, its font of evil. She thought of how Ben, when he was older, might respond to this blackening of her character: surely he would read his father's books one day (and probably Bob's, too, when he learned what they were about), and then what? She felt sick on this account, truly sick.

"This is just lies, Bob," she complained, "nothing but false-ness. How could he do it? It's amazing — one of the most ill-tempered, deeply vicious pieces I've come across. He doesn't even have the courage to say what he really thinks . . . to air his ugly little ideas about women, for instance, the conse-quences of their 'liberation,' and so forth. He puts it all on my head, instead. Pretends to be telling the truth, but every word's a falsehood, a glaring lie. Either he's gone off the deep end or he's always been a kind of monster, as you once said. A great hypocrite. I don't understand it. Why befoul your own life? Why? You don't murder the truth."

Bob quite agreed with her, and yet he was calming, he put things in perspective. Not to be excusing anyone, of course, but she needed to recall Rick's recent struggles, his sudden loss of his powers: the profound disruption on every level caused by his two years of dire illness. When Rick became sick, he experi-enced for the first time feelings of failure, of inadequacy, and under the influence of these shocking sensations (actually new to him) his personality began to crack. Maybe even more than most mortals, Rick Mansure was an assemblage of customary behaviors: of impressive achievements, remarkable capacities, but with something nebulous at the core. Out of the confronta-tion with this core of himself, this essential formlessness, had come a profound fear, in Bob's opinion.

"Nothing like real confrontation, though," he added, warming to his own analysis. "Not a real knowing. It only went so far, then grabbed for anything that came to hand.

When I heard that his therapist, Klepper or whatever his name is, was encouraging him to be more assertive — whatever the hell *that* could mean in connection with Rick — well, then I knew something was dreadfully wrong. The idea that Rick has been victimized by his closest friends, his family — that just amuses me. Sure he's had some hard times, sure it's sad about his parents, his blighted upbringing and all that. But give me a break. Rick is the guy who just cannot be bettered, cannot be overcome. You don't get over on him, no matter what. That's what Rick's all about . . ."

In the book, Catherine was seen as fleeing her husband's illness, declining to comfort or nurse dependably; she was depicted generally as a grown-up child, a self-absorbed seeker after bogus "true feelings." The affair with Bascomb was mentioned only briefly, as only the latest in a string of betrayals (spiritual, if not sexual). For years she had conducted a questionable relationship with her husband's best friend, according to the book; who, for his own part, had exploited personal attachments for dubious literary purposes.

"*I* think," Bob concluded, "that he's made his misogyny quite clear enough. And for that reason alone, I'd advise him not to publish. It hardly matters that he slanders you, or me, or any number of others. But his ugly little ideas are all over the thing. He'll only harm himself, do permanent damage to himself as a writer. People will think of him as a crank after this."

Catherine strongly disagreed; she thought that Rick's unashamed frankness would find sympathy with many readers. "People are ready to hear this stuff, Bob, and it reads very well, you have to admit. It's intense. It doesn't apologize for what it is, and it knows what it wants to say, knows it to the last word. It's the story of a man triumphing over a frightening illness, among other things, and people eat that up. I predict another great success. Something on the order of *Escambeche*, or bigger."

Bob wondered how Maryanne, who was famously sensitive to all real as well as imagined slights against her sex, would respond. Would this put Rick beyond the pale for her, as she had been beyond for him? What effect, if any, was this likely to have on their new relationship — their recently established professional connection? Seeing Catherine's puzzled look, he hastened to disclaim any detailed knowledge beyond what Catherine undoubtedly already knew herself: that Rick had recently approached their mutual friend and asked her to handle his side of the divorce, and that Maryanne, while protesting, had finally agreed to do so. After lengthy discussions about the kind of outcome Rick envisioned, she had become convinced that she could act for him in good faith, that her friendship with Catherine would not be compromised. Apparently, Rick intended to be "grown up" about the whole thing — generous, nonpunitive, and so on. Perhaps his writing of this foul hatchet piece had gotten all resentment out of his system.

"Oh no, I doubt that," Catherine said after a moment, feeling rather stunned. She had heard nothing from Maryanne about this; their discussion of a few weeks before would have seemed to preclude it. "My God — I haven't even filed the papers yet. Well, I guess I have to get a lawyer now, don't I, Bob? Are you sure about all this? Did she really say that? Well, you know, it's pretty funny. Because he doesn't like her, not at all. He hasn't been able to make himself say two words to her in almost five years . . . but why go that way, what for? I mean, aside from its being really nasty, gratuitously unkind. Making one of my oldest friends turn away from me, to make me feel even worse. To show me how alone I am. Then again, it could be a ploy to make me think we can settle this thing casually, just among friends, you know . . ."

"I guess it's really started now," Bob said. He scratched his head, looking sheepish. "The divorce, I mean. Now it's really begun."

B*efore she returned* to Oregon, Muriel hoped to see her nephew, Ben; so the two sisters drove down the peninsula on a Wednesday, having arranged beforehand to pick him up after school. It was a cloudy, blowing day. Catherine felt encouraged, thinking that it might rain, but the forecast was for clouds and nothing more: the drought was firmly in place, the authorities said, it could not be broken. Having missed out on rain all winter, the region was certain to remain dry at least till October. Everyone and everything would have to survive on what was already there — already there on the ground.

They found Catherine's son, and his aunt, whom he had always liked, presented him with a large wrapped package. Ben tore it open in the school parking lot. The tall, shockingly redheaded woman (Muriel) and her slightly smaller, slightly less redheaded sister stood on either side as the dark-haired boy hurriedly exposed a box of Rollerblades. His eyes narrowed briefly, otherwise his expression changed not at all. Catherine had to remind him to say thank you.

"I like them," he said a moment later. Then in his high, uninflected voice, "They're cool."

Catherine had seen Bascomb's truck in the school lot. Soon he came out of the entrance trailing Mary Elizabeth, and Catherine called out to them. Bascomb looked stricken. He stopped dead in his tracks, having only her voice to go on, nothing yet to see. But soon he returned to himself. He sauntered across the pavement, herding his daughter before him. He was wearing a blue windbreaker today, which Catherine had given him.

When introduced, he shook Muriel's hand slowly. Then he turned to Catherine, and his austere, somewhat imperious expression took on a different meaning, became an ironic version of itself. He held Catherine's eyes, and Muriel stood off to the side of them, watching. After a moment Muriel's own expression relaxed.

"Muriel remembers you . . . even if you don't remember her."

"She does?"

"Yes," the sister put in, "I heard you play once. It was here at a local bar. You were in a band. I went down there with Catherine."

"Oh, I remember that night," he replied with a self-mocking tone, as if there were something embarrassing about the event. "Yes, and Catherine too . . . and a few days afterwards, she said that she'd heard me play. And that she liked my music. I fed off that for about six months, as I remember."

"Oh — but you must get complimented all the time," Muriel countered, unwilling to allow this false modesty. "You're a wonderful musician. I remember being very impressed. Really carried away."

"Well, thank you. But I know just how good I am . . . but thank you anyway. No, not so often . . . and hearing it from someone I didn't know, someone who had no particular reason to say anything to me — that made a difference. It made me believe that good things could happen, even to me, if only I put my music out there. Let it go in the world. That it would find its way sometimes."

"But don't you think good things are likely to happen to you, in general?" Muriel wondered, with a look of amused penetration.

Bascomb became shy. Would this woman be trying to analyze him — was she hoping to get at something important, something hidden? "Oh, but they're not *likely* to happen," he finally said. "They do sometimes, but no, they're not likely.

And afterwards you always see how extraordinary they are. What incredible accidents. I had to play out of my head that night, you know, for no particular reason . . . and Catherine had to be there. And then a week or so later, she happened to give me a ride in her car. To tell me things . . . no, not likely at all, I'd say. Good things aren't likely, they require too many coincidences. Lucky break on top of lucky break. You see the hand of Providence in them, being a little too clever."

Muriel thought that this was perhaps stretching things a bit. "Women go for musicians all the time, you know. And then they like to talk to them afterwards. It's an old, old story. At least in our family it is." And as she said this, she blushed rather extravagantly, young-girlishly. Which caused Bascomb to warm to her, or at least to her embarrassment.

"Well, but did you know," he said, "I met Catherine before. Years and years ago. And I drove myself crazy trying to think of how to get to her again. But I wasn't bold enough, I guess. Then, when conditions were finally right . . . when 'Fate' decreed that we were ready . . . well, I couldn't get away from her, or she from me. I saw her everywhere, even up at her lake. Swimming naked she was, like a shocking, outrageous nymph . . . but what had put me there? I wondered. Right in those bushes, on that particular day? Why was *I* given that glorious vision to enjoy? It didn't seem real somehow, didn't seem earned. You know — Fate leaves the strings on us puppets sometimes. Fate is insincere, mostly."

Muriel suggested that they all go somewhere, have a cup of tea. There was only one restaurant in Cuervo, and it was usually closed in the afternoon. But they drove down there anyhow, just to make sure. The town's commercial district consisted of a single general store, the health food store, a post office, the restaurant (yes, closed), and four bars, and once again they found themselves marooned in a nearly empty parking lot. Ben put on his Rollerblades, and he attempted to skate off on them. Then he fell. Mary Elizabeth watched alertly — she, herself, would be sure to do better if given a chance.

Bascomb invited them all to his house then. Catherine said they would like to come, but they had planned to see Gerda, who had recently come home from the hospital. But Muriel wanted to see Bascomb's house — she had conceived a particular curiosity about it, she said. Catherine had described it to her in mysterious terms, and as a connoisseur of rustic cabins she was eager now to have a look. And so they went.

Lurching up his driveway, in the car with Catherine and Ben, Muriel sighed and said, "Yes — now I see. Now I see."

"You see what, Muriel?"

But she would only smile to herself. She seemed convinced of something now, absolutely decided.

Bascomb brewed them a pot of strong tea. It tasted of honey and black currants, but not the kind of currants he gathered in the forest, something less rankly purple-tasting. His house was cold on this gloomy, windy, clouded day. Muriel examined his bookshelves carefully as he built a fire, then she noticed his violin, which was sitting in an open case, covered with a soft cloth. She wondered aloud whether he still played music in the bars, whether it was possible to earn a living that way — just playing here and there whenever the spirit moved him.

"No, not really possible. You have to be looking for jobs all the time . . . and I haven't been serious enough, thorough enough. I only play when that group of friends asks me, or when somebody hears about me. But we've got a few dates coming up this summer. We'll see how that goes — maybe we'll be famous."

"But can you ever support yourself," Muriel persisted, "even if you worked all the time, got every job that came along? Would it even be possible? Is it realistic?"

Bascomb seemed vaguely amused. He would allow her this probing, this cross-examination, if she insisted on it. "If you're asking me whether I can support Catherine . . . well, the answer's no, I guess. I probably can't, not right now. But I want her to live with me, so I'll have to find something, won't I? I may have to leave the canyon to do it. There's not much around here, so I'll probably have to go."

"I wasn't asking anything of the kind," Muriel quickly demurred. "And I'd hate for you to have to leave. It's such a perfect little nest you have here . . . a woodsy dream. When you get inside, you see how it's just right — just human size, exactly. I think every woman in the world has dreamed, at one time or another, of living in a place like this . . . with the right sort of man, of course. And Catherine will be earning her own living now. Isn't that right, Catherine?" And turning toward her silent sister she said, "Aren't you sick of having men support you, Cath? Doesn't that get tiresome and impossible after a while?"

"Oh, whatever you say, Muriel. Whatever you tell me — that's how it has to be."

And then they all laughed, since, of course, she was only fooling.

≈ ≈ ≈

Two days later, as Muriel was getting ready to go to the airport from her hotel, she told Catherine what she really thought about Bascomb.

"The fog that envelops you . . . oh, the sheer dreaminess of it. Wonderful, in a way . . . like some storybook romance. But it's being played out in real time, Catherine. That's what he was trying to say to us, I think, when he talked about these 'coincidences,' Fate being too obvious, and all that. He knows it's unreal. I can tell that he loves you, as far as a man like that is capable of loving someone . . . and you've fallen for the dream of it, the image of love. When you see a young girl do that out of ignorance, well, you hold your breath, hoping she won't be hurt too much. But you're not a girl, Catherine.

You're a woman now, and a mother. You don't go into something like this at your age, I think . . . openly courting destruction. It's a kind of sickness at this point."

Catherine was silent for a moment, a little shocked as she contemplated this unequivocal, compelling declaration. "But I thought you liked him, Muriel. You responded to him. I could see it. What was it you said — that he was perfect for me, because he was perfect for just about anyone?"

"Oh, exactly. He's one of these special men, these romantic paragons. Someone with an instinct for it — a gift for love. His whole life is about that, I think, and nothing else . . . it's a kind of performance. He's beautiful, of course, and so self-contained, so wounded-seeming. And your woman's heart just swells at that, it leaps up, it wants to go out to him. The sadness of him . . . the sad sexiness. The musical soul. He isn't real, Catherine, he's a dream. A man like that knows only one thing — how to play that romantic role. He's desperately in love with you because he's desperate to find himself, through you . . . and you activate him, you give him a pretext. But someday, the pretext finally wears out. And then there you are. Married to a dream man. To a performance."

Catherine could only shake her head. She was offended, and her instinct was to leap to Bascomb's defense. It was easier to speak of this, of her sister's misunderstanding, her gross misperception of him, than of her own feeling of insult.

"You only know what you see, Muriel, you can't feel for me, not now. I don't know why you want to distort him so . . . he isn't dreamy or false, not in any way you might understand. I suppose I should try to triumph over this, not let myself feel that something important has happened, something terribly right for me. Even something 'fateful,' as he likes to say. You always imply that I'm so ignorant . . . thoughtless, unaware. But I'm completely conscious now, I swear I am. Conscious with all my love for him — with my living, desiring body, that wants only him. And I'm not sure why I'd be wiser if I ignored that."

"Catherine — I'm sorry," Muriel said in a half-placating tone. "I know I'm speaking out of turn. You're a grown woman, after all . . . you must know what you want. I just felt I ought to say something. I'm your sister, your big sister, and I've got some ideas. Maybe that's all they are. I wish you every happiness, you know I do. I'd love to have a man look at me the way he looked at you the other day, in the parking lot . . . but never mind. Be joyful, and be in love."

In the end, Catherine felt disappointed — it was as if Muriel actually didn't care. She had only wanted to get on the record with this — to lodge an official protest, which they might refer to one day if things didn't work out. Then she dropped the matter conclusively. She mounted the steps of the airport shuttle bus, her arms full of bags and parcels. When she found a seat, she waved to Catherine almost absentmindedly. The bus drew slowly away.

That *June,* when Catherine was still living in San Francisco, she received a long letter from Bascomb. He had gone to play music at a bluegrass festival in Oregon. After describing the difficulties and pleasures of performing with his friends, he urged her to join him (the festival was being staged in the town of Modoc, Oregon, near the California border, with air service to a field fifteen miles away).

"I hate it here," he wrote, "the landscape frightens me. You keep expecting a hawk to come out of the sky and snatch you up, the prairie's so bare and endless. Someone just told me that it isn't really prairie — it's high desert, all sagebrush and greasewood, and other beaten-down stuff. Very cold in winter. Bleak and searing in summer. 'With a beauty all its own,' I'm sure.

"There was an Indian war here a hundred-some years ago. The restaurants all have displays of arrowheads and spear points, and half the people have Indian faces. They look amused about something. A tiny, swift old woman walked by me half an hour ago on the street, making no sound, and I felt like the shadow of that great hawk passed over me. I think she must be a witch. I followed her, but she wouldn't let me see her face again, no matter what I did. Her black shawl was like a shadow she was wearing. Her face was beautiful, awful — astonishing. A dried-up peyote button sort of face. Very witty and evil.

"I don't see why they fought the Indians for this land, though; let them have it, let them get what sustenance they can from it. Yesterday, we played at ten in the morning, the first band scheduled, and as I was walking up onto the stage, which is out in a field, I had a moment of pure terror, wondering what was I doing here, would I remember how to play even a note. The sky went whirling all around me, and my mind went up, it sort of came apart. But in the end I did remember how to play a note. And the feeling was enjoyable after a while — so raw, so fierce.

"Everything feels that way to me now, a little bit, and I think it's because of you. Because you've taken me apart, you've torn me down; you've gotten right to the end of me, and I'm not the same anymore. I feel everything in my bones now. The sky over us, the music, the weird, x-raying sun — it all flowed through me, shocked me. It left me glowing, the way I sometimes glow with you, when we make love.

"I think we'll always have to be this way, though, because I can't go back to the other, to feeling things halfway. I can't live quietly anymore — I can't be half asleep. It all started, I think, when I first touched you — little thinking of what I was doing, of course. That small part of you that I know now, that I can actually hold with my own body — just to touch it nearly destroyed me, finished something in me. It brought me way down, to the basis of myself. And now I've put myself back together, I feel fine, I feel good, but with a kind of trembling in everything. A raw, hopeful aliveness.

"I'm not concerned about the future, not at all. I know that I can do whatever I have to, anything to make the life with you. I have that feeling of inevitability, as you know — as if something had revealed itself, shown itself to be a little on our side, to be making a mystery for us. I believe in that, absolutely. Or maybe what I believe in most is this touch of tenderness between us, this small flame we kick into being, just between us. That's enough to believe in, don't you think? And that's where the future will come from. That tenderness. That flame.

"The festival ends on the eighteenth, a Sunday, and then we could go away together. There's a town not far from here, only a couple of hundred miles north. Everyone says it's very quiet there, very beautiful. If you came up to be with me, we could go there together. It's in a great forest, they say, on the eastern slope of the Cascades. In a bit of the ancient, uncut forest remnant, the real old wilderness. Two rivers join just below the town, they actually run through it. We could hike up into the mountains, or just go there and stay a while. There must be some motels.

"Mary Elizabeth can stay on at her grandmother's, and your son can do without you for another week. I don't see what's stopping us, really — something that someone said, the way they described it, made me think that this was for us. Maybe we'll see the future from that place. The water coming out of the Cascades is very cold, very pure, they say, and we can swim in the rivers if we're brave enough; although I'm not looking to be cleansed, to be 'purified' with you, quite the opposite, in fact. We can make love there, I figure, as much as we want. Maybe we can even fuck the future into being — see it clear from that place.

"I'll be playing for three more days, but after that I'm done. So why don't you come up and join me? And we'll go away somewhere. Maybe to that town — I have a good feeling about it, I know I want to take you there. I want to make love to you there, in the forest."